BRIAN FLYNN
THEY NEVER CAME BACK

BRIAN FLYNN was born in 1885 in Leyton, Essex. He won a scholarship to the City Of London School, and from there went into the civil service. In World War I he served as Special Constable on the Home Front, also teaching "Accountancy, Languages, Maths and Elocution to men, women, boys and girls" in the evenings, and acting in his spare time.

It was a seaside family holiday that inspired Brian Flynn to turn his hand to writing in the mid-twenties. Finding most mystery novels of the time "mediocre in the extreme", he decided to compose his own. Edith, the author's wife, encouraged its completion, and after a protracted period finding a publisher, it was eventually released in 1927 by John Hamilton in the UK and Macrae Smith in the U.S. as *The Billiard-Room Mystery*.

The author died in 1958. In all, he wrote and published 57 mysteries, the vast majority featuring the super-sleuth Antony Bathurst.

GW00538119

BRIAN FLYNN

THEY NEVER CAME BACK

With an introduction by
Steve Barge

DEAN STREET PRESS

Published by Dean Street Press 2021

Copyright © 1940 Brian Flynn

Introduction © 2021 Steve Barge

All Rights Reserved

The right of Brian Flynn to be identified as the Author of the Work has
been asserted by his estate in accordance with the Copyright, Designs
and Patents Act 1988.

First published in 1940 by John Long

Cover by DSP

ISBN 978 1 914150 69 2

www.deanstreetpress.co.uk

INTRODUCTION

"I believe that the primary function of the mystery story is to entertain; to stimulate the imagination and even, at times, to supply humour. But it pleases the connoisseur most when it presents – and reveals – genuine mystery. To reach its full height, it has to offer an intellectual problem for the reader to consider, measure and solve."

Brian Flynn, *Crime Book* magazine, 1948

BRIAN Flynn began his writing career with *The Billiard Room Mystery* in 1927, primarily at the prompting of his wife Edith who had grown tired of hearing him say how he could write a better mystery novel than the ones he had been reading. Four more books followed under his original publisher, John Hamilton, before he moved to John Long, who would go on to publish the remaining forty-eight of his Anthony Bathurst mysteries, along with his three Sebastian Stole titles, released under the pseudonym Charles Wogan. Some of the early books were released in the US, and there were also a small number of translations of his mysteries into Swedish and German. In the article from which the above quote is taken from, Brian also claims that there were also French and Danish translations but to date, I have not found a single piece of evidence for their existence. The only translations that I have been able to find evidence of are *War Es Der Zahnarzt?* and *Bathurst Greift Ein* in German – *The Mystery of the Peacock's Eye*, retitled to the less dramatic "Was It The Dentist?", and *The Horn* becoming "Bathurst Takes Action" – and, in Swedish, *De 22 Svarta*, a more direct translation of *The Case of the Black Twenty-Two*. There may well be more work to be done finding these, but tracking down all of his books written in the original English has been challenging enough!

Reprints of Brian's books were rare. Four titles were released as paperbacks as part of John Long's Four Square Thriller range in the late 1930s, four more re-appeared during the war from Cherry Tree Books and Mellifont Press, albeit abridged by at least a third, and two others that I am aware of, *Such Bright Disguises* (1941) and *Reverse the Charges* (1943), received a paperback release as part of John Long's Pocket Edition range in the early 1950s – these were also possibly abridged, but only by about 10%. They were the exceptions, rather than the rule, however, and it was not until 2019, when Dean Street Press released his first ten titles, that his work was generally available again.

The question still persists as to why his work disappeared from the awareness of all but the most ardent collectors. As you may expect, when a title was only released once, back in the early 1930s, finding copies of the original text is not a straightforward matter – not even Brian's estate has a copy of every title. We are particularly grateful to one particular collector for providing *The Edge of Terror*, Brian's first serial killer tale, and another for *The Ebony Stag* and *The Grim Maiden*. With these, the reader can breathe a sigh of relief as a copy of every one of Brian's books has now been located – it only took about five years . . .

One of Brian's strengths was the variety of stories that he was willing to tell. Despite, under his own name at least, never straying from involving Anthony Bathurst in his novels – technically he doesn't appear in the non-series *Tragedy at Trinket*, although he gets a name-check from the sleuth of that tale who happens to be his nephew – it is fair to say that it was rare that two consecutive books ever followed the same structure. Some stories are narrated by a Watson-esque character, although never the same person twice, and others are written by Bathurst's "chronicler". The books sometimes focus on just Bathurst and his investigation but sometimes we get to see the events occurring to the whole cast of characters. On occasion, Bathurst himself will "write" the final chapter, just to make sure his chronicler has got the details correct. The murderer may be an opportunist or they may have a convoluted (and, on occasion, a somewhat over-the-top) plan. They may be working for personal gain or as part of a criminal enterprise or society. Compare for example, *The League of Matthias* and *The Horn* – consecutive releases but were it not for Bathurst's involvement, and a similar sense of humour underlying Brian's writing, you could easily believe that they were from the pen of different writers.

Brian seems to have been determined to keep stretching himself with his writing as he continued Bathurst's adventures, and the ten books starting with *Cold Evil* show him still trying new things. Two of the books are inverted mysteries – where we know who the killer is, and we follow their attempts to commit the crime and/or escape justice and also, in some cases, the detective's attempt to bring them to justice. That description doesn't do justice to either *Black Edged* or *Such Bright Disguises*, as there is more revealed in the finale than the reader might expect . . . There is one particular innovation in *The Grim Maiden*, namely the introduction of a female officer at Scotland Yard.

Helen Repton, an officer from "the woman's side of the Yard" is recruited in that book, as Bathurst's plan require an undercover officer in a cinema. This is her first appearance, despite the text implying that Bathurst has met her before, but it is notable as the narrative spends a little time apart from Bathurst. It follows Helen Repton's investigations based on superb initiative, which generates some leads in the case. At this point in crime fiction, there have been few, if any, serious depictions of a female police detective – the primary example would be Mrs Pym from the pen of Nigel Morland, but she (not just the only female detective at the Yard, but the Assistant Deputy Commissioner no less) would seem to be something of a caricature. Helen would go on to become a semi-regular character in the series, and there are certainly hints of a romantic connection between her and Bathurst.

It is often interesting to see how crime writers tackled the Second World War in their writing. Some brought the ongoing conflict into their writing – John Rhode (and his pseudonym Miles Burton) wrote several titles set in England during the conflict, as did others such as E.C.R. Lorac, Christopher Bush, Gladys Mitchell and many others. Other writers chose not to include the War in their tales – Agatha Christie had ten books published in the war years, yet only *N or M?* uses it as a subject.

Brian only uses the war as a backdrop in one title, *Glittering Prizes*, the story of a possible plan to undermine the Empire. It illustrates the problem of writing when the outcome of the conflict was unknown – it was written presumably in 1941 – where there seems little sign of life in England of the war going on, one character states that he has fought in the conflict, but messages are sent from

Nazi conspirators, ending *"Heil Hitler!"*. Brian had good reason for not wanting to write about the conflict in detail, though, as he had immediate family involved in the fighting and it is quite understandable to see writing as a distraction from that.

While Brian had until recently been all but forgotten, there are some mentions for Brian's work in some studies of the genre – Sutherland Scott in *Blood in their Ink* praises *The Mystery of the Peacock's Eye* as containing "one of the ablest pieces of misdirection" before promptly spoiling that misdirection a few pages later, and John Dickson Carr similarly spoils the ending of *The Billiard Room Mystery* in his famous essay "The Grandest Game In The World". One should also include in this list Barzun and Taylor's entry in their *Catalog of Crime* where they attempted to cover Brian by looking at a single title – the somewhat odd *Conspiracy at Angel* (1947) – and summarising it as "Straight tripe and savorless. It is doubtful, on the evidence, if any of his others would be different." Judging an author based on a single title seems desperately unfair – how many people have given up on Agatha Christie after only reading *Postern Of Fate*, for example – but at least that misjudgement is being rectified now.

Contemporary reviews of Brian's work were much more favourable, although as John Long were publishing his work for a library market, not all of his titles garnered attention. At this point in his writing career – 1938 to 1944 – a number of his books won reviews in the national press, most of which were positive. Maurice Richardson in the *Observer* commented that "Brian Flynn balances his ingredients with considerable skill" when reviewing *The Ebony Stag* and praised *Such Bright Disguises* as a "suburban horror melodrama" with an "ingenious final solution". "Suspense is well maintained until the end" in *The Case of the Faithful Heart*, and the protagonist's narration in *Black Edged* in "impressively nightmarish".

It is quite possible that Brian's harshest critic, though, was himself. In the *Crime Book* magazine, he wrote about how, when reading the current output of detective fiction "I delight in the dazzling erudition that has come to grace and decorate the craft of the *'roman policier'*." He then goes on to say "At the same time, however, I feel my own comparative unworthiness for the fire and burden of the competition." Such a feeling may well be the reason why he never made significant inroads into the social side of crime-writing, such as the Detection Club or the Crime Writers Association. Thankfully, he uses this sense of unworthiness as inspiration, concluding "The stars, though, have always been the most desired of all goals, so I allow exultation and determination to take the place of that but temporary dismay."

In Anthony Bathurst, Flynn created a sleuth that shared a number of traits with Holmes but was hardly a carbon-copy. Bathurst is a polymath and gentleman sleuth, a man of contradictions whose background is never made clear to the reader. He clearly has money, as he has his own rooms in London with a pair of servants on call and went to public school (Uppingham) and university (Oxford). He is a follower of all things that fall under the banner of sport, in particular horse racing and cricket, the latter being a sport that he could, allegedly, have represented England at. He is also a bit of a show-off, littering his speech (at times) with classical quotes, the obscurer the better, provided by the copies of the *Oxford Diction-ary of Quotations* and *Brewer's Dictionary of Phrase & Fable* that Flynn kept by his writing desk, although Bathurst generally restrains himself to only doing this with people who would appreciate it or to annoy the local constabulary. He is fond of amateur dramatics (as was Flynn, a well-regarded amateur thespian who appeared in at least one self-penned play, *Blue Murder*), having been a member of OUDS, the Oxford University Dramatic Society. General information about his background is light on the ground. His parents were Irish, but he doesn't have an accent – see *The Spiked Lion* (1933) – and his eyes are grey. Despite the fact that he is an incredibly charming and handsome individual, we learn in *The Orange Axe* that he doesn't pursue romantic relationships due to a bad experience in his first romance. We find out more about that relationship and the woman involved in *The Edge of Terror*, and soon thereafter he falls head over heels in love in *Fear and Trembling*, although we never hear of that young lady again. After that, there are eventual hints of an attraction between Helen Repton, but nothing more. That doesn't stop women falling head over heels for Bathurst – as he departs her company in *The Padded Door*, one character muses "What other man could she ever love . . . after this secret idolatry?"

As we reach the halfway point in Anthony's career, his companions have somewhat stablised, with Chief Inspector Andrew MacMorran now his near-constant junior partner in investigation. The friendship with MacMorran is a highlight (despite MacMorran always calling him "Mr. Bathurst") with the sparring between them always a delight to read. MacMorran's junior officers, notably Superintendent Hemingway and Sergeant Chatterton, are frequently recurring characters. The notion of the local constabulary calling in help from Scotland Yard enables cases to be set around the country while still maintaining the same central cast (along with a local bobby or two).

Cold Evil (1938), the twenty-first Bathurst mystery, finally pins down Bathurst's age, and we find that in *The Billiard Room Mystery* (1927), his first outing, he was a fresh-faced Bright Young Thing of twenty-two. How he can survive with his own rooms, at least two servants, and no noticeable source of income remains a mystery. One can also ask at what point in his life he travelled the world, as he has, at least, been to Bangkok at some point. It is, perhaps, best not to analyse Bathurst's past too carefully . . .

"Judging from the correspondence my books have excited it seems I have managed to achieve some measure of success, for my faithful readers comprise a circle in which high dignitaries of the Church rub shoulders with their brothers and sisters of the common touch."

For someone who wrote to entertain, such correspondence would have delighted Brian, and I wish he were around to see how many people have enjoyed the reprints of his work so far. *The Mystery of the Peacock's Eye* (1928) won Cross Examining Crime's Reprint Of The Year award for 2019, with *Tread Softly* garnering second place the following year. His family are delighted with the reactions that people have passed on, and I hope that this set of books will delight just as much.

Steve Barge

CHAPTER I
THE DISAPPEARANCE OF 'LEFTY' DONOVAN

ANTHONY Bathurst looked up and regarded Emily with some amount of mystification.

"You say that this lady insists on seeing me now?"

Emily nodded. "Yes, sir."

He glanced at his wrist-watch. "It's a quarter to eleven, Emily. Time all good Christians were in bed—to say nothing of indifferent ones."

"Yes, Mr. Bathurst, I know. I told her that she should have made an appointment with you. But she seems in such distress, sir, that I promised her I would ask you on her behalf. I hadn't the heart to turn her away. For one thing," added Emily with shrewd diplomacy, "she's wet through to the skin. It's a terrible night."

Anthony Bathurst went to the window and looked behind the blind across London. Emily was undeniably right. There was no exaggeration in her statement. A soaking rain which, earlier in the evening, had been a pernicious mist, had now entered its kingdom and set up a climatic condition of supreme misery. Anthony shivered at the mere sight of it. He walked back to his arm-chair by the fire. Emily proceeded to consolidate her position.

"If you could see her face, Mr. Bathurst . . . the state she's in . . . I feel sure you . . ."

Anthony waved a hand in her direction. "You win, Emily," he said quietly. "I present you with the sponge. Bring the lady up."

"Thank you, sir . . . and if I may say so, I'm grateful to you."

Emily disappeared on her errand with alacrity. Anthony prepared to receive his visitor. He heard Emily's voice on the stairs, and then the sound of ascending footsteps. Emily tapped on the door and at his invitation ushered in the lady who had called upon him so late.

"This is Mr. Bathurst," Emily said to her; "will you please come in?"

The girl in the background obeyed. Emily, flushed and successful, returned to her own haunts.

Anthony surveyed his visitor as she came towards him.

"Sit down . . . will you . . . and . . . er . . . make yourself quite comfortable. Come near the fire."

The girl took the chair he had indicated. She was certainly wet through as Emily had stated. Her clothes, utterly saturated, were clinging to her skin. Her hat was drenched and her gloves soddened. The water showed even in her hair. She was pretty by some standards. Dark appealing eyes haunted by fear and anxiety were companioned by heavy coils of dark hair. In normal conditions an almost insolent air of bravado would have been attractive. But now her face held pallor only, save for the lips which were bravely red and well shaped.

"Take your time," said Mr. Bathurst.

He walked to the sideboard. She heard the chink of glass. When he came back to her side he said "and drink this."

The girl made no demur. She took off her gloves and drank. The spirit brought a fleck of colour into her cheeks. Anthony sat opposite and waited for her to speak.

"Forgive me worrying you, sir. Especially seeing that it's so late. I'm sorry. But I'm pretty well all in and . . ."

She stopped. The tears which her voice held had mastered her words. Her voice surprised him. There was a rich quality about it although her accent was the accent of the working classes. Anthony put her down as Irish but he was wrong as he was to discover before the interview finished. Again he waited for her to recover herself. She dabbed at her eyes with the back of her fingers.

"I've come to you, sir, on the recommendation of an uncle of mine, a Mr. Bryant. He lives—or he used to live—down at Upchalke in the West Country. He always says how kind you were to him some years ago when his wife was murdered."

Anthony nodded sympathetically.

"I remember him and his trouble quite well. He was a good fellow. But tell me all about yourself and your present anxiety."

"My name is Flora Donovan."

Anthony flattered himself that his judgment of her nationality by her speech had been correct but in this direction he was destined for speedy disillusionment.

"It sounds an Irish name . . . and I suppose it is, but really I'm Scotch myself. I was Flora Gillespie before I married . . . my husband is 'Lefty' Donovan. He, of course, is Irish."

As she spoke the name, she gazed at Anthony anxiously. His eyes caught sight of the thin circlet on her wedding finger. He heard her repeat the name 'Lefty' Donovan.

The spoken name stirred a chord in his memory. 'Lefty' Donovan was one of the most promising heavyweights in the country. Indeed, he might be fairly described as almost the leading white hope to wrest in due time the championship of the world from the hands of the 'Brown Bomber,' Joe Louis.

But Flora Donovan was telling her story.

"We have been married three years . . . he's the boxer . . . I expect you've heard of him . . . and no girl could have wished for a better husband. Also . . . I have the dearest little girl . . . I'm telling you these things so that you may understand properly what our home life was like."

Anthony nodded again.

"I understand. Don't worry, you're doing splendidly. All those things help."

Flora Donovan shook her head helplessly. More tears kept her silent again. Finding courage she went on with her story.

"Today is the seventeenth of November. My husband has been missing now for exactly a week. I think that he must be dead. I'm sure that he must be dead. I can find no other explanation."

"Tell me all that has happened," prompted Mr. Bathurst quietly, "right from the beginning."

"I will try to. But it isn't easy. 'Lefty' had a letter that morning at breakfast time. That would be on the tenth of November. He seemed in two ways about it."

She paused.

"Tell me exactly what you mean, It's vitally important."

"He was pleased . . . and at the same time he was puzzled. And that's all I can tell you. Because that's all that I know."

Anthony felt a sense of dismay at the meagreness of the information. The blank wall had come all too quickly.

"What happened then, Mrs. Donovan? Surely your husband spoke to you about it? Said something?"

She nodded.

"Yes. 'Lefty' said that he'd had a grand offer but that it was so good he thought there must be something 'phoney' about it. You know what I mean?" she added anxiously.

Anthony smiled.

"Yes. That's all right. I understand. Go on."

"'Lefty' finished his breakfast almost without saying another word, put on his mackintosh and went out. Smiling and happy but quiet as though he were considering something. Kissed me and little Norah, the baby. He hadn't a care in the world. I'm sure he hadn't. That was the last time I saw him," she concluded simply.

Anthony leant forward to her eagerly.

"What was the letter like?"

"I think . . . I only caught a glimpse of it from my end of the table when I was pouring out the tea . . . that it was written on a piece of paper from an ordinary exercise book."

Anthony gestured his disappointment.

Flora Donovan continued.

"It was a 'grand offer.' I remember that 'Lefty' used those actual words to me. But I can tell you nothing more. When I asked him for more details, he sort of put me off. Please help me though, for if ever a woman needed help, I am that woman."

Anthony rose and paced the room. Suddenly he stopped and turned to her.

"Was your husband in training?"

"Yes. He always kept himself fit."

"But was he in *actual* training? As he would be, let us say, if he had a fight coming off a week or two ahead?"

Her answer was simple but direct.

"He had a fight just ahead. In about a month's time to be exact. At the Belfairs Stadium. He was matched against Phil Blood and would have actually started special training this week. There was a fairly big purse at the loser's end."

"Who's his trainer?"

"Sam Whitfield."

Anthony sat down and noted the name.

"His manager?"

"Jack Lambert."

Another note by Anthony.

"Now tell me where you live, Mrs. Donovan. I don't think that you've mentioned it so far."

"At Wimbledon. 22 Ploughman's Lane. Near the Stadium."

"Thank you, Mrs. Donovan. Now what have you done about all this besides coming to me?"

"I went to the police the same night. In the ordinary way, 'Lefty' would have been back that same day at midday."

"He gave you absolutely no indication of any kind as to where he was going?"

"No. Not the slightest. Just said 'out' as he often did. I was beside myself . . . from midday onward . . . when he did not return I mean . . . and when the evening came I just couldn't stand the strain and suspense any longer. So I put on my hat and coat and went to the police."

Anthony determined to test the issue.

"You have hidden nothing from me?"

She met his eyes with the utmost candour and frankness. "Nothing at all, sir."

"You had no quarrel of any kind with your husband?"

"Never," she replied proudly. Anthony saw the flash in her eyes.

"There was no other attachment?"

"For 'Lefty,' you mean?"

He nodded.

"Never on your life, Mr. Bathurst. He's a 'one-girl' man. And I'm a 'one-man' girl. That's the reason I'm so dreadfully worried. There's only one thing which could stop him coming back home. If he were dead."

She spoke the words white-faced and trembling.

Anthony was grave.

"And yet I can think of another reason, Mrs. Donovan. You'll agree with me too, when I tell you what it is."

"What is it you mean, sir?"

She looked at him in blank wonderment and acute anxiety.

"If he were being kept a prisoner somewhere and couldn't get back to you. Forcibly detained."

"Who would do that? And why should anyone do it? He's as straight a man as ever lived. Nobody's got anything on 'Lefty'."

"That's only as far as you know. Did he discuss most of his affairs with you, Mrs. Donovan?"

She nodded.

"Pretty well everything."

"And yet you admit that he only mentioned this particular letter you speak of in general terms? Gave you no details at all?"

"I know. I thought at the time that he would tell me about it afterwards."

Anthony was sympathetic.

"I expect he intended to. Now coming back to that letter . . . did you notice the postmark?"

Flora Donovan shook her head.

"No. I never looked at it. You see . . . when it came . . . it didn't matter to me . . . did it? All I know about it is that the envelope was a blue colour. A deepish sort of blue."

"H'm. There are no money difficulties, I suppose?"

"No, sir. We're not rich but we've never wanted for anything. 'Lefty's' steady and reliable. Always lets me have enough housekeeping money for our requirements. He's never once kept me short."

"Any post come for your husband since he disappeared?"

Flora Donovan shook her head.

"No, sir. Not a line."

"Who's looking after your little girl now?"

"A neighbour, sir. I told her I simply must go out this evening and she promised to mind little Norah. She's helped me before in that way. I suppose I must be getting back. But I feel a little better now that I have told you. All the same, I'm so afraid! For all our sakes. There's the baby besides me. I'm afraid that 'Lefty's' dead."

Her lips twitched convulsively.

Anthony found words of comfort for her.

"While there's life there's hope . . . and no news is good news which means that we aren't going to accept the worst until we know that the worst is inevitable. What's the matter, Mrs. Donovan?"

Anthony had suddenly noticed that the girl was staring straight in front of her with a strange expression in her eyes. "What is it?" he repeated.

"That blue envelope I mentioned to you, sir . . . I've just thought of something."

"Tell me," said Anthony ". . . please."

"I expect you'll think me fair daft not to have remembered it before but I've been that worried. I seemed to lose the power to think at all . . . but it's just come to me that when 'Lefty' went out . . . he gave the blue envelope to the baby to play with. She's able to make little lines with a pencil . . . something like big letters . . . and do you know, sir, I think I can see that blue envelope in the tray at the front of her high chair."

"If you're right, Mrs. Donovan . . . it's the best news you've as yet told me. That envelope may give me a starting-point."

She wrung her hands as she stood and faced him.

"Oh, if only I'd remembered it before and had thought to have brought it with me. It might have made all the difference."

This time the tears dropped from her eyes unchecked. Anthony made a quick decision.

"Don't you worry about that, Mrs. Donovan. That's an omission which can be very quickly mended. I'll tell you what—I'll come with you now and get the blue envelope. Assuming that the little girl hasn't damaged it too far beyond repair."

His eyes smiled at her and she caught something of his confidence.

"Oh, thank you, sir—saying that—you give me hope that I thought I could never have again."

"Wait here five minutes while I get my car. When I'm ready I'll tell Emily . . . that's my maid, who brought you up, to return the compliment and bring you down. I'll be waiting for you. Let's see . . . Wimbledon, you said, didn't you . . . well that won't take us very long . . . you just sit there in that chair and possess your soul in patience."

Mr. Bathurst was already moving quickly. She heard him on the staircase. When Mrs. Donovan heard the car draw up outside it happened almost simultaneously with Emily's arrival in the room again. Anthony made the pale-faced girl comfortable at the back. He started the car.

"You know, Mrs. Donovan," he said over his shoulder as it glided off, "I have known a postmark in the past tell me a very great deal. What do you say about this one?"

"I hope so, sir," she said.

"Here's hoping, too," replied Anthony Bathurst as he peered into the rain and darkness.

The car made the pace.

CHAPTER II
THE POSTMARK ON THE ENVELOPE

WHEN Anthony turned the car into Ploughman's Lane, it was raining even harder than before. The soft saturating drip of it had changed into a stinging lash and whereas before it had soaked your clothes insidiously and with malignant malice it now attacked you boldly with such sharp strokes that the mere wetness of it hit you much harder than previously and rebounded from you.

"Tell me the house, Mrs. Donovan," said Anthony, "so that I can pull up."

She nodded and at once issued directions.

"The one on the left—you can see it. With a light."

Anthony understood her and pulled up the car outside the appropriate house. A tall girl with a mop of fair hair and light blue eyes opened the door to Mrs. Donovan's soft knock. She looked with surprise at the car drawn up at the gate.

"It's all right, Mrs. Hayward," said Flora Donovan in explanation. "I'm back and thank you so much. How's—"

The fair girl anticipated the question.

"S'sh. The baby's all right. Don't worry. She's fast asleep. She whimpered a bit about an hour ago . . . but I went up to her and I got her off again. I'll slip out now quietly. That's all right. You'll do as much for me one day perhaps. See you in the morning."

She put her finger to her lips and slipped away. Flora Donovan pointed to an arm-chair.

"Sit down, Mr. Bathurst, please. Baby's high chair's in the back room. Her toys are all in there as well. If the blue envelope's anywhere about it will be in there. I'll go there now and see if I can find it. You don't mind stopping in here for a moment or two, do you, sir?"

"Carry on, Mrs. Donovan. I'll wait here in hope and patience."

With her face still wearing the far-away look he had noticed previously, Flora Donovan slipped out into the back room. Anthony could hear her moving about in there. Her footsteps were quick and decisive.

The room in which he sat was neat, tidy and above everything homely. Mr. Bathurst found more than ordinary pleasure in the sight. For one thing, it helped to confirm the impression of Mrs. Donovan which he had already formed. It helped to corroborate, too, a good deal of what she had told him. He heard more rapid movements and then the soft thud of something falling on the floor. The door of the room opened and he saw Mrs. Donovan come in. She held something in her hand. Anthony saw at once that it was a piece of crumpled blue paper. An envelope. *The* envelope! She was smiling at him. It was the first time he had seen her really smile. Besides smiling, she was listening.

"Just a moment, sir. I thought I heard the baby moving," she explained.

Anthony reassured her.

"It was only the rain on the windows."

Anthony went to the table where she smoothed out the blue envelope and held it out to him. The handwriting on it was thin and spidery.

"Not the handwriting," Anthony considered to himself, "of an educated person as the term would be generally applied and understood."

The address read 'Mr. Lefty Donovan, 22, Ploughman's Lane, Wimbledon.' Anthony's eyes went to the place of the postmark. It was plainly 'Barking.' He pointed to it.

"Barking, Mrs. Donovan, in Essex. We at least know now where the written offer came from. May I have this?"

"The envelope? Oh . . . of course . . . sir. Take it with you by all means."

"Now—tell me—because this is important. Did your husband have any friends or acquaintances at Barking, Mrs. Donovan?"

Flora Donovan shook her head at the question.

"Not that I know of, sir. I never heard him tell of any. I can't remember that he ever went there."

Anthony sat down again and looked into the remains of the fire. It had fallen low and the room was decidedly cold. The wife of 'Lefty' Donovan stood at his side, still, and suffering. Suddenly Anthony shivered. The girl showed instant sympathy.

"You're cold and wet, sir. Let me get you something. I shouldn't have dragged you out."

Anthony laughed it off and waved away the offer.

"I'm all right, Mrs. Donovan. The damp caught me for a second, that was all. I'll tell you what you *can* do for me, though, while I'm here. Give me the addresses of Lambert and—er—Whitfield, your husband's manager and trainer, will you? I meant to ask you for them when you were at my place but it slipped me. I shall have to get into touch with both of them."

Flora Donovan gave him the required information. Anthony noted it in his diary. Then he added as though he had come to a decision within himself.

"Did your husband gamble at all, Mrs. Donovan? To any extent, I mean?"

She shook her head without the slightest hesitation.

"No, sir, hardly at all. He might have a few shillings on a big race sometimes, like the Derby or the Grand National. But he never made anything like a habit of it."

"I see. Now another question. Any idea how much money he had in his possession when he went out on the morning of the tenth of November?"

"Not exactly. I couldn't give a figure and feel that I was being absolutely accurate. But I'm pretty certain in my own mind from what I know of the previous weekend and what he spent then that it would be under a pound. If I *had* to answer, I should say somewhere about fifteen shillings. Between fifteen shillings and a pound."

He nodded again at the information.

"I see."

Rising, he shook her by the hand.

"I'll get back to my own place, Mrs. Donovan. And I am glad we haven't wasted our time. We know more than we did. And I promise you that everything I can do, I will do. Where's the nearest 'phone that I can get you on if I should want you in a hurry?"

"Three houses away, Mr. Bathurst. Number sixteen. The name's Cannon. When you ring, ask for me, sir. They don't mind."

"What's the 'phone number?"

"Eight two . . . I'm not sure. It's silly of me. I ought to have . . ."

"Never mind. I'll look it up. It won't take me a second. The name's Cannon, you say, and I know the address. That's O.K. then. Good night, Mrs. Donovan and keep your chin up."

The last memory he had of her was of her white face and dark hair framed in the doorway as she closed the door behind him.

Anthony drove back to his flat deep in thought.

"I don't like it," he muttered to himself. "I don't like any of it. He's either being prevented from going home . . . by force . . . or else he'll never go home again . . . and if that's the case, I don't want the job of telling his missus. All the same though—I'd like to know 'why'."

He was still thinking over the problem when he got into bed. But whereas he slept, Flora Donovan did not.

Chapter III
THE NEWSAGENTS BY THE QUAY

ANTHONY drove down through the city along the East India Dock Road through Canning Town and East Ham into the Borough of Barking. He was able to park the car near the site of the old Abbey not unknown to William the Norman. He had made the journey more than once before and knew something, therefore, of the district in which he now found himself. He had purposely come in the early evening for the following reasons. There were more people about then than later, especially in and out of the shops. Inquiries attracted less attention then than when the shops were comparatively empty.

It was his idea that the blue envelope which had come to 'Lefty' Donovan and which he now carried in his pocket, had been purchased at an ordinary newsagent's, rather than at a more authentic stationer's.

Anthony decided to stroll round the streets of the Borough of Barking towards the older and poorer part of the town. With his back to the Abbey, he turned to the right. From the character of the various buildings which he passed, he judged that he was travelling in the direction of the old town quay.

The rain of the previous night had given way to a murky mist and a 'Regulator' of semi-derelict trams, which stood forlornly in the middle of the road, buttoned up his greatcoat to the chin and huddled himself against a high wall for shelter. Every few minutes a tram arrived at a funereal pace to what was evidently a terminus and another started going westward even more slowly.

A small newsagent's window on the other side of the street attracted Anthony's notice. He crossed over to it and looked at the wares it displayed. It seemed to stock most things from imitation hand-cuffs to ancient boat-race favours and bore the name 'H. Sand-sprite.' But neither notepaper nor envelopes seemed to be part of its stock-in-trade.

Mr. Bathurst walked on. But for the electric lights at reasonable intervals the place would have been dismal indeed. From where he was now, he could see the outline of the wharf and the general conditions of the quay. He could even discern the shape of a boat moored alongside. Probably it had carried timber in its hold. Here to be sure where he stood was an old-world setting, with a strong hint of the Low Countries.

It was at this precise moment that Anthony found a shop of the exact kind for which he had been looking. A newsagent's, with a window full of paper books, postcards, balls of string, paper fasteners and clips and, above all, to his intense gratification, many samples of cheap quality notepaper and envelopes.

Anthony pushed open the door and went in. A clanging bell announced his entry. A tall, lanky girl whom he judged to be in her 'teens came from the back of the premises to attend to him.

"I want a few envelopes and some sheets of notepaper, please."

"What colour would you like, sir?"

"Oh . . . I don't know. . . . I'm not over particular. May I glance at a few samples?"

"Certainly, sir. We have the ordinary white or cream-laid paper or if you prefer it, you can have grey or a blue-tinted paper. Those shades are very popular just now. With, of course, the envelopes to match."

"Thanks. I don't mind a blue. Something like this, if you have it."

He produced the envelope that had been posted from Barking to 'Lefty' Donovan. The girl looked at it appraisingly.

"Yes, I think that I can match that, sir. As a matter of fact we stock that particular make."

Anthony grinned at her. There were comfort and good-fellowship in that grin and the lanky girl recognized the fact. More than that— she responded to it. Anthony knew that this response was there, waiting for him to develop it. He gestured towards the used envelope.

"As a good saleswoman, you'll be telling me next that not only do you stock that particular brand, but that you recognize the hand-writing on the envelope as well. And I shall reply, 'Come come, little lady—that's just a trifle *too* steep.'"

There was challenge in his tone and intended challenge at that and the girl, now thoroughly on her mettle, cocked her head side-ways at the Donovan envelope. To Anthony's joy the eyes began to bulge from that same head. He knew now for a certainty that his shot had been a lucky one and had gone straight home.

"Yes," she cried excitedly, "I can even do that. I do recognize the handwriting and that's a fact."

"It's more than that," returned Anthony with ostentatious admir-ation in both voice-tone and look, "It's a most amazing coincidence . . . besides being a tremendous tribute to your powers of observa-tion. Well . . . let's put it to the test . . . tell me the name of the writer and then I can see if you're right or not. Not pulling my leg. After all, you must prove your claims, you know."

He smiled at her again. She gave him the name he so urgently desired to hear.

"Joe Bellamy or 'Banjo,' as they call him round here. Well—am I right?"

Anthony smiled sympathetically.

"You most certainly are, young lady. And I heartily congratulate you. I would never have believed it. Give me a dozen sheets of notepaper and the same number of the blue envelopes. When I see 'Banjo,' I'll tell him of the extent of his reputation."

He laughed merrily and the girl behind the counter added her laugh to his.

"How much do I owe you?" asked Mr. Bathurst.

"Sixpence, if you please, sir."

Anthony found the required coin and handed it over. Then he tried another bow at a venture.

"There's one thing about old 'Banjo'," he said, "there's no mistaking him, is there? Once you've seen him you'll never forget it. I mean he's distinctive, isn't he? You can pick him out in a crowd."

The girl looked at him with? certain amount of wonderment. For a split second he thought that he had made a *faux pas* and that this second shaft had missed the mark. The girl's face cleared, however.

"You mean that swelling on his neck? I wondered at first. What do they call those things—the proper name, I mean? I can never remember the word."

It was a 'sitter.' Anthony took it one hand.

"Don't you mean a 'wen'?" he remarked.

The lanky girl nodded in confirmation. Quickly and with decision.

"Yes. That's it—a 'wen'."

Anthony smiled at her, wished her good evening and turned to the door. Outside the shop, he waited to look in the window again.

"What a stroke of luck," he communed with himself, "with an added *soupçon* of 'finesse'. There's one thing—I know where I go to from here which I certainly didn't know before."

He walked towards the brighter lights of the town itself. He already had a plan in his mind. Unless he were very much mistaken, Bellamy would be a man who could be easily traced. Especially in a place of the character of Barking. Anthony came to a hostelry which promised both comfort and refreshment.

He made his way to the saloon bar, where he ordered a tankard of beer. The apartment was crowded. Anthony waited for his chance to present itself. Eventually, a short, compactly-built, middle-aged man found a place at the bar at Mr. Bathurst's side. Very soon he had beer on his moustache.

Anthony watched him for a few minutes in an attempt to size him up. A commonplace colloquialism broke the ice and led the way to what became almost a conversation. Anthony skilfully steered it into the particular channels which suited him. At length he clinched the issue.

"By the way," he said almost casually, "do you happen to know a man named Bellamy? I believe he lives near here—'Banjo' Bellamy he's called as a rule. Fellow with a wen on his neck."

"Know him well," said the middle-aged man with pungent satisfaction, "he's a Barking man born and bred. Been in the town all his life. Everybody round here knows him. He might be in the 'four-ale' bar at this very moment. There are more unlikely things than that, mister."

"Go on. As far as I can remember he used to live just along there by the—"

Mr. Bathurst paused with subtle artistry—-as though he had temporarily forgotten an unimportant detail. His companion entered the trap almost eagerly. The jaws closed on him.

"By the town wharf. That's right. The third house on the right as you come up from the quay. 'Banjo's' grandfather lived there in the days of the big explosion. It was a wonder the old boy wasn't blown to bu—glory—with the rest of them. Too artful, I expect."

Anthony ordered two more beers. It was a gesture of generosity. He intended to dispose of his own more rapidly than he had disposed of its predecessor. On the whole he had done a most satisfactory evening's work. He was undecided, however, as to his next step.

He drank up, wished his new acquaintance 'Good night' and sauntered back to the vicinity of the quay, the stationer's shop and the abode of 'Banjo' Bellamy and his grandfather before him.

The third house on the right as you walked up from the wharf. A mere hundred yards away now. Anthony slowed down his pace. The whirring of a gramophone record came from the open window of a house nearby. Anthony's ears caught the words of the song "When the Broadway Baby says good night, it's early in the morning." . . .

At that moment he found himself outside the house which by all dead reckoning should be the house of 'Lefty' Donovan's correspondent. 'Lefty'—'Banjo'!

An idea came to him as he considered the associations of the two sobriquets. Was Bellamy, by chance, an old 'pug'? And in that connection linked with Donovan? There were more improbable things than that.

The house he looked at was small and squalid. Not a light showed from it. Mr. Bathurst wondered concerning Bellamy's *'entourage.'* As he wondered he made up his mind. He had his man's name, he had his man's house and also certain details of his man's appearance—he would take no further action for the time being.

Thus decided he started to walk back to the place where he had left his car. He had gone but a few yards when a burly figure came towards him out of the mist and darkness. Anthony saw that it was a solidly-built man who wore a dark, plum-coloured pullover high to his neck.

To Anthony's surprise this man stopped abreast of him. He held an unlighted cigarette between two fingers.

"Excuse me, mister," he said in a voice from which the milk of human kindness had been drained, "but could you oblige me with a light? I've run short of matches."

Anthony at once plunged his hand into his overcoat pocket. Coincidentally, something very much akin to a well-filled sandbag hit him on the point of the jaw. As he fell, his last conscious thought was of the face in front of him. On the side of the neck there was a large wen!

CHAPTER IV
THINGS BEGIN TO MOVE

ANTHONY Bathurst does not know how long he was 'out.' For several reasons. When he came back to consciousness he was still lying on the pavement but it was a different slab of pavement from that which he had struck so forcibly at the hands or rather fist of Comrade

Bellamy. His head throbbed unceasingly and the point of his jaw felt as though it had been kicked well and truly by Blue Peter himself.

As he lay on this new portion of pavement, he seemed to be partly supported by a wall about three feet in height and the sound of voices came to him from but a short distance away. It had become very dark. He scrambled to his feet and listened. The surroundings were quite unfamiliar to him but he felt certain that the noise of hilarious conversation that he could hear was coming from a 'pub' which must be close at hand.

A few seconds later his idea was confirmed. He had taken a few paces towards the building when a singularly fruity voice floated down the road.

"Good evening, Mrs. Leslah . . . hah yah . . . two tankards of bittah please, and an ounce of 'Cut Golden Bah.' Thank yah."

Anthony looked at his watch. It had stopped—probably at the moment when Bellamy had struck him. Mr. Bathurst smiled ruefully. Ah, well—tomorrow was also a day and he might have the pleasure of meeting Mr. Bellamy again. The first job he had to do at the moment was to discover exactly where it was that friend Bellamy or his auxiliaries had so considerately brought him. He was not long in finding out. A small Post-Office gave indications that the district was Gidea Park. The actual spot where either Bellamy or Bellamy's agents had deposited him was midway between two public-houses.

"This precious stone," murmured Anthony to himself, "set in the silver sea. Two precious stones!"

Men have been known before to stagger and fall when leaving establishments of this nature. Anthony stood outside the ramshackle Post-Office and deliberated. A man approached. He attempted to take stamps from a machine outside the Post-Office. Anthony heard him curse because the machine was empty.

Eventually Anthony resolved to hire a car and return to the parking-place in Barking where he had left his own. The squaring of accounts with Bellamy would have to wait for a future occasion. Actually he was able to find a garage and be back by his own car within the space of half an hour. This accomplished, he drove at once to his flat. Once here, he went immediately to the telephone. He wanted more than a word with Chief-Inspector Andrew Mac-

Morran of Scotland Yard. He was pleased to hear MacMorran himself answer the ring. For once in a while, the Inspector's voice was music in Anthony Bathurst's ear.

"Who's there?"

"Bathurst," returned Anthony.

"Good Lord. That's the very last name I was expectin' to hear. I thought you'd gone abroad or something. And what have you got to say to me at this time of the night?"

"Busy, Andrew?"

"Ay. More or less. Chiefly more. Crime's flourishin' these days. What's your private trouble, Mr. Bathurst?"

Anthony told him first of all of 'Lefty' Donovan's disappearance and of Flora Donovan's distress. MacMorran clicked his tongue. Anthony heard it distinctly. He proceeded to tell the Inspector more. Of the blue envelope and where it had led him.

"Of course," said MacMorran, "if you *will* try to do these things off your own bat—you'll get precious little sympathy from me. One of these days you'll run your head against something that'll hur-rt you."

Anthony chuckled.

"O wise and upright judge! An Andrew come to judgment! As a matter of fact, you old ruffian, I did this evening. Only it wasn't my head. It was my chin." Anthony went on to recount what had happened to him from the moment Bellamy had stopped him and asked him for a light. MacMorran guffawed down the telephone.

"Eh—but that was too bad. Takin' you for a sucker like that."

"Never mind about that, Andrew. Tell me what you know of the Reverend 'Banjo.' That is, if you know anything."

"That's askin' me. I can't manage to recall anything—and that's a fact. The name's unfamiliar."

"Well—do something for me, then. At once. And trust me with regard to it. As you have so often in the past. Put a couple of your best men on his tail. Pronto. Unless I'm very much mistaken, Bellamy is mixed up in a spot of exceedingly dirty work."

"H'm. Don't know about that. You haven't a rare lot to go on, Mr. Bathurst—now have you?"

It was obvious from the reply that the Inspector was dubious. Anthony's voice became grave. The Inspector was suitably impressed.

"Well, Andrew, I'm going to say this. I don't think that Donovan will ever go home again to his wife and child."

"You don't? What do you mean exactly by that remark?"

"Just this. Nothing more and nothing less. I think that Donovan's dead. Do you get that?"

"Eh—don't say that. It isn't like you to look on the black side."

"Nevertheless, I do think so," replied Anthony with dogged emphasis.

"You're hintin' at murder, Mr. Bathurst? Is that the idea?"

"You've said it, Andrew. I'm very definitely hinting at murder."

MacMorran let go a prolonged whistle.

"Eh—but I don't like the sound of that."

"Well then, do as I ask you. Send a couple of men down there—*now*. I'll tell you exactly where it is. Now is that a bet?"

"Give me the details and I'll consider it."

"Listen to me then, you super Didymus."

Anthony detailed directions. MacMorran noted them. Anthony rang off and then, the line having cleared, dialled another number. A woman's voice answered him.

"Is that Mrs. Cannon? . . . will you be good enough to ask Mrs. Donovan to speak. Mrs. Donovan at Number Twenty-Two . . . oh, certainly . . . I'll wait for her with pleasure."

When Flora Donovan came, Anthony was quick and explicit.

"Any news for me, Mrs. Donovan? It's Bathurst this end."

She told him 'none.'

"Not a word of any kind." Her voice held a cold resignation.

"I'm sorry. But don't despair yet. You mustn't—for 'Lefty's' sake keep your chin up. By doing so it may be that you will help 'Lefty.' Now I want you to listen to me carefully. Have you ever heard your husband mention the name of Bellamy? Think very carefully."

Her answer came to him in the negative.

"You're quite sure you haven't?"

"Certain, Mr. Bathurst."

"Ever heard him speak of the name 'Banjo'?"

There was a pause. Anthony had the strange fancy that he could almost hear her thinking. But her reply came at last. Similar to her previous answers. The name 'Banjo' was entirely unfamiliar to her.

"All right," responded Anthony. "Never mind—I was just testing an idea of mine—and don't be discouraged. I'll try to ring you some time to-morrow evening . . . unless I get through to you before, of course. Which, in that case will mean good news for you. Good night, Mrs. Donovan." Anthony hung up. But he shook his head gravely as he did so. The lump on his jaw was sore and exceedingly tender. He decided to go to bed. He went to bed.

Five minutes after midnight, he was awakened by his 'phone ringing. He crawled out of bed to answer it. He was rewarded for the effort. MacMorran was at the other end.

"You," said Anthony, "are more than inconsiderate. You are almost sadistic. No punishment would be too appalling for you. I was asleep."

"Listen, Mr. Bathurst," said the Inspector. "I'm sorry and all that to disturb you, I'm sure . . . but you'd rather know than not know."

"All nice girls would, Andrew . . . I'm surprised at you ringing me to tell me that."

"Listen," cut in MacMorran doggedly. "I sent two men down to Barking immediately following our previous conversation. I listened to you—you see—after all. Two *good* men. Drummond and Markham. Both used to that particular kind of work. What do you think they found when they got there?"

"I'll try one. The cupboard was bare. How's that, Andrew?"

"You're right in one. Your old school friend Bellamy had gone . . . lock, stock and barrel."

"I'll bet the last was the most important from his point of view. Quick work though, Andrew. Don't you agree?"

"Quick! My conscience! This is Bellamy—that was."

"Did your chaps make any enquiries?"

"Only one *very* discreet one. I told them to watch their step and be careful. At the pub opposite. 'The Three Curlews.' Bellamy moved about nine o'clock. So they were told. He had little to go with him. A small van turned up and exit Bellamy. We're trying to trace the van now."

"No grass on his soles is there, Andrew? Seems to be as quick with his feet as his fists."

"That's just about what I thought."

"Oh, you did, did you? Well snap out of it and think of something else for a change. What about 'Lefty' Donovan now?"

"You saying that brings me to something else." MacMorran's tone changed.

Anthony at once reacted to the difference. He knew his Mac-Morran inside out. He could hear MacMorran speaking again.

"I'm going to read you something I've dug out from our files. I had something like a brain-wave and turned them up. The first is a police message which originally came from the authorities up in the Midlands. Are you fit? Right! 'MISSING. TED BAILEY. AGE 24. HEIGHT 6 ft. 1½ in. WEIGHT 12 st. 11 lbs. Dark hair. Mole on chest. Brown eyes. Teeth regular. Well-cut features. Well-known Boxer, not only in the Midlands district but all over the country. The missing man left his home at 22 Tresadern Street, Northampton, at 10 o'clock in the morning of Friday, February 16th last and has not been seen since. Will any person who . . .'"

"Cut the blah," said Anthony quietly, "and tell me the rest. Something's coming back to me about that case—"

MacMorran at the other end obeyed.

"Nothing more was heard of Bailey in any shape or form until the 27th of the same month. A period of eleven days. I'll read that to you as well from the newspapers. 'Missing Boxer Found Drowned. The body of Ted Bailey, the missing Northamptonshire boxer was washed ashore at Worthing to-day. It was clothed in flannel trousers and open-neck shirt and bore every appearance of having been in the water for some days, as the face and the upper part of the body bore many signs of severe mutilation.' Now hear what was said at the inquest. 'Dr. Grandison, the local Divisional Surgeon, gave it as his opinion that these marks and cuts on the body had been probably caused after death by the body having been struck into by either a rowing-boat or possibly having been washed against the iron supports of Worthing pier.' There were what he described as 'lacerations.' There was no direct evidence forthcoming as to how Bailey got into the water. Doctor Grandison upon being further questioned by the Coroner thought that Bailey, who is reported to have been but a moderate swimmer, may have committed suicide by jumping from the end of the pier. The jury returned a verdict of 'Found Drowned'."

Anthony was silent.

"Well?" asked MacMorran.

"And that," said Anthony quietly, "took place nine months ago."

"It sure did."

"I wonder . . . if that motor-van that moved Bellamy went south."

"It's no good wondering," said MacMorran, "go back to bed and sleep on it. You can't do better than that for the time being. I'm just off home . . . to the missus."

"Good night, Andrew. And many thanks."

Anthony hung up once again. Sleep, however, was far off. The cold white pain which had showed on the face of Flora Donovan had crept towards him. Had been creeping towards him now for nearly two days. . . . It was going to get him. Get under his skin. Anthony Bathurst clenched his teeth, then he shook his head with a gesture of hopelessness. He must be at work first thing in the morning. See MacMorran and ask him . . . if he had been able to . . .

CHAPTER V
LOOSE ENDS

THE morning brought Anthony no consolation. Enquiries of Mac-Morran by telephone elicited the further disturbing news that his two plain-clothes men had been unable to obtain any clue of value as to the identification of the small motor-van which had been employed to transport the goods and chattels of Bellamy from Barking in Essex to an unknown destination. They reported, however, that Bellamy was a bachelor who had lived 'on his own' for many years and had little to take with him in the shape of worldly goods when it came to the question of a quick 'get-away' from anywhere. Nobody knew to whom the van had belonged or the number plate that it had carried and it was even suggested that it might well be the property of Bellamy himself. Markham, however, had gone to the local licensing office, administering the Road Fund, and had satisfied himself that this suggestion of Bellamy's possible ownership was unfounded. Bellamy, according to the office records, was the owner of a driving licence but not of a vehicle. That is, of course, as far as any official registration went. This news made Anthony more impatient than ever. So much so that he decided to get at the heart of things and call on Donovan's manager, Lambert.

Flora Donovan had given him an address in Fleet Street. When he got there, he found that Lambert had a room over a tailor's shop. Anthony ascended the somewhat dingy staircase, walked down a corridor partly covered with a length of cheap coconut matting and knocked on a door which bore Lambert's name.

The man who invited him to enter was stout, jovial and rubicund. His face was built over a tier of chins. His eyes were black like currants pushed into dough. He sat in his shirt-sleeves at a desk littered with papers. A telephone was at his elbow. To Anthony's eye he looked more like a sub-editor than anybody else. Anthony introduced himself at once. He made no bones about the purpose of his call.

"In the matter of 'Lefty' Donovan," he added quietly.

Jack Lambert pushed back his ample chair, heaved up his ample abdomen and stared at him in surprise.

"May I sit down?" enquired Mr. Bathurst cordially.

"Sure. But I thought you were somebody else. Somebody I was expecting by appointment. Just about this time, too." Lambert consulted a large watch. The action was ostentatious. "I can spare you exactly three and a half minutes. Not a second more."

"That's most charming of you. One can do a lot in that time. Even in the same number of seconds—upon occasion."

Lambert grinned at the pleasantry, but the grin was not one of geniality.

"What's your business?" he barked.

"I told you. I thought I'd made myself perfectly clear. In the matter of 'Lefty' Donovan. Due, I believe, to meet Phil Blood at the Belfairs Stadium about the middle of next month. If my information be correct."

Lambert grunted.

"Not much information about it. Matter of common knowledge."

"All the better," returned Anthony; "in that case we need make no secret of our conversation. Which will suit me very well. I said just now '*Due* to meet'."

Lambert glared.

"I heard what you said and I know very well what you mean. But I'm not putting the shutters up yet. That's not Jack Lambert's way. 'Lefty'll be back to-day most likely. If not to-day—well then, by to-morrow. If not by to-morrow—by the end of the week. What's the use of screaming before you're hit? Don't believe in it. Never did. Do you? And by the way, mister, I didn't catch your name properly— where exactly do you figure in 'Lefty' Donovan's outfit?"

Anthony carelessly crossed a leg as he answered the question.

"Suppose we say, for want of a better association . . . Scotland Yard."

Lambert's pudgy fingers caressed his chin . . . uncertainly.

"And . . . er . . . by the way . . . as you just said, Mr. Lambert . . . my three and a half minutes are just up . . . may I take it that . . . ?"

"Go on," returned Lambert curtly. "I'm listening."

"Thank you," said Anthony, "now in that case we can talk intelligently. Both of us, that is. Something I'd like to know. What does Whitfield think about things?"

"Couldn't tell you. Not one of my accomplishments, reading people's thoughts."

"What does he *say*?"

"'Lefty' wasn't in strict training," returned Lambert sullenly. "He wasn't under Sam Whitfield's care night and day. Sam wouldn't be playing nursemaid—not until next week."

"Interesting—but it hardly answers my question."

Lambert shrugged his bulky shoulders.

"Sam Whitfield's worried same as I am. Same as we all are. No good sayin' he isn't. But he knows no more than I do, which is nothing. All the same—that doesn't stop me having ideas." Lambert thrust his hands into his trousers pockets and stared at the floor.

"What do you mean?" asked Anthony with direct emphasis.

"Well—why do men leave home? Haven't you ever heard?" Lambert leered unpleasantly. "Maybe they prefer blondes."'

"Somehow," said Anthony, "I don't think so in this particular case. Good men sleep at home." He spoke deliberately.

"You never know," pronounced Lambert.

"Neither do you," returned Anthony ever so pleasantly. Lambert seemed a little taken aback at the unexpected rejoinder.

"Surely," went on Mr. Bathurst, "there are financial interests at stake? No fight at the Belfairs, I suppose, will mean a loss to somebody?"

"It will," replied Lambert gloomily, "me included."

"So you won't talk?"

"Nothing to say, Captain, at the moment. 'Lefty' Donovan's gone. He'll either come back—or he won't—and that's all there is to it. Search me for anything more. And that's flat. Scotland Yard or no Scotland Yard."

Anthony smiled—but he was anxious all the same. He rose from his chair. As he did so, he heard voices from below. A strident voice dominated the other. Anthony could hear words plainly. "Very well, I'm going up." Anthony waited. Mainly because he had noticed that Lambert showed distinct signs of uneasiness. As he stood there expectant, the door of the room opened and a man entered.

He would have attracted attention anywhere, but actually Anthony knew him directly he came into the room, from the many photographs he had seen of him in the press. The man was Sir Cloudesley Slade, the celebrity who, with Lord Lonsdale, was perhaps the most popular figure in the sporting world of the day. Tall and thin, with fierce light-blue eyes and a large jutting nose, two deep lines made ravines in his cheeks. His hands were thrust hard in his pockets and his hat was tilted at the back of his head. The blue eyes were deep-set and commanded with a truculent domination whatever he looked at, whether it be person or inanimate object. He regarded Anthony almost insolently but at the same time there was a rough and rugged cordiality in the insolence.

"I want you, Lambert," he said in the same strident voice Anthony had heard before, "and this is the time I arranged. Now what the hell are you up to?"

"Very good, Sir Cloudesley," said Lambert, "I am at your service. As always, Sir Cloudesley. But perhaps . . . er . . . I—"

"Perhaps what," cut in the tall man—"I don't understand."

Lambert shuffled to his feet and propped himself against his table.

"This gentleman here . . . is from Scotland Yard."

Sir Cloudesley was round like a flash.

"Scotland Yard," he barked . . . "again I don't understand. What have you been doing, Lambert? Lost your dog or something?"

Anthony repeated the phrase that he had used to Lambert.

"In the matter of 'Lefty' Donovan."

Sir Cloudesley lifted his eyebrows. This time there was no doubt about the insolence.

"What has the Yard to do with 'Lefty' Donovan?"

"Let us say that it is interested in the matter of his disappearance, on behalf of Donovan's wife. A missing husband, you see, is as important as a missing heavyweight."

Slade turned to Lambert.

"Explain to me, will you, Lambert? I'm frankly in the dark. I don't like being in the dark. It don't suit me."

"I was about to, Sir Cloudesley. That's the main reason I asked you to call here this morning. It's like this. Donovan's gone. Vanished. Clean as smoke. Not a breath or a squeak of him for over a week. I felt in the circumstances you ought to know. That's the dope I had for you."

"You thought I ought to know," repeated Sir Cloudesley slowly and ominously—"now that's bloody good of you."

Lambert was obviously nervous. More now than he had been at the time of Sir Cloudesley's entrance. Anthony waited.

"What have you done?" demanded Slade. His face bristled with fierce impatience and his eyes gleamed with aggression.

"Nothing," replied Lambert.

"Nothing?" bawled Slade.

Lambert shook his head weakly.

"What could I do?"

"Well there's one thing—if you blew your brains out, there'd be no mess to speak of to clean up. And where the hell do I stand while you numskulls are so busy doing nothing? I suppose a cool five thousand's chicken feed to you—eh?"

Lambert shrugged his shoulders with a gesture of helpless resignation. He was badly scared—that was plain. Slade stormed on. His rage increased.

"And how long have you known these joyful tidings—eh, Lambert?"

"Since last Thursday, Sir Cloudesley."

"And who told you, may I ask?"

"Sam. Sam Whitfield. He rang me last Thursday evening. Said he was by way of being worried. He'd heard nothing from 'Lefty' since the Monday afternoon previous. So he had got into touch with Mrs. Donovan—and she had put him wise."

"I see. And you, I suppose, have sat on your great fat backside ever since?"

This time Lambert judged it prudent to keep silent. Sir Cloudesley Slade removed his hat and sat down. He wiped his forehead with a handkerchief. Anthony could see that despite his bold front, the news had disturbed him. Again Anthony waited for the next move. Rather surprisingly, it came from Slade to him.

"The point is, my dear Mr. Policeman in Disguise, that if I don't produce a man to beat Blood on the twelfth of next month, I stand to lose a little matter of five thousand Jimmy o'Goblins. As Mister Lambert here and Mister Whitfield know—as well as I know it myself. And do you know—I'd have banked the whole of my fortune on 'Lefty'. On his character and personal integrity, I mean. A blasted skirt, I suppose—when we get to the rights of it. That's why his missus has got the wind up. Ten to one on it."

Anthony shook his head.

"I don't think so, Sir Cloudesley, somehow. But since you've been good enough to tell me so much—perhaps you wouldn't mind telling me a little more. Your wager is, I presume, a side-stake?"

Slade shook his head.

"Not exactly. I'm keen on the fight game and dearly like a gamble. I think Blood's going downhill and was prepared to back my opinion. I've thought that of him for a long time now. Lambert here came in with me, and 'Snick' Jefferson promoted the scrap."

"Whom's your own bet with, Sir Cloudesley?"

"Marcus Secretan. He nominated Blood. I expect you've heard of Secretan. Tons of money. Festoons of jewellery. Hairy heels. Have I said enough?"

The blue eyes gleamed.

"I see. That information may prove to be of assistance to me. As a *quid pro quo*, I may now be able to pass certain news on to you. Donovan had a letter on the morning of his disappearance. He told his wife that this letter contained an offer. An attractive offer. Upon receipt of it, Donovan went out almost immediately. Donovan didn't come back. Donovan hasn't come back. What's it feel like to you, Sir Cloudesley? I confess I'd like to know."

Slade started up.

"Sink me . . . do you hear this, Lambert?"

Lambert looked at him hopelessly.

"That's Mrs. Donovan's story, Sir Cloudesley. I don't know that we need attach too great an importance to it. After all, she's a woman and—"

Sir Cloudesley Slade's voice broke in upon him like the crack of a whip.

"What the hell are you talking about, Lambert? A woman! What do you expect Donovan's wife to be? A box of kippers? Why wasn't I informed of this business before? Why has it been kept from me until now? Am I Donovan's chief backer or not? Tell me that. Whose money's at stake? Mine or Robinson Crusoe's?"

Lambert made yet a further helpless gesture with his hands. At this stage of affairs, Anthony deemed it sound policy to ask a question.

"Your bet, Sir Cloudesley. About producing a man to beat Phil Blood on the twelfth of next month. Does that mean Donovan only, by actual nomination—or would any man fill the bill from your side of the picture?"

Slade turned and stared at him curiously.

"Damn it—that's an idea. I hadn't thought of it in that light. It must be a man round about the weight and of course not a past champion or belt-holder. But why do you ask? I don't quite see. What's your point exactly?"

Anthony smiled at him easily.

"I just wanted to know where you stood—precisely. That was all."

Slade became grave again.

"All the same . . . it's as broad as it's long, I'm afraid, when you get down to brass tacks. So far as my knowledge goes, Donovan's the only man in this country who stands an earthly against Blood. I know every man in the game—and I'm aware of that all right. There's a boy at Bath—Mike Jago—but I fancy he wants another two years before he'll come to his full strength. He's a bonny fighter but there you are."

Lambert sat at his table like an animal caught in a trap. Waiting for the finale that it knows is inevitable. His eyes held a hunted look. On the other hand, Sir Cloudesley's blue eyes were looking into the distance.

"Let's get back to this Donovan disappearance business," he said at length, "looks to me as though he's been nobbled. Good and proper. Like in the old days. Been got at. Dirty work somewhere. And not necessarily at the cross-roads."

He selected a cigar from his case with infinite care, bit off the end with an almost impudent relish and stuck the cigar in the corner of his mouth.

"Don't like it," he went on as he struck a match. "I'll tell you what my great-grandfather used to say. Sir Hugo Slade he was, and knew every bit of what he was talking about. Been a Corinthian in his early days. 'Put your money on a horse or a dog or a—but never on a man. Why? He can talk! Never back anything that can open its mouth to speak. If you do, you'll be let down as sure as eggs are eggs. I've heard my father quote that dozens of times. Looks as though it would have paid me to have taken his advice. Donovan's been decoyed. Not a doubt of it. Very likely he'll never see the ring on the twelfth—let alone climb inside it in a dressing-gown."

He glared at each of his listeners as though inviting their opinions. Anthony tangented.

"You mentioned a Bath boy a moment or so ago, Sir Cloudesley. As a highly promising heavyweight. Mike Jago. I keep in touch with the fight game myself . . . just a little . . . on the surface. Wasn't there another very likely lad supposed to be coming along in the news a short time ago? I can't recall his name at the moment. Let me see now . . . what was that boy's name? . . . I had it on the tip of my tongue a moment ago. . . ."

Anthony rubbed his hand across his forehead as though in an effort of remembrance. Sir Cloudesley nodded in obvious approval.

"I know the chap you mean very well."

Lambert was biting at the butt end of a pencil. His fingers drummed nervously on the table in front of him. Slade went on.

"The man you're thinking of was Bailey—the Northampton boy. Ted Bailey. A nailing good boxer, too. I had the luck to see him fight two or three times. I saw him beat Denny Moran at Dreamland in five rounds about this time last year. Lovely scrap from start to finish. No huggin' and clinchin'—but real slap bang all the way. Oh yes . . . he was good . . . very good. But he came to a bad end."

Anthony shook his head.

"I can't recall . . . what happened to him . . . it's eluded me."

Sir Cloudesley shrugged his shoulders.

"I know what you're thinking of. It came to me directly you mentioned his name. The poor fellow committed suicide. Down at the seaside somewhere."

"That's it," cried Anthony. "He jumped in the water. After being reported missing for some time. I remember the circumstances now. Yes, sad . . . very sad."

Sir Cloudesley was frowning heavily.

"This talk's all hot air. Not getting us anywhere. Damned useless, all of it. Simply wasting our time. What the hell's Ted Bailey got to do with 'Lefty' Donovan? No connection at all. Nothing whatever to do with each other."

"Both boxers, Sir Cloudesley," remonstrated Anthony quietly . . . "and both promising lads. Of the heavyweight class."

As Anthony Bathurst spoke, Slade swung round on to Lambert who sat in his chair following every word that was spoken with unmistakable indications of anxiety.

"Did you know Ted Bailey at all, Lambert? Did he ever steer your way?"

Lambert shook his head.

"Never, Sir Cloudesley. Never met him. Knew *of* him from reports—naturally. He was coming along nicely—that lad. All the best judges were agreed on that. Terrible pity."

"So you never ran across him yourself? Your misfortune, Lambert. You missed a treat. Secretan himself was very . . ."

He paused suddenly and the cigar cocked up in his mouth. It seemed that he was considering a possibility that had just presented itself to him. He leered impishly at Anthony.

"Not altogether inconvenient for friend Secretan—eh—if Donovan fails to appear on the 12th prox? Damn my eyes—I'm too slow to catch cold—I hadn't thought of it like that."

He licked his lips—almost hungrily.

"I wonder. Marcus Secretan Esquire . . . if I thought you'd pull a fast one on me like that—I'd—"

He broke off with surprising abruptness and shot out a hand towards Anthony.

"You see it's like this. Although I know Secretan well, and meet him frequently, I don't like him. I'm afraid I'm a creature of likes and dislikes. Take after my mother. Can't help it. Born in me, I suppose. This business has made me think. And think darned hard! Lambert!"

The man addressed jerked himself into some measure of attention.

"Yes, Sir Cloudesley."

"Listen to me, Lambert. With both your ugly ears. I don't intend to weigh out that five thousand quid without a struggle. No, sir! And I'm looking to you to help me. Not that I think you're a lot of good. Frankly, I don't. I was never one to call a spade a bloody shovel. But you're better than nothing. Just a little. I'm not lying down to have my pockets rifled by any 'Four by Two.' You've got to get 'Lefty' Donovan back—at all costs. That's your job. And if you fail it'll be the worse for you. D'ye hear me, Lambert?"

"Yes, Sir Cloudesley. I hear. But how can I?"

Lambert spread his hands helplessly.

"I haven't a shred of evidence to work on. You're asking a pretty big thing of me, Sir Cloudesley."

Slade glared at him almost vindictively.

"I didn't know that you were a blasted Croesus, Lambert. I seem to be acquirin' knowledge. I should have thought that you would have wanted to put up a scrap for your share that's going west as much as I do. If you don't, of course, and you can afford to throw your few hundred down the drain—well, that's your funeral."

He relapsed into a strange sullenness and sat there with folded arms. Lambert glanced across at Anthony. The glance held both criticism and resignation. Anthony, however, had no comment to contribute. For a man with a watching brief and speculative at that, he hadn't done at all badly. Slade came back to his former condition of exasperation.

"I'm just beginning to wonder if Secretan knew anything when he made the wager. I have an idea the swine seemed over-eager at the time. I suppose that should have shown me the red light."

He rose and walked up and down the room impatiently, his hat tilted on the back of his head and his hands thrust deep into his trouser pockets. He reminded Anthony of a fierce eagle. Lambert's trepidation was most obviously increasing. He watched Sir Cloudesley's movements with a look of fascinated fear. More than once he opened his mouth to speak and then seemed to think better of it. Suddenly and almost challengingly—the telephone bell rang. Lambert looked uncertainly at Sir Cloudesley Slade.

"Damn it all, man," cried the latter impatiently, "answer the thing. Don't sit there gaping at it."

"Y-yes, Sir Cloudesley. . . . I w-will."

Lambert picked up the receiver.

"Lambert speaking . . . yes . . . yes."

Anthony and Sir Cloudesley Slade watched him with something more than merely ordinary interest. They saw large beads of perspiration show suddenly on Lambert's forehead and his face screw up into an epitome of incredulity. Then the sweat began to run down his forehead.

"What?" they heard him say . . . "you don't mean that? You can't. I can't believe it . . . it's impossible." Then he stopped again and began to listen afresh.

"All right, Sam. I'll see to that. Sir Cloudesley's here with me now. Yes . . . in my office. I'll tell him at once. Though God knows what he'll say to me."

Lambert replaced the receiver with shaking hands. When he looked up, his eyes wavered as they met the fierce gaze of Sir Cloudesley Slade.

"Well," demanded the latter, "what's the trouble now? What are you going to tell me? Nothing good, I'll be bound."

Lambert shook his head weakly.

"Lefty's dead," he said in little more than a whisper. "His body's been found on the beach at Littlehampton in Sussex. Sam Whitfield's just had the news from his missus. The police have been to her."

Slade's face showed both incredulity and horror.

"'Lefty' Donovan dead," he muttered—"I can't believe it. It's—it's . . ."

Anthony's voice broke in upon them.

"How was he killed, Lambert? Did Whitfield tell you?"

Lambert shook his head again.

"No. He doesn't know very much yet, he says. All he knows is that 'Lefty's' face is badly cut about and his neck . . . as well . . . and . . ."

Lambert paused in his story. The two others seized on his indecision. It was Anthony Bathurst who translated it into words.

"And what? What else was there?"

Lambert spoke slowly.

"According to Sam Whitfield . . . the police are very puzzled about something. Something very strange. Near 'Lefty's' body, there are two curious footprints in the sand. The police can't make them out at all."

Anthony pleated his brows.

"Why not? Of what sort, then, are these footprints?"

"I don't know, Mr. Bathurst. But from what I can make of it—out of what Sam said—they couldn't have been made by anything human."

As he spoke, Lambert slumped forward and collapsed on the table in front of him.

An oath broke from Sir Cloudesley Slade.

CHAPTER VI
THE MARKS ON DONOVAN

"THE local police, for once in a way," said MacMorran, "seem to have done the right thing."

"Sent for you, do you mean, Andrew?" replied Anthony Bathurst. "Is that the idea?"

MacMorran eyed him severely.

"How d'ye mean exactly?"

"Don't call upon me to explain," returned Anthony. "It will mean—*inter alia*—a loss of valuable time." His eyes twinkled.

"I intended to convey to you the fact that they had called in the 'Yard.' You of all people, remembering certain past experiences, should be grateful."

"Oh—I am, Andrew. Profoundly. In fact, nobody could be more grateful. And I'm going to remember one other thing—above all others."

"To keep your eyes open and your mouth shut?"

"No. Not that, Andrew. That would be two things. Just this. That in this affair I represent the interest of Flora Donovan, the murdered man's widow. Who came to me for help and who went empty away."

Mr. Bathurst spoke with bitterness.

"It's no good you feeling sore over that. No man can do impossibilities. You did your best—and it wasn't good enough. That's all there is to it. We all have to put up with that."

"Exactly," responded Anthony. "I did my puny best—and it wasn't good enough. You've put it very well, Andrew. And if you want to know—that's exactly what hurts me."

The Inspector was openly scornful.

"If you never get worse hurt than that in this game you won't have to worry."

Anthony shook his head.

"That's very nice of you, Andrew—but all the same—"

MacMorran became severely practical and interrupted him.

"The Commissioner wants us to go down in the car. You got his message, I take it?"

Anthony nodded.

"That's why I'm here. My car's outside now. I'm ready when you are."

"That suits me. Come along then."

Anthony punched the pace directly they were clear of the London area. They made the seaside resort of Littlehampton in under two hours. An Inspector of Police was waiting for them at the Police Headquarters to which Anthony had driven. MacMorran at once introduced himself and his companion. The local officer was tall and heavily built, with a wealth of thick black bushy hair, some of which fell on his forehead.

"My name's Lilley," he announced rather shamefacedly, "but you mustn't blame me for that. It was also the name of my father. Inspector Lilley! Now which would you rather do first—see the body of Donovan—or go down to the foreshore where the poor fellow was found?"

As he put the question, MacMorran looked in Anthony Bathurst's direction.

"What would you say, Mr. Bathurst?"

Anthony turned towards Lilley.

"Have you the report of the autopsy yet? From your Divisional Surgeon?"

Lilley nodded.

"Oh—yes. There was no special need for it, really. Cause of death was too obvious. Does your question mean that you want to see it?"

"We'd like to see it of course, but don't bother about that now. It can wait. If it's all the same to you, we'll first of all have a glance at Donovan's body."

Lilley nodded again. He seemed, Anthony thought, from his preliminary contact with him, to be excessively anxious to please. Any idea of placing obstacles in their way, a condition which Anthony had encountered in the past in similar circumstances, seemed absent from this Inspector Lilley.

"He's in the mortuary . . . not far from here. Just at the back of the building. I'll have you there in a jiffy. But I ought to tell you he's—" Lilley paused abruptly.

"He's what?" enquired MacMorran with sharp insistence.

Lilley shrugged his shoulders.

"He's by no means pretty to look at. I'm a fairly tough case—but I tell you I didn't linger when I took my first look at him. In fact one of our sergeants very nearly chucked a dummy when he saw this chap on the slab." Lilley shook his head with a hint of doubtful appreciation.

MacMorran drooped an expressive eyelid towards Anthony Bathurst. Lilley jingled a large bunch of keys as he beckoned to them to follow him. They did so and passed through a monotonous succession of doors of varying sizes. Most of these' doors had to be unlocked and then locked again by Inspector Lilley. Eventually they came to the mortuary.

"We've nearly always got a full house here," remarked Lilley as he entered. The remark savoured of professional pride, akin to the pride of the Income Tax collector who counts triumphantly the number of his distress warrants. "You see," he added in explanation, "bein' a seaside town, so to speak, we collect a certain amount of 'undesirables,' as you might say, who from time to time do themselves in. Drownin' 'emselves as often as not. Apart from those that put a cushion in the gas-stove. They're just humdrum cases." He closed the door behind them and repeated the technique of carefully locking it again. "This way, will you?"

Anthony and MacMorran went with him.

"He's over here in this corner. If you stand back a bit. I'll get him out for you."

Lilley pulled at a handle and a long slab-tray slid out towards them. On it lay the body of a man covered with something that looked like a light sheet. The face was completely covered. Lilley flicked back the face-covering. Anthony looked carefully at what he saw revealed there.

"He's not been washed yet . . . by orders," said Lilley, "so that you chaps could see him just as we found him."

The blood was dried and crusted on Donovan's face. Lilley's warning to them had had ample justification. On each side of Donovan's neck, too, there were severe lacerations that were almost gaping wounds. Anthony's brow furrowed as he looked at them. Lilley bent and turned down more of the sheet-covering to show Donovan's chest and shoulders. From MacMorran there came a sharp exclamation of dismay and even horror. For on the chest and shoulders there were the same terrible lacerations and slits as on the face and neck. Anthony bent down to examine the wounds more closely.

"Never seen anything like this," commented MacMorran.

Lilley clucked approval of the statement.

"Just what I said when I first saw him."

"Look here," said Anthony, "at this."

He pointed to Donovan's left ear, or rather the flesh fragments that remained of it. For, if the truth be told, it hung in torn shreds that were just pink ribbons of embroidered flesh and little more. And a pink that was gradually changing into a waxy yellow tint, the ghastly hue of death. Anthony heard the breath come slowly from MacMorran's half-parted lips.

"That's bad," muttered the Inspector—"bad."

Lilley watched them both closely as he spoke.

"What's the doctor say?" demanded Anthony.

"Death from loss of blood—there's severance of the carotid artery for one thing. In itself quite enough to be going on with."

Anthony looked again at Donovan's body.

"He was a grand fellow. Physically. Look at his muscles and general development. His missus didn't exaggerate when she told me about him. Kept himself as fit as a fiddle. And now look at him." Anthony went on and purposely misquoted. "For behind the hollow crown that fronts the mortal temples of a man, keeps Death his court. And there the antic sits, scoffing his state and mocking at his Pomp—"

He stared once more at the tearing wounds. Then he turned to MacMorran.

"Come over here, will you, Andrew?" he said quietly.

MacMorran obeyed him. Went to Anthony's side.

"What were the words I quoted to you before we came down here? That Lambert had said to me in his office. What he got on the 'phone from Sam Whitfield?"

"What—with regard to the marks on the sand?"

"Ay, Andrew. Just that."

"That they couldn't have been made by anything human."

"Exactly, Andrew." Anthony pointed to the wounds on Donovan's body. "Think of that statement in conjunction with those marks of horror there."

"I am thinking," returned MacMorran, "and I don't mind admitting that I'm fair scared of all of it."

"Now have another 'think'—this time in the terms of Ted Bailey of Northamptonshire who, after disappearing for some days, was found dead on the beach at Worthing, with mutilations of the face and the upper part of the body. *Je ne l'aime pas, Monsieur André.* As with you—it frightens me." Anthony turned away and stood with his back to Donovan's body. MacMorran rubbed the side of his cheek. Anthony swung round to him again.

"Worthing! And this is Littlehampton! But a few miles apart. Notice that. What devilry are we facing now, Andrew? What devilry is it that has brought a horrible death to two grand boys?"

"These wounds," contributed MacMorran in a detached sort of way, "look to my eye as much like gigantic scratches as anything else." He appeared not to have heard Anthony's previous questions. "Yes," he repeated half to himself and half to his audience. "I'll say that again with even greater confidence—gigantic scratches."

"And scratches," responded Anthony, assimilating the idea, "in the same terms as were the marks on the sand—not made by any human being."

MacMorran gave him an uneasy glance. Anthony went on.

"And there's something else, Andrew. Have you noticed the *cleanness* of the wounds? Underneath where the blood has dried on them? They might almost be knife-edge slices, all of them. There's no suggestion of dirt or discoloration on the top of Donovan's left shoulder. See there, Andrew! See what I mean?"

Lilley cut in with a relevant statement.

"As a matter of fact, the Divisional Surgeon has remarked on that, Inspector MacMorran, in his report. The same point struck him directly he looked at the body. You'll find it all in there when you read it."

Anthony nodded approval. MacMorran then saw that something else had riveted Mr. Bathurst's attention. And that this something was vital and important MacMorran could tell by the sudden gleam that had come in Anthony's grey eyes. Mr. Bathurst spoke.

"Come here again, Andrew—and you too, Inspector Lilley, will you—look closely at these wounds which MacMorran here has just described as scratches. Do you notice anything peculiar about them?"

MacMorran and the local Inspector peered more closely at the 'scratches' on the dead man. After a moment or so's examination in this way, MacMorran clinched the issue with a shake of his head.

"Tell me," he said laconically.

Anthony proceeded to explain his point.

"Look carefully at these marks on the face just to the right of the point of the jaw, near the chin. Look at them carefully. Doesn't anything about them strike you as being a trifle strange?"

Again the two Inspectors shook their heads.

"No?" said Anthony, "then I'll try to show you what I mean." He put a finger, close to the marks on Donovan's jaw. There were at least three of these plainly defined. "Don't you see that the top or upper portion of these scratches seems to be wider and deeper than the lower or bottom part? See what I mean?"

The two men nodded assent. Anthony continued.

"Good. That's more or less established then. Now—consider this. Proceeding from a starting-point which we may, quite happily as it happens, call 'scratch.' Supposing I scratch at your face with the nails of my fingers, or an animal does the same thing, or say a large bird of the eagle, vulture, or lammergeyer type, in which direction would the scratch be? Normally, that is?"

Anthony waited quietly for the reply. The two answers came to him almost simultaneously.

"Downwards."

"Exactly," commented Anthony, "downwards and in that case, the deeper part of the wound is usually towards where the scratch ends and not where the scratch begins. Here we find the reverse condition. Therefore, I deduce that they were caused by a movement that was made in an upward direction. Now, gentlemen, what could that have been reasonably?"

Lilley made a somewhat tentative contribution.

"I have known certain animals strike upwards with their back feet or back legs when cornered or held in a particular way. An infuriated cat will, for example."

Anthony nodded.

"Yes. I'll concede that. A cat will use its back legs in that way. I've had experience of it. They're strong and powerful. But I can't imagine a cat having made marks on a man's face of this kind. Round his head, neck, face and shoulders. Not to mention his chest. His chest is the lowest part of his body to have received a wound. Get me, Lilley?"

Lilley nodded. He appeared to be thinking hard. Suddenly Anthony went back to the body under an obvious emotion of excitement.

"Something else, Andrew. For you to explain to me. If Donovan were attacked at close quarters, as he *undoubtedly* was, from the nature of his wounds, why in the name of all that's sane and sensible didn't he defend himself? That's what I can't get over. Why didn't he put up a fight against his assailant? Whoever or *whatever* it was."

This time MacMorran nodded. It was evident that he agreed with Anthony.

"You're going by the condition of his hands and wrists—eh?"

"Not a mark on 'em, Andrew."

"So I see."

"Nary the tiniest of tiny scratches! Donovan put up no fight at all, Andrew. Why?"

"Perhaps the opposition was too overwhelming."

"Or . . . maybe . . . too dreadful."

This last from Inspector Lilley.

"Yes," agreed Anthony, by this time roused to contention. "I'm prepared to accept all that but at the same time only so far as it goes, and I'm going to say that it's all wrong. Or in other words it doesn't fit."

Lilley shook his head in disagreement.

"It might. We can't tell. We don't know all the circumstances. And because we *don't* know all the circumstances—"

Anthony swept him aside with scant ceremony.

"But say what you like—it's all wrong, man, circumstances or no circumstances! Let us use our brains on it. Donovan was a *fighter*. Used to a scrap. Experienced in a struggle. Liked 'em no doubt—otherwise he wouldn't have gone in for the fighting game. Are you going to tell me that a man of his kind and of his nature, would submit to this treatment that we know he received, without any resistance? Because, if you are, it won't do for me, Inspector Lilley."

The local Inspector shrugged his shoulders with resignation.

"All right, Mr. Bathurst—have it your own way. I would accept your argument had the circumstances been normal. But they're *not* normal and to my mind that makes all the difference. I'm sorry and all that."

Anthony shrugged his shoulders as Lilley had and cast in another direction. He spoke to MacMorran.

"I'm going to test your memory, Andrew. Let's get back to the death of Ted Bailey of Northampton. Another hope of the boxing world. What were his hands and wrists like? Any idea?"

"No. It wasn't ever my own case from a police point of view and I contented myself with its rough details. But I can easily find out for you. Remember to remind me when we get back to town."

"D'ye know, Andrew, I haven't been in the Northampton district since I looked into that little problem of 'The Peacock's Eye.' I'm strongly tempted to make a return visit."

MacMorran eyed him doubtfully.

"Why do you say that? It's not like you to rush things or jump at conclusions."

Anthony spoke deliberately. "I never rush things, Andrew, and I scarcely ever jump at conclusions. You can make of that whatever you like."

Lilley endeavoured to catch MacMorran's eye—but failed.

"By the way," said Anthony, "what clothes was Donovan wearing when he was picked up?"

"An ordinary brown tweed suit. I can show it to you if you like. It's all here. Beyond some particles of sand, as you would expect, there was nothing of any kind to excite suspicion."

"Put this poor fellow back where he came from, then, and show me his suit."

Lilley did as requested. The tray slid back into place. Lilley spread out a coat, waistcoat and trousers of brown Harris tweed. Anthony and MacMorran went over them with a small tooth-comb. Mac-Morran's keen eyes missed nothing. Lilley's statement couldn't be shaken. A little sand—nothing more.

"What was in the pockets?" asked Mr. Bathurst. "Anything?"

Lilley consulted a list that he took from his pocket.

"A little money—to be exact—tenpence ha'penny, a photograph of a girl and—this is rather unusual, I suppose—two champagne corks."

"Interesting," remarked Anthony, "highly interesting—may I see them and the photograph?"

"Certainly, Mr. Bathurst. Here they are."

Lilley passed them over to him. Anthony looked first at the two corks. He read words printed on the bottom of one of them. 'Champagne de Castellane—Epernay.' The tin cap was still on the head of the cork. Anthony then looked at the second cork. It was in similar condition.

Anthony read the description. 'Fournie et Cie, Epernay, France.' Little pieces of each cork appeared to have broken away from the bases—mere tiny fragments.

"H'm," said Anthony, "interesting and possibly instructive. One can't say at the moment. Means waiting for it. Let me look at the photograph though, will you, Inspector, please? That may tell us something. I have strong hopes that it will."

Inspector Lilley handed over the photograph. Anthony examined it curiously. It was of a young girl of ample proportions as far as he was able to judge. She seemed to be the possessor of much hair, large eyes and a big mouth of prominent teeth. The eyes struck Anthony as being hard and staring. As his glance went to the photographer's name an exclamation was forced from him. For the name of the photographer was 'East, 22 St. Andrew's Terrace, Northampton.' MacMorran and Lilley responded to the exclamation in different ways.

"What is it?" asked Lilley. "What do you think you've discovered?"

MacMorran, on the contrary, said nothing. He held out his hand quietly for Mr. Bathurst to pass him the photograph.

"Consider the town of the photographer, Andrew," remarked Anthony. "Consider its way and be wise." He rubbed his hands briskly and went on. "Things are warming up for us, I fancy. Once again I find my thoughts turning in the direction of the late Ted Bailey. By the way, Inspector Lilley, did *you* come into contact with that case at all? Bailey's body was washed ashore at Worthing. A few miles from here. The suggestion was that he had committed suicide by jumping off Worthing Pier. Personally, I don't think he did—although I admit I have often wanted to myself. Those pigeons are so extraordinarily lugubrious in the rain. And it always rains at Worthing when I happen to be there. Did you happen to touch the case, Inspector?"

Lilley shook his head.

"No, Mr. Bathurst. The Worthing people had it to themselves. I remember the affair quite well, of course. In the early part of the year. Created a bit of a stir in the district at the time."

Anthony turned to MacMorran.

"That photograph, Andrew, you have there . . . what profession, trade, or calling would you give the lady? Formed any opinion in that direction yet."

MacMorran nodded.

"I have, Mr. Bathurst. And I'll give it to you in one. Barmaid! What's your own opinion?"

"My opinion, Andrew, coincides with yours. A neat-handed Phyllis! Dispenser of the wine of the country. Venue? Somewhere near Northampton, county town of Northamptonshire. 'Such as hang on Hebe's cheek, and love to live in dimples sleek.' Were you with me, Andrew, on that historic occasion when a barmaid addressed the Commissioner of Police as 'Angel Face,' or was it another of the Force?"

MacMorran chuckled.

"Not guilty, Mr. Bathurst—but I'd have loved to have been there, and seen the Guv'nor's dial."

From Lilley there were coming manifest signs of impatience. He did not know his Bathurst to the extent that MacMorran did.

"Well, gentlemen," he said as MacMorran handed the photograph back to him, "you must make up your mind . . . is there anything else I can do for you while we're in here . . . or shall we adjourn?"

"Inspector Lilley," said Anthony, "you may harbour no regrets. You have done well. For one thing—you have given me much food for thought. Indeed, I feel extremely confident that we shall solve our little problem after all. Will you now take us along to the spot where the body of Donovan was found?"

"Certainly, Mr. Bathurst," said Inspector Lilley. "I've been waiting for that. Come this way, will you?"

CHAPTER VII
THE MARKS ON THE SAND

ANTHONY Bathurst, with his two companions, walked through the old-fashioned streets of Littlehampton.

"How far?" enquired Mr. Bathurst.

"A little more than a quarter of a mile," replied Inspector Lilley. "The body was found on an extremely quiet stretch of the beach, near the water. It's a desolate spot altogether. Outside a few courting couples, and even that very occasionally, ordinary people don't go there. Especially at this time of the year. In the summer, of course, it would be a bit different. But now—it might just as well be the Sahara desert."

"Tell me, Inspector Lilley," said Anthony, "who found the body of Donovan? I can't remember that I've heard."

"One of the local boatmen. He's by way of being a bit of a character in the town. Proper old-stager, Phil Perkins by name. His trade's quiet in the winter months, so he does a bit of walking to pass the time away. You know what I mean—in between opening times. Coming back from one of his jaunts he ran across the body."

"What have you done down there?" asked MacMorran.

Lilley grinned at the implication.

"How do you mean?"

MacMorran by this time had noticed the grin.

"Was it too near the water's edge? Is that the idea?"

"It was, by a long shot. The tide had washed all the marks out within an hour."

"What were you able to get?"

"Drawings of the three marks that were by the body. I've been waiting for you to ask me about them."

"We'll have a look at them when we get back," said Anthony. "As a matter of fact, I'd prefer to see the actual terrain before I look at the copies of the marks."

They walked for another quarter of an hour along the parade. Suddenly Lilley stopped in his tracks.

"Here we are." He pointed downwards. "Just down there, between those two low-lying points of rock."

Anthony's eyes followed the direction of Inspector Lilley's pointing finger.

"Come down," he said curtly.

MacMorran and Lilley followed him on to the sand.

"Show me where the body was."

Lilley demonstrated with his hands.

"Head where?"

Lilley indicated.

"Feet?"

Lilley with his hands again.

"On his back?"

"No, Mr. Bathurst. He was lying with his face on the sand, with his left arm flung across his mouth."

"What!" exclaimed Anthony. "Do you hear that, Andrew?"

MacMorran nodded.

"Ay! Strikes me as being rather peculiar."

"I should say so, Andrew!"

Anthony turned his back to the waves of the sea and gazed shoreward.

"Midway, Andrew, or about midway between two sloping descents; from the promenade to the beach. That fact, at least, is interesting to know. Don't you think so?"

MacMorran nodded. Anthony walked back to the parade. From there he was able to survey the road. After a moment or so's hesitation, he returned to MacMorran and Lilley.

"I'm ready now, Lilley, to have a look at those marks you've prepared. I've kept them to the end purposely. Had I seen them to begin with they might have influenced me too much. That condition I desired to avoid. Lead on, Lilley, will you please?"

Back at the Police Station, Lilley produced the drawings of the three marks.

"Before I look at these marks, Lilley," said Anthony, "where were they exactly in relation to the position of the body? Which side of it?"

"Towards the sea."

"Between the sea and the body do you mean?"

"Yes, Mr. Bathurst." Lilley bent down and solemnly inspected a polished toe-cap.

"These drawings are exact copies, I assume, of the marks on the sand?"

"Exactly. There are three drawings there in all. You will see that they represent in every instance the outline of an extremely large claw. The only difference in them is that they are slanted a little differently."

Anthony nodded his understanding.

"In which direction were the marks travelling? As far as you could judge?"

"Two towards the body from the edge of the water and one from the body towards the sea. That is to say in the reverse direction. This mark was the nearest one to the sea."

"Thank you, Inspector. MacMorran—come here, will you; what do you make of these marks?"

MacMorran looked hard at the drawings.

"Looks suspiciously like a bird track to me."

"Good. I shall be delighted then, Andrew, to draw upon your fund of natural history. Name your bird, do you mind?"

Anthony grinned. MacMorran responded to the challenge.

"Well, from the size of the mark, something like an ostrich, I should say, if I *had* to answer."

"Now, now, Andrew—think. Stir up the old grey matter. Has an ostrich claws?"

MacMorran scratched his cheek.

"I thought it had. Am I wrong?"

"You are, Andrew. In the many processes of evolution, the claws of the ostrich have changed their character. The result is that the fighting weapon of the ostrich is a claw no longer. It has gradually become a hoof."

Lilley intervened.

"But that argument only goes for the ostrich, Mr. Bathurst. What about other members of the bird family? The big birds—I mean."

"Such as?" enquired Anthony with sweet insistence.

Lilley shrugged his professional shoulders.

"Well—I'm like Inspector MacMorran—forgotten most of my natural history. But I could mention . . . er . . . eagles and vultures . . . and er . . . the emu and the cassowary and—"

"Good, Lilley. You're doing remarkably well. You've left Mac-Morran at the post. Absolutely outclassed him. But let me point out to you, my dear Lilley, before you go any further, that like the ostrich, the emu and the cassowary both have the hoof in the family. As for eagles and vultures—and the others you mentioned—"

This time it was Mr. Bathurst's turn to shake his head and shrug his shoulders. He returned to look again at the three drawings. MacMorran saw him shake his head twice. The Chief Inspector came across with another question. When he heard it, Lilley's eyes flashed with satisfaction and he nodded his approval.

"Are there any other big birds, Mr. Bathurst? Big enough to attack and kill a man? Could you give me any names?"

Anthony shook his head gravely and gave question for question.

"Still extant do you mean, Andrew?"

"Of course. What else could I possibly mean?"

"Just this, Andrew. I must call your attention to the fact. Have you thought of the size of the foot that this claw would fit?"

"Ay. Naturally. What did you think I said ostrich for—in the first place?"

"A hoof, Andrew! A hoof every time! Your ostrich might have put its head in the sand for very shame—not its claw."

Lilley seemed to divine the gravity behind Anthony's statements.

"What are you hinting at exactly, Mr. Bathurst? Don't you think you'd better tell us?"

"Well, Inspector, I am no star in natural history—far from it in fact—but all the knowledge that I have in that direction suggests to me that a creature whose foot was fitted with a claw of that size, must have trodden this land of ours when those rocks we looked at just now, that the tide had left uncovered for a time, were nothing more than soft ooze and slime."

Lilley gaped at him open eyed.

"Do you mean years and years ago—1066 and all that?"

"Certainly at least ten million years ago, Inspector, and much more likely a little matter of one hundred million." Anthony handed round his cigarette case and carefully selected one for himself. There was a silence as he made this astounding declaration. This heavy silence was maintained. Lilley's voice came through it.

"What was the name of that period? I'm interested."

"It might have been the Cretaceous. I'm not sure and may be drawing a huge bow at the wildest venture. But the Cretaceous would have been one of the periods."

MacMorran also thirsted for information.

"And what was the name of the dear little bird with plates of meat such as you've described?"

Anthony hesitated.

"Again, Andrew, I'm not too sure. You mustn't ask me too many questions. But I've an idea at the back of my mind that my bird wasn't a bird. It's just occurred to me." MacMorran grinned at Anthony's pleasantry.

"Don't tell me," he responded in the same vein, "that it was a Boyle Roche."

Anthony laughed.

"I fancy that my bird was more of a reptile."

"I've known several like that," muttered Lilley in ungallant reminiscence. Anthony went on.

"The name of it, I think, was the Pteranodon. But I'm not sure."

"Did it attack men and women?" enquired Lilley anxiously.

"In all probability, if we accept what our scientists tell us, there were none to attack. The first man you see, came millions of years later."

"I do see."

"Let me answer your question, however, in another way, which I imagine will serve your purpose. Had there been men in the salad days of the Pteranodon they would have fallen easy victims to the brute. We must presume in the first place that they would have been unarmed."

Lilley whistled lugubriously.

"Not so good. I shan't fancy a stroll along the beach this evening. Or on any other evening—come to that." MacMorran glanced at Anthony anxiously.

"Do you associate yourself with those sentiments, Mr. Bathurst? I can't help thinking of Mrs. MacMorran—"

Anthony closured him with a shake of the head.

"No, Andrew, things even as I see them aren't as bad as all that. The Pteranodon wasn't born to blush unseen and waste his presence on the seaside air. There was nothing furtive or stealthy about his methods. Let's attempt to measure him up. You must imagine wings with something like a thirty-feet spread, and a beak about four feet in length that would go through you like a bayonet."

Lilley shivered and looked uneasily behind him over his shoulder. Anthony continued:

"The creature was related, probably, to that other charming fellow—the Dinosaur—but the Pteranodon, my *protégé*, was the lord of the ether. Much more so, I'm afraid, than either the modern 'Spitfire' or 'Hurricane'."

MacMorran became severely practical.

"But where are we getting to with all this natural history stuff? That's what I want to know. Is it leading us to the murderer of 'Lefty' Donovan? Or are we just playing around? Because you aren't putting it into me that this ancient monster has flown out of oblivion to kill a man like Donovan and then flown back again. And that's said to you, Mr. Bathurst *and* to you, Inspector Lilley."

It was evident that the Chief Inspector was a trifle nettled. Anthony took it upon himself to reply.

"I'm not attempting to put it into you as you suggest, Andrew. I am merely saying this. If Inspector Lilley's drawings are correct—or even reasonably accurate—no bird in existence at the present time ever left a claw print of those dimensions. Either on the beach here or on the sands of Time itself. And that's said to you, Monsieur Andre."

MacMorran, under the onslaught, adopted the line of least resistance. He turned his attack towards Lilley.

"Are those drawings of yours accurate, Inspector Lilley? Can you swear to them? To a fine point of accuracy?"

Lilley was dogged in his own defence.

"Absolutely."

"You are positive?"

"Positive."

MacMorran turned to meet Anthony's accusing eyes.

"There you are, you see, Andrew. Lilley's sure of his ground. And there *have* been pre-historic survivals, you know. Certain monsters of the water have endured—and if of the water why not a creature of the air?"

"*Hot* air," muttered MacMorran with undisguised contempt— "*and* that's the most sensible phrase that's been used since we've been here."

There was another period of oppressive silence. Lilley broke it. His questions may have been crude but Anthony understood the essential emotions which prompted the man to ask them.

"I've been wondering—could a creature like that have been shut up anywhere—kind of imprisoned—and suddenly got out?"

Anthony thought for a moment before he committed himself by answer.

"I suppose such a contingency as that might happen. I can imagine 'imprisonment' possibly—using your own word—in a vast cavern of a kind and then something like a violent volcanic disturbance taking place and creating an exit for the creature."

Listening against his will, MacMorran snorted with disgust and disapproval.

"Utter rubbish. I'm absolutely surprised at you, Mr. Bathurst, talking in such a wild way. I thought you were a sane and sensible person."

"Just a minute, Andrew—before you completely dispose of me and throw me to the lions. What about the Loch Ness monster? Remember the sensation it caused? A lot of people claim to have seen it, you know. Including two members of the Church of Scotland."

"A lot of daft idiots are always seeing things. They have to. As others take alcohol or sit on Committees. It's the breath of their existence."

"And besides the Loch Ness monster—which is the best example of the kind I can think of during comparatively recent times—there is also the persistent legend of the roc and that curious story that came from somewhere in the North of England about a hundred years ago. Quite creditable witnesses claimed to have found the tracks after a night's fall of snow of a huge creature with a great pendent tail. This monster was supposed to have flown over houses and other even larger buildings and to have left a trail in various places very similar to that which is facing us here." MacMorran shook his head decisively.

"I don't believe it—and that's that. And nothing on earth would induce me to accept such a daft story."

Anthony smiled at the Inspector's uncompromising attitude.

"Do you know, Andrew, I don't believe that's the first time I've heard you speak like that."

"Verra likely. And if you persist in tellin' me more tales of mystery, horror and pure imagination—it won't be the last. Not by a long chalk!"

MacMorran's jaws closed with a snap. Anthony shrugged his shoulders and turned to Inspector Lilley of Littlehampton.

"There you are, Inspector Lilley, you see how things are. Nothing will move him. He won't have your 'death-bird' at any price. You'll have to think of something else."

Lilley shook his head dolefully.

"I wish I felt the same way about things, Mr. Bathurst. But I don't! And that's a fact. If you want to know—I'm dead scared at what you've been telling me. And that's a fact, too!"

When Anthony and MacMorran left the premises, Inspector Lilley was still looking like a man who had been embraced by a shuddering ghost.

Chapter VIII
STAR MERRILEES

SOMEWHERE about sixteen hours later, the telephone rang in Anthony Bathurst's flat. By a stroke of good chance he happened to be in and was able, therefore, to answer it. The voice that came to his ear was feminine. At the first moment of hearing it, Anthony expected that it was Flora Donovan who had called him. But he immediately discovered that this idea of his was wrong. The voice that spoke to him was different altogether from Flora Donovan's. For one thing it was not of Wimbledon, it was of Mayfair.

"Is that Anthony Bathurst?"

Mr. Bathurst admitted the truth of the matter.

"Would it be convenient for me to see you—on something of the gravest and most vital importance?"

Mr. Bathurst frowned and requested more wealth of detail. The voice came through to him again.

"If I mention the name 'Donovan' to you—does that clarify the matter sufficiently?"

Anthony was at once the victim of hesitation. He decided to finesse. His answer was guarded.

"Partly, perhaps. But certainly not sufficiently. May I enquire whom I have the honour of addressing?"

"That can wait. It isn't really of the slightest importance. If I told you my name, I doubt whether it would convey anything to you."

"I might be the better judge of that, don't you think?"

A low musical laugh came to him down the telephone.

"How like a man! Do you know—that reply of yours has forced me to a decision."

"Not an unpleasant one, I hope. I should hate to think that."

"That depends. On the point of view. Actually the decision is an invitation. And a rather nice one at that. Does that sound better? Will you dine with me this evening?"

Again Anthony hesitated. The girl at the other end of the line sensed the hesitation.

"*Aren't* you the reverse of flattering? What are you afraid of, particularly? That I'm a hag? My dear Mr. Bathurst, I give you my solemn word of honour that you can dismiss any idea of that kind. Self praise? I can assure you that I am attractive, charming, witty, and not even unintelligent. Well—and what does the great detective say to that?"

"Attraction may be of two kinds. Charm—like beauty—lies in the eye of the beholder. I have even heard people claim that there are two numbers of *Punch* that are witty, and as for 'intelligence'—well, it's a word the teacher in the elementary school applies to the least backward of his pupils."

"Oh—what a perfectly icy shower! Wait until I get my breath back. Still I'm not of the kind that crumples when chair-legs are waved at me. And in addition I'm superbly confident about myself. What do you say to my invitation?"

"First of all, where is the rendezvous?"

"Well—my own idea was Murillo's. How does that appeal to you?"

"There are certainly worse places," conceded Anthony.

"Name one of them—and the invitation still stands." Anthony smiled at the aptness of the riposte.

"I don't know that I want to do that. Actually I am rather attracted by Murillo's."

"Right, then. Don't. Murillo's it is. What time shall we say? Seven-thirty sharp?"

"You wait a minute. I haven't accepted yet. Although you evidently take it for granted that I'm going to."

"I feel certain that you won't be so ungallant as to refuse. You couldn't be. Seven-thirty pip emma at Murillo's, then. That's O.K. with me."

Before he could reply, Anthony knew that she had hung up on him. Thoughtfully he rubbed the ridge of his jaw. "We progress," he muttered—"and what's more, I haven't the least idea of who she is, what she's like, or how I shall recognize her when I see her. It reminds me rather of Lilley's reaction to the Pteranodon."

HQ glanced at his watch and realized that he now had to dress for dinner. He rang for Emily and gave her certain instructions.

He arrived inside the foyer at Murillo's at seven-twenty-nine precisely. Immediately a tall girl, exquisitely gowned, bore down upon him. She was golden—almost Madonna-like in her charming fairness. Anthony at once mentally described her as a luminous personality. Her face, though, held a quality which he found difficult to understand. Perhaps it came from the set of her lips. Her eyes were remarkable . . . they asked and challenged you to assess her. Frankly—but deliberately. Anthony thought of an auctioneer asking for a higher bid for what he knows beyond any question to be a most valuable article. The shimmering nature of her gown, allied with her own golden fairness, made him think of a tall, lambent flame. Her eyes flickered over him critically and a slight smile ameliorated somewhat the slightly hard lines of her lips. Anthony knew at once that this girl was beautiful in an unusual way, and already many heads had been turned in their direction.

"I shall not say 'Mr. Bathurst' enquiringly, because there is no need. Already I embrace certainty. I feel sure that it's you."

She gave him the tips of her fingers. He smiled at her.

"You have the advantage of me. I can't reply in the same vein. In my case, you see, I don't know what 'you' signifies."

A little low laugh escaped her and the eyes flickered over him again.

"I am Star Merrilees. Does that tell you anything?"

The significance of the name came home to Anthony at once. He knew that he was in the company of the reputedly brightest of the Bright Young People. For some months her name had hit many headlines in the Press.

"Yes," he answered, "that tells me something. I think it almost tells me enough."

"I don't know that that's a compliment." The mouth was a little harsh again.

"My dear young lady, it wasn't intended to be." Anthony was definitely defensive now.

"There is an attractive table," she said lightly, "in the Diadem Room. A table that has always appealed to me. I took the liberty of 'phoning Murillo himself after I had spoken to you, and making arrangements. I asked him to reserve it for us. I suggest that you escort me there. In your best 'Joy to the Brave' manner. Yes?"

Anthony smiled and obeyed. She indicated the table that was waiting for them. They took their seats.

"I hope," said Anthony, "that you have not ordered?"

She shook her head. "Of course not."

"Good. I am delighted. Your value is immediately enhanced."

"Thank you, Mr. Bathurst."

"It's a man's job."

"I entirely agree with you."

He ordered. Each course, as it was nominated by him, was referred to the lady by a movement of Anthony's head and approved by her before the waiter accepted and noted it. With the arrival of the oysters, Anthony endeavoured to break the first sheets of vital ice.

"Eggs," he said, "must be broken before omelettes can be made. Trite perhaps, but undoubtedly true, for all that. Supposing we agree that the password for us tonight is 'Edna Lyall'?"

She was all light and flame and luminosity—but she furrowed her brow at his remark.

"Edna Lyall? I don't know that I understand you. Didn't she write goody-goody books or something for our grandfathers and grandmothers before our Baptism?"

Anthony grinned at the sally.

"She did. Most successfully. And not only before our Baptism. *Inter alia* she wrote *Donovan* and *We Two*. I fancy that the one was the sequel of the other. I haven't read them. I've merely seen them on shelves. Well—here are 'We Two.' Which makes me so much more interested in the matter of 'Donovan.' Do I make myself clear?"

Anthony waited for her. She calmly swallowed her remaining oyster before she answered.

"Do you know, Mr. Bathurst, I find you terribly attractive. I do really—and I had no idea I was going to feel like this."

Anthony flashed a quick glance at her. He was surprised to feel sure within himself that there seemed more in her remark than the merely conversational and flattering convention.

"Donovan," he said severely. "Just Donovan."

She waited for the waiter to finish what he was doing before she spoke again.

"Yes—Donovan," she repeated. "Donovan—and why I'm so worried. Why I asked you to meet me here this evening and why—oh—all of this."

"Now," returned Anthony with deliberate provocation, "you begin to interest me. I almost said 'at last.'"

She remained calm under the taunt.

"I shall ignore the obvious discourtesy," she observed quietly.

"And talk about Donovan?" Anthony spoke hopefully.

Star Merrilees inclined her golden head. "Let me tell you this. I am engaged to be married."

Anthony looked pointedly towards the fingers of her left hand.

"Presumably," he replied.

"That," she said understandingly, "is not always an infallible guide. I might tell you I have known extraordinary cases of girls—"

"They don't matter. Don't let us waste time. Time that is valuable. Tell me about Donovan."

She raised what remained of her eyebrows. "*Must* you rush me? I ought to tell you that I always do far better when I'm left alone to travel at my own pace. I am engaged to be married to Godfrey Slade. I met him in April and we understood each other almost at once."

The surname made all the difference to Anthony's reception of her statement. Star Merrilees went on:

"You may be feeling surprised as to why I made that statement so early in our acquaintance, but you have already met Sir Cloudesley Slade, Godfrey's father. One of our famous sporting baronets."

There was sarcasm in her tone. Anthony duly noted it and wondered still more.

"You are aware, too, that my father-in-law-to-be had matched a man named 'Lefty' Donovan for a biggish purse against the redoubtable Phil Blood and looks like losing much more than he can afford to lose now that this Donovan man has been . . . shall we say . . . removed from the sphere of action? All this you have already been told. But I want you to understand that you haven't been told all. The annoying man who will relieve my future Papa of his hard unearned income is a certain gentleman named Marcus Secretan . . . who started life, I believe, sweeping out a tobacconist's shop in Hackney and then making cigarettes out of the mixture. That fact hurts old Slade and Godfrey so acutely that unless I step in and do a quick bit of thinking my Godfrey's going to get hurt a good deal more. And, incredible though it may seem and sound to you in these modern times, I happen to love Godfrey Slade."

Anthony looked at her intently.

"I love Godfrey Slade," she continued almost defiantly, "because he's so gloriously strong and fit. A man—if ever there was one. Physically, I think he's the most perfect specimen of manhood I've ever seen. I love him so much that I'm going to do my darndest that he doesn't get hurt. Not for all the beastly filthy money in the world."

She stopped abruptly.

"If I may be allowed to comment," said Anthony, taking quick advantage of the pause, "you are still a trifle enigmatic."

The mouth was definitely harsh now. "Perhaps I am. Perhaps even I intend to be. After all, we have never been introduced."

"Tua culpa," murmured Anthony.

Star Merrilees shook her head impatiently. "I suppose I *had* better be more explicit otherwise there is but little point in my saying anything. But *you* are to blame for my own personal anxiety. There—now you know! Actually I hadn't intended to tell you that." Again she paused as the waiter appeared with another course.

"I?" said Anthony in surprise. "May I enquire as to the exact meaning of that statement? How am I to blame?"

"You may. I know what I'm talking about. Because you were the person who put the mad idea into Sir Cloudesley's head to find a substitute for 'Lefty' Donovan. And *that's* the matter that is making me lose my sleep at nights. Observe I didn't say my beauty sleep."

"Putting two and two together," said Anthony, "I *think* I begin to understand. Although when I made the suggestion to which you refer I was entirely unaware that Mr. Godfrey Slade had any pretensions in the direction that you seem to be indicating."

"That demonstrates the mistake of talking without knowing your book. Godfrey won the Public Schools Middle Weight Championship one year, and the year after he followed up that success by winning the Public Schools Heavy Weights. I sound like an almanack, don't I? He is considered, let me tell you, Mr. Bathurst, to be 'a very promising lad'."

Anthony nodded. "I am beginning to understand even better. But surely, Sir Cloudesley Slade wouldn't be mad enough to put him up against a man of Blood's class?"

Star Merrilees shrugged her white shoulders.

"I don't say that he will. At the moment I think it's more Godfrey's own idea than Sir Cloudesley's. That's the main trouble. As I said just now, you put the general idea into Sir Cloudesley's head—and Godfrey has fastened on to it and won't let go of it. You see—financially, it's a pretty serious matter for the old man."

"Very serious?"

"I don't say that—but quite serious enough—believe me."

"I see. I had already formed that opinion myself." The waiter came with champagne in an ice-bucket. Anthony decided to force the issue.

"Now, apart from the information you have already given me, what can you tell me about Donovan himself?"

She shook her head in quiet denial.

"Nothing?"

"Nothing at all—I'd never heard of the ghastly man until he got himself murdered. What makes you ask me?"

"My question was foundationed on hope. I can't forget, you see, that you used the name 'Donovan' when you suggested that I should meet you here this evening. I am not too pleased that your action smacks of false pretences." Anthony waited for her reaction to his challenge. He noticed that she flushed a little.

"That may be true. But it's only partly true and I want your help. That was the only weapon I had in my power to use with you. I knew that if I mentioned the name 'Donovan' to you I should at least excite your curiosity and that you ought to rise to the bait."

"You are, at least, frank."

"I must be. I know full well that I shall get no help from you unless I am absolutely frank."

"Accepting that, then, what help can I give you?"

She leant over to him with eager earnestness.

"You must stop Godfrey from being smashed up. Battered and mutilated. You see, I know him so well. I know how headstrong he is. Once he makes up his mind to fight, nothing on earth will stop him. You have already met Sir Cloudesley. I know that—because he mentioned it when he came home. Godfrey's as obstinate as his father—every bit. I want you to use your influence with the old man. He *mustn't* let Godfrey fight. What *you* tell him will make a great difference to him. Much more than anything I can say. *Now* do you see what I mean?"

Anthony looked at her deliberately—full in the face.

"Miss Merrilees, before we talk any more, let us understand one another. You have been frank. Now it's my turn for frankness. I am in this case on behalf of a girl named Donovan. Wife of 'Lefty' Donovan—and mother of his child. Donovan—a thoroughly decent chap, I should say—was decoyed from his home and murdered. I intend to get that murderer if it's the last thing I ever do. Shall I tell you more?"

"Please. Besides being attractive—you have begun to interest me."

"Some months ago, another fine young fellow went the same way as Donovan has gone."

Anthony paused. To notice that Miss Merrilees had become deathly pale.

"Again," he said, "would you care to hear more of this other instance?"

"Yes," she whispered, "of course. How can you possibly stop now?"

"It would be, I admit, profitless—to say nothing of tantalizing. This other young fellow's name was Bailey, Ted Bailey. He came from the Midlands—Northampton, He also disappeared one morning. Very much in the same way as 'Lefty' Donovan did. Some time afterwards, his body was found on the beach at Worthing. It had been washed ashore. There were severe injuries to the face and chest. Again—note the similarity to Donovan. And—if I may stress the point—Worthing is not terrifically far from Littlehampton."

"No," she murmured, "that's just what I was thinking."

"Inevitably there was an inquest on young Bailey from North-ampton. There was no evidence as to how his body came to be in the water. The result was that the jury returned a verdict of 'Found Drowned.' The Littlehampton jury, however, will not be able to return that verdict in the case of 'Lefty' Donovan."

She shook her head.

"You are assuming that I know as much as you do yourself. I don't. All I know is that Donovan is dead. That his body was discovered at Littlehampton. I know no details."

"You will do—by the time you leave me to-night. At any rate, you will have a better idea of what we are up against. Of the evil forces that are arrayed against us."

"You may flatter yourself that you have already succeeded in doing one thing, Mr. Bathurst. You have frightened me most effectively. I came to you for help in respect of Godfrey. Instead of getting any, or even the promise of any, I shall go away with more anxiety and more personal apprehension."

There was a tinge of bitterness in her voice but he knew that it was allied to fear. Anthony instinctively recognized the presence of each of these qualities. He knew that he must soften his heart towards her before she left him that evening. He leant over the table, therefore, and spoke with a greater sympathy than he had previously shown.

"Don't misunderstand me, Miss Merrilees. I wouldn't have that for the world. I have not yet said that I'm refusing to help you."

There were harder lines round her mouth as she answered.

"Not in so many words, perhaps, but as good as."

"No. That isn't true. Don't look at it like that. Please. Look here! I'll make you a proposition. You can please yourself whether you fall in with it or not. But listen to it first of all. Bring Godfrey Slade to see me. You and he can come together. Either at my flat—I'll give you the address before I go to-night—or we can all three have some grub together somewhere. Even here again. It would suit me all right. I should like to talk one or two things over with him in your presence. What do you say?"

For some seconds Anthony was uncertain as to how she had taken his suggestion. Doubt showed plainly on her face. Eventually her face cleared.

"All right, then. I will. That's on. Perhaps it may turn out to be a good idea. Godfrey's obstinate—as I told you—but I think I can persuade him to come along."

"Thanks. That's good of you. Give me a ring when you have the arrangements ready and I'll fall in with them whichever way you choose. A few hours' notice will do for me. After all, you know my telephone number, don't you?"

Anthony Bathurst smiled as he put the question to her. For the first time that evening, Star Merrilees seemed to be a little discomfited. Where she had before been a little anxious, she was now bordering on the uneasy. But she quickly recovered her normal confidence.

"Yes," she smiled back, "as you say—I know your telephone number."

The waiter brought Mr. Bathurst the bill.

"What would you like to do now?" asked Anthony of his companion.

"Have you your car here?" she asked.

"I have."

"Well, then—if it wouldn't be troubling you too much I should like you to drive me straight home. Do you mind . . . terribly?"

Anthony shook his head. "Not at all. I have an idea at the back of my mind that I'm being honoured. But tell me first of all where 'home' is."

"Little Stanwick Street. Number 22. You are quite sure you don't mind? I'm not spoiling your evening?"

"My dear Miss Merrilees," said Anthony, "on the contrary, I ought to regard myself as one of the luckiest of men. Even though a certain Mr. Godfrey Slade may be the luckiest. I shall be ready for you in the foyer within ten minutes."

"In that case, Mr. Bathurst," replied Star Merrilees in almost exactly the same tone as he had used, and with her glorious eyes flickering over him, "I shall be waiting there for you."

Chapter IX
THE BAILEY WHO DIDN'T COME HOME

IT WAS twenty-four hours after yet another hurried conference between the Littlehampton Police and the 'Yard,' when Anthony Bathurst walked out of Northampton station into the courtyard. He was greeted with a wind that blew upon him with chill and malevolent hostility. The time was early evening. He commented upon the nature of this wind to the driver of the taxi which he hired to take him from the railway station to the police station.

"Yes, sir," said the driver, "you're quite right—it is a bit on the nippy side. No two opinions about it. Enough to freeze the . . . er . . . ears off a brass monkey. Due East, you know, sir. We get the East wind down in these parts pretty regular. More often than's welcome. And do you know the real reason why it blows so cold?"

Anthony immediately admitted his ignorance.

"Well—I'll tell you," continued the taxi-driver preparatory to taking up his position, "it isn't everyone knows this—it blows straight across here from the East Anglian coast. If you look at the map, you'll see that there's nothing in the way. Got a clear road! It's all flat between here and the coast. Comes behind the old Boston stump. That's worth knowing now, isn't it?"

Anthony agreed that it most certainly was. The driver became more confidential than ever. He placed his face close to Anthony's and delivered himself once again of a valuable opinion.

"And what's more, there's very few what know that. My old grandmother told me about it when I was a nipper. Couldn't have been more than five, I couldn't. And what that old girl didn't know wasn't worth knowing."

"I suppose not," returned Mr. Bathurst, "voluminous—no doubt."

The driver got the vehicle under way. Anthony hadn't visited Northampton for some years. The last occasion had been in connection with his investigations of that curious problem of 'The Peacock's Eye.' When his driver deposited him outside the police headquarters, Anthony took a quick glance at his face and decided to risk putting a direct question to him.

"What sort of a place is Northampton for sport these days?"

The driver, realizing the unusual generosity of the tip that had been handed to him, expanded liberally.

"Sport?" he echoed, "sport?" he repeated—"you're askin' something of me, Guv'nor, aren't you? The old 'Cobblers' are well down the Third Division table, the little old county has won one match in the County Championship in the last 'undred years—why it's enough to make 'Fanny' Walden take to knittin'. Sport—you've said it, Guv'nor," he concluded dramatically. "You must be takin' a mike at me."

"But that's only football and cricket, what about other sports—boxing, say?"

"Well, there's a few likely lads knockin' about these parts—but not a lot as you might say. Though we certainly 'ad one star until a few months ago—when we lost 'im in very tragic circumstances. You arskin' reminded me of it. Did you ever 'ear of Ted Bailey, sir?"

"Ted Bailey! I rather think I did. The name certainly sounds familiar to me. Ted Bailey! Wasn't there something in the papers about him some little time back?"

The driver nodded cheerfully.

"Found drowned," he said with relish. "All bashed about, too. Round the 'Chevy Chase' and all across the 'Bushel.' Cut to blazes. Some of the town folk reckoned as 'ow he done himself in but I don't. Never on your life. I reckon he spoke out of his turn and somebody what was nearly a gang knocked him for six. Now—he *was* a likely bloke with the mittens, if you like—and looked like going a long way in the game."

"Great pity," concurred Anthony, cherishing the hope that the driver would enlarge still more on the subject. He was not to be disappointed.

"I never knew him myself," continued the taxi-driver, "I didn't use the same house. I usually pop in the 'Dog and Partridge.' Ted Bailey used to get in the 'Black-Faced Ram.' That's a little boozer down the road there."

The driver stabbed with a plump finger. "On the right of the road. About a quarter of an hour's walk from here. Stands on a corner. You can't miss it. Not far from where Rouse, the 'Blazing Car' murderer, popped up from the ditch and got spotted by them two fellers what was walking home from the dance. On the fifth of November that was. Remember it, sir? Didn't 'arf cause a sensation round 'ere."

Anthony intimated that he did and considered at the same time that it might not do for him to be inordinately curious with regard to the dead Bailey. He had already picked up a valuable snatch of information of which he intended to make full use as soon as he was able. The taxi-driver touched his cap, backed his vehicle and started his unprofitable journey back to the railway station.

Anthony waited for a few moments before making his next move. The cold was intense and his face under the relentless onslaught of the wind felt stiff and board-hard. He swung into a sharp walk with the intention of altering the programme he had mapped out. He would leave his visit to the police authorities until after he had been to the 'Black-Faced Ram.' With a bit of luck he might pick up one or two morsels of even more valuable information in the bar of that establishment. At any rate, the effort would be well worth trying. His experience had taught him the value of the local hostelry when it came to a matter of private news-gleaning. Also, his intended visit to a certain photographer's could wait till even later.

Twelve minute's sharp walking brought him to the sign of the 'Black-Faced Ram.' This proved to be a low-roofed house of the old-fashioned type. Flaring gas jets showed bright points of flame through the blurred windows. Judging by the buzz of conversation which came from within, the 'Ram' was already well patronized. The regular noise of the beer-engines was audible on the wintry air. Mr. Bathurst opened the door that was marked "Saloon." He was surprised at the number of people he found in there. There were at least two dozen, in knots of threes and fours, chiefly men, and they were dotted round the apartment in an equal term of distribution. The saloon was comfortable, if somewhat on the gaudy side as regards decoration.

Anthony walked to the bar and ordered. A barmaid, with red nails, a supercilious mouth and heaped-up hair well henna-ed, served his drink. Equipped at last, he retired to a table. He knew that his first task must be to listen to all the various snatches of conversation that came his way. If this failed entirely to produce anything, which was what he expected, he would be compelled to select the psychological moment and force the pace himself. He pulled out an evening paper he had purchased at Bletchley and read diligently. For a considerable time no remark was made by any of the occupants of the saloon which Anthony could by any means regard as hopeful or even encouraging. Then something happened. A game of 'Darts' started in a corner of the apartment. It struck Anthony that he might, with advantage, place himself in a position which would be close to the players. He thereupon walked over to another table carrying his glass with him. He soon saw that each of the players possessed skill much above the average. The game was an ordinary 301 up, beginning and ending on a 'double.' One of the players, a tall lanky chap with a fair drooping moustache and an unusually high collar, went out with 157 scored with three darts. Treble 19, Treble 20 and 'Double Top.' A burst of clapping from the onlookers signalized the success. Anthony deliberately joined in the contribution of applause. It was a good move on his part. By so doing, he effected an immediate and welcomed identification with the 'Darts' party.

"Like a game, sir?" asked the tall man—"for a pint of ale apiece?"

This was the opening which Anthony had desired.

"Certainly," he replied, "though I haven't the slightest doubt that you're much too good for me. Still, I shall be delighted to hand over your share of the stakes."

His prediction was quickly verified. In a comparatively short time he proved a moderately easy victim for this local champion. A return game followed—with a similar result. The lanky man sat at a table and disposed of his tankards of triumph with unconcealed relish.

"Spoils of the chase," grinned Anthony as his opponent replaced the second tankard on the table in front of him. "I'm rather afraid," Anthony continued as he seated himself again, "that I'm not quite in your class as a darts player. Still—that can't be helped. Every man to his trade."

"That's all right, sir," returned his conqueror. "I expect there are plenty of games at which you could take my trousers down—well and proper. But 'Darts,' you see, 'appens to be my special 'obby. Spend most of my spare time at it. So there you are. Makes all the difference."

The man who had played with the tall man at the beginning overheard what had been said and joined in the conversation.

"Ay," he said with a wag of the head, "old Tom here throws a pretty nifty dart. We all know that, 'ere at the 'Ram,' to our cost. More or less keep 'im in wallop we do—the artful old devil! So you needn't feel too ashamed, sir, because Tom Lessons 'as taken your number down. You're in good company."

"When I want my revenge I shall have to have the gloves on with him," responded Anthony with a laugh, "then perhaps we could cry 'fifty-fifty'."

The man who had been referred to as Tom Lessons looked at Anthony with undisguised admiration.

"I can see you're pretty fit, sir, and that I shouldn't stand an earthly with you with the gloves on. I'll give you that much before we start. I'll freely admit I shouldn't like to argue with you. You look altogether too useful for a bloke like me."

Lessons paused as though he was remembering something. Anthony waited for it. Sure enough it came.

"A pal of mine, though, who used to use this 'ouse pretty regular, would ha' been a different proposition for you. A very likely lad he was—and no error."

"Oh," said Anthony scenting the imminence of the battle, "and who was that, may I ask?"

Lessons shook his head as though reminiscence were distasteful to him.

"A man well known in the boxing world. Ted Bailey. Knew him well. Lived only a few doors away from him. Unhappily—just as his future looked all bright and rosy—the poor fellow came to a nasty end."

Anthony nodded decisively.

"I remember it. Not so long ago at that. Committed suicide somewhere, didn't he? In the early part of the year? Or am I confusing him with somebody else?"

"No, sir," replied Lessons, "you're absolutely on the spot. You're on the right man. Although I don't know," Lessons began to speak more slowly, "speaking for myself and as one who knew Ted Bailey from A to Z as you might say, that I agree that it *was* suicide. But never you mind that—you're thinkin' of the right fellow." Lessons concluded with a nod of the head.

"Really," said Anthony, with a strong show of interest, "and what grounds have you for your idea? Let me see now, wasn't Bailey's body picked up at the seaside somewhere? Or am I wrong this time and really confusing him with somebody else?"

"No. You're still right. That's the Bailey case you've got hold of. Worthing was the place where the body was found. Young Ted was supposed to have done himself in by jumping off the pier. Jumpin' off the pier, my foot!" Lessons spat in contempt.

Anthony persisted.

"And why don't you agree with the suicide theory, Mr. Lessons? I think you were going to tell me."

Lessons rubbed his top lip before he spoke.

"Well—in my opinion, Ted Bailey wasn't the sort of bloke to do such a thing. A man doesn't go to the length of bumping himself off unless he's got a good reason. Now—does he? Am I talkin' sound common-sense or not?" Lessons turned to Anthony for his corroboration.

"I should say that you are undoubtedly talking common-sense."

"Very good, sir. Then we understand each other to be going on with. When they first came to me with the yarn that my pal Ted had done himself in by jumping off the pier at Worthing, do you know what I said?"

"I have no idea, Mr. Lessons."

"I said—'take a run and tell that yarn to the marines'."

"You did?"

"I did, sir, without the slightest hesitation. For one thing, Ted Bailey was a good plucked 'un what could take it. 'E never screamed. You get my idea?"

"Yes. But that point isn't necessarily convincing. On what are you basing that conclusion?"

"Ever seen Ted in the ring?"

"Never."

"Well—there you are. He could take punishment with the best of 'em. I've seen Ted fight dozens of times and never once have I seen him show a streak of yellow. See my meaning, sir?"

"Yes—but again, I don't necessarily agree with you. Look at it this way. Courage as we understand it is such an inconstant quality."

Lessons looked a little perturbed. Anthony understood the conditions of his doubt.

"Let me put it to you this way. A man who will face heavy shell-fire with the utmost equanimity may be scared stiff of cats. I have actually known an example of that. I knew a man who shivered if a cat came within a yard of him. I can see that you know what I mean."

Lessons nodded in agreement. Anthony continued his argument.

"Now from that position we arrive at this. Bailey may have been as brave as a lion when he had the gloves on but a personal crisis in his life, of a very different kind, may have completely broken down his defences—and found him totally wanting. With the result that he does what many another man has done before him—he crumples up and takes what he considers the easiest way out—destroys himself."

Lessons shook his head.

"With some men I know—I might have agreed with you. But not as regards my 'old china' Ted Bailey. No, sir!"

Anthony smiled at his persistence. Lessons proceeded.

"I suppose you reckon I'm prejudiced—but I don't think I am. Knowin' a man means a rare lot. I knew Bailey—you've never met him. I was his constant companion. Makes all the difference."

Lessons spat on the floor for emphasis.

"I'm prepared to grant you that," replied Anthony.

"Another thing," Lessons appeared to have thought of an additional argument—"Ted Bailey was in love at the time he conked out. As much as any fellow I've ever seen. No—more than any fellow I've ever seen. Can't say fairer than that, can I? Ted was hooked up with the prettiest girl in the town. Generally admitted! Even by the girls themselves. Her name was Stella Molyneux. She was a good-looker, I can tell you. A bit above Ted—from a social point of view, too. Quite the classy sort. No parents living. Had come in for a good bit o' dough from them. She and Ted would have been married by now, I reckon, if nothing 'ad 'appened to 'im. And you would have had a rare job to find a handsomer couple. Could ha' walked a thousand miles and failed. Both of 'em as smart as paint! Now are you still going to tell me, sir, that Ted Bailey committed suicide—when there he was, all merry and bright? His career openin' right in front of him, full of promise and all that and Stella Molyneux waitin' for 'im just round the corner, as you might say? Because, if you are, it won't do for me. Not if you argue with me for a month of Sundays."

Lessons shook his head again gravely.

"Just a minute," said Anthony, "before I reply to that, I'll order another round. I'm sure you can drink another beer."

He went to the bar again and ordered. Lessons remained at the table and waited for him. The evening was proving more than usually profitable for him.

"Well, sir," he said, upon Anthony resuming his seat, "and what have you to say to me now? Have I made any impression on you?"

Anthony smiled at him again.

"Something that will, I think, probably surprise you. This! I entirely agree with you!"

Lessons thrust out his hand. "Shake, sir," he said eagerly. "That sounds good to me—I feel as though I've done my old pal a real good turn. That's how it strikes me. That I've got somebody to believe in him against the odds. Just as I do myself. Because I reckon suicide's a cowardly act. It's just dodging the issue. Somehow I can't piece it up with what I call a true Britisher. And that's what Ted Bailey was—all the way through."

Lessons shook hands with Anthony and then drank beer with both obvious and audible enjoyment. Anthony spoke again as though an idea had just come to him.

"Where exactly did Bailey live? Near you, you said, didn't you?"

"I did. Ted lived in Tresadern Street same as what I do. I'm at Number 14. He was at Number 22. Four doors in from me. Lived with his old mother and sister, 'e did."

"I suppose they moved away from there after his death?"

Lessons shook his head. "No. Not they. They stuck to the old place—and will, I expect, till they carry the old girl out feet first. Decent old body—Mrs. Bailey. One of the old school. My—wasn't she proud of young Ted! 'Ad good reason to be. Lovely fellow! Over 6 feet— between twelve and thirteen stone stripped to the skin—and only 24 years of age. Corks—was 'e fit! I'll say. Wish I was 'arf as fit." Lessons drank more beer.

"And what happened to the young lady in the case? Miss Molyneux?"

"Young Stella? Well—it's funny you should ask that—'cause a peculiar thing happened with regard to her. Very soon after Ted's affair, she went away."

"Went away? How do you mean? Left the district?"

"That's exactly what I do mean. She cleared away suddenly. And what's more—nobody seems to know where she went to—or what's become of 'er. Seems as though she wanted to forget the place altogether and everybody in it. As far as I know, nobody's 'eard a word of 'er or from 'er."

"Perhaps it's understandable if, as you say, they were so wrapped up in each other. Took it badly."

"Still," argued Lessons, "you'd ha' thought she'd 'ave kept in touch with somebody, now wouldn't you?"

"It would have been reasonable, I suppose. But there you are— you never know—and you mustn't attempt to lay down rules of life or conduct for other people. Different temperaments react in different ways when circumstances are difficult and trying. One man sits down under a strain and endures what comes. Another runs away from it. Just as I suggested concerning Bailey. A third sails in and fights hard with all the courage imaginable. And yet—before the time of trial actually comes—no one knows for certain what each of those three men will do when the time of trial does come. That's my point, Mr. Lessons."

"I agree with you, sir—generally speaking. And you agree with me over Ted Bailey—so we'll call our little argument square. Fifty-fifty—eh?"

Lessons grinned as he came to this judicial and eminently satisfactory conclusion.

"Well," said Anthony, "I must be getting along. What do you say to one for the road? You won't refuse me, I'm sure."

"Well—I won't say 'no,' sir—seeing that you've asked me—although I shan't be leaving here for some little time yet. Make it a pint of mild and bitter this time—if it's all the same to you, sir."

When Anthony made his departure from the 'Black-Faced Ram' he found himself wondering if the photograph he carried in his pocket was anything like Stella Molyneux, the girl who had so suddenly disappeared. According to Lessons's arbitrament of Beauty . . . he didn't think it could be . . . but, there, as he told himself once again . . . Beauty lies in the eyes of the beholder.

Keeping his eyes well open he soon found a turning with the name-plate Tresadern Street. He made his way to Number 22. It was a smallish, unpretentious house of the villa type. Anthony walked up to the front door and knocked. Receiving no answer to his summons, he knocked again. He heard footsteps coming to the door. A girl opened the door to him. The electric light that was burning in the passage shone on and showed up her face. Anthony had to prevent himself from stepping back in astonishment. It was the face of the girl whose photograph had been found on the body of 'Lefty' Donovan!

CHAPTER X
THE HOUSE IN TRESADERN STREET

WHEN Anthony had recovered from his first shock of surprise, he heard the voice of the girl speaking to him. He saw that she was staring into his face.

"Who is it? What is it you want?"

"If I could be permitted to have a few words with Mrs. Bailey, I should be extremely obliged."

"Who are you?" asked the girl again from the doorway.

Anthony had prepared himself, and made certain explanations. The girl evidently accepted both him and them. Her next words, however, occasioned him further surprise. Although he has admitted more than once since that, considering all things, they should not have done.

"I will tell my mother what you say. She's upstairs. Will you please come in and wait."

So the girl whose photograph had been found in 'Lefty' Donovan's pocket was none other than Ted Bailey's sister. The skein of the problem was becoming more involved than ever. Anthony was shown into a small room of the parlour type. The girl who had admitted him disappeared for a few moments, to return with a thin, anxious-looking woman evidently in the middle fifties. Her face was lined, and her hair prematurely greyed. She held her arms folded as she looked at him. Anthony was glad to think that he had the photograph with him. It would give him a magnificent opportunity to establish his credentials and open his enquiry.

"Sit down, sir," said Mrs. Bailey, "and tell me why you have come here. Is it about my son?"

Anthony produced his card of identity fortified by the completely illegible signature of Sir Austin Kemble, Commissioner of Scotland Yard. Mrs. Bailey looked at it and handed it back to him.

"I am glad you have come," continued Mrs. Bailey, with simple candour, "although as I expect you know, the police have already been here many times. But I know that Ted was killed by somebody and I want the truth established. My Ted never killed himself."

Anthony chose his next words carefully.

"Now, listen to this, Mrs. Bailey. The body of a man was found recently on the shore at Littlehampton, in Sussex. Littlehampton, as you are probably aware, is not far from Worthing. This man who died at Littlehampton was a distinguished boxer."

The girl stirred in her chair uneasily. Anthony again continued without turning to look in her direction.

"But what I think will probably interest and concern you more than anything else, is the fact that this photograph was found on the dead man's body."

He put the photograph on the table so that both of his auditors could see it properly. A choking gasp came from the lips of the girl. Her mother's face, as she gazed at the photograph, held the ashen pallor of faintness. The girl spoke:

"Who was this man that was murdered at Littlehampton? Tell me his name, please."

"His name, Miss Bailey, was Donovan. He was known to his intimates as 'Lefty' Donovan."

She nodded understandingly. "Yes, I know. I have heard of him." She turned to her mother. "He was even better known than Ted in the boxing world—what this gentleman says is perfectly true."

"It would help me," said Anthony, "if you could suggest any explanation of his having your photograph with him."

"In one way, the explanation is simple," replied the girl. "My brother had the photograph with him. I had it taken at East's, and he had carried it about with him for months."

"Yes," nodded Mrs. Bailey, "that's the explanation, all right. Winnie has hit on it."

Anthony felt a strong feeling of satisfaction as she spoke. He knew now what he had previously but suspected. The murderers of Ted Bailey were the murderers also of 'Lefty' Donovan. He immediately translated this knowledge into words.

"That fact, I think, ladies, proves conclusively that your son and Donovan were victims of the same people. Miss Bailey's photograph was taken from your son and then planted by them in Donovan's pockets. The reason, at the moment, is not obvious."

"I think you are right, sir. They took Winnie's photo off Ted when they killed him."

Anthony nodded. "I wonder whether you would be good enough to answer one or two questions that I should like to put to you. Do you mind? Your answers may help me materially."

The mother took it upon herself to answer him.

"Not at all, sir. We shall be only too pleased to answer you."

"Firstly, then, have you ever heard your son speak of or refer to anybody named Bellamy?"

Mrs. Bailey shook her head. Anthony turned to the girl at her side with a look of interrogation. Winnie Bailey did as her mother had done. She shook her head. Neither showed the slightest hesitation. Anthony tried again.

"He *might* have mentioned the name of 'Banjo' Bellamy. Does that help you at all?"

Again they shook their heads.

"No," said Mrs. Bailey, "I never heard Ted mention that name, either. It's one that I should have remembered."

"And you, Miss Bailey?"

"No, sir. Never. I never heard the name. And Ted wasn't one to be secretive. He told us nearly all his business. I should say we were in his confidence with regard to most things. Would this man Bellamy have been a boxer, do you think, sir?"

"To *do* with boxing, I fancy, in some capacity or other. Still—never mind—I want to take you back to the morning of the day your son disappeared."

Mrs. Bailey nodded that she understood. "That was on the sixteenth of February, sir. When Ted received a letter. It was a Friday. Ted had been spending the previous weekend with some friends at Bedford. Cousins of ours, they are, really."

"Tell me what happened then, on the morning of the sixteenth, will you, when this letter that you mentioned came? With as many details as far as you are able to remember them after this lapse of time."

Winnie Bailey took up the story while her mother was hesitating.

"Ted had the letter by the morning post."

"Just a moment, Miss Bailey. Did you see this letter? Did your brother show it to you?"

"No, sir."

"Did you see the envelope in which this letter came?"

"No, sir. And nobody else saw it, either. Nobody but Ted. The police asked us both about that. As a matter of fact, Ted put it in his pocket. When he went out, I should say he took that letter with him. There's not the slightest doubt that he did."

"Did he make any remarks about this letter he had received? At breakfast, say?"

"Yes," cut in the elder woman eagerly, "I can answer that at once. He did. To me. My daughter, here, may not have heard him. I think she had gone out of the room at the time. He was pleased about the letter. Said something about it being 'a grand offer.'"

Anthony was struck by the similarity of the Bailey to the Donovan circumstances. This phrase which had been spoken by Mrs. Bailey was the precise phrase which Flora Donovan had used to him when she had first come to him for help.

"So that he was *pleased* to receive this offer, such as it was—eh?"

"Yes, sir. Without any doubt, sir. Pleased as Punch. As far as I could see, Ted thought that a big chance had at last come his way. Not only big—but also unexpected."

"And he went out?"

"He went out, sir."

"Giving you no indication of any kind as to where he was going or as to how long he would be?"

Mrs. Bailey shook her head again. "None at all, sir. But I'll swear that Ted meant to be back for lunch that same day. I can't prove it, of course—but I'd swear to it from his manner. You know how it is, sir, a mother can tell these things with a son that she's brought up and who's lived with her for years. It's a sort of instinct she has, I suppose."

The daughter intervened in support of her mother's contention.

"I must say that I agree with my mother, sir, with regard to that point. I'm as certain as can be that when my brother Ted went out that morning he fully intended to be back with us at midday. I told the police that—several times. They kept on asking me about it."

"Your opinion is invaluable, Miss Bailey. I promise you that I shall keep it in mind. Perhaps you could help me as well in relation to another matter? I refer to a lady of your brother's acquaintance—a Miss Stella Molyneux."

As Anthony spoke, mother and daughter exchanged glances. Mrs. Bailey eventually answered his question although it had been directed towards her daughter.

"Have you any news of Stella, sir?"

"No fresh news, I'm afraid. On the other hand, I rather wanted information about her from you."

Mrs. Bailey shook her head. "You will be disappointed. We have not heard a word of Stella since she left Northampton. When you mentioned her name we thought that you might have heard something concerning her which you wanted to pass on to us."

"No. I know nothing. How long was it after your son's death that Miss Molyneux disappeared?"

"About a week, sir. Certainly not more."

"It was a complete surprise to you when she went?" Mrs. Bailey nodded. "Well—after the news of Ted's death came through to us, we didn't see a lot of Stella. She kept away from here. That was natural, I suppose. But we didn't expect that she'd go right away from the place without saying a word to us. Still—that's exactly what did happen. She went all right."

"And you haven't heard from her since?"

"As I said—not a word, sir. And nobody in Northampton has, sir. Nobody!"

"You've no idea or even suspicion as to where she's gone?"

"Not the slightest. Her father and mother were both dead. She was alone in the world, as you might say, and could therefore please herself. And I know nothing about any relations she may have had or gone to in any other part of the country."

"Your son was going to marry her?"

Again Mrs. Bailey nodded. "They would have been married some time this year, sir. That was an understood thing. Either at Easter or in the summer, I expect it would have been."

He saw that Mrs. Bailey was now near to tears.

"Do you happen to have a photograph of Miss Molyneux handy? If you have—I should like to look at it."

Mrs. Bailey shook her head at the request, and looked enquiringly at her daughter. But Winnie Bailey shook her head as her mother had done before her.

"I'm sorry to disappoint you, but we haven't such a thing in the house. My brother had a small snap of her, but I don't know what he did with it. I'm certain it's not here. I haven't seen it since his death, and I don't remember seeing it for a long time before that."

"That's a pity. I should like to have seen a photograph of Miss Molyneux. Never mind. It can't be helped. Could you give me a description of her. Just a rough one—shall we say?"

Mrs. Bailey came into the conversation in answer to this question. Anthony thought that she seemed eager to justify her son's choice.

"Stella was a lovely girl, sir. There's no arguing about that. One in a million. My Ted and her made a lovely couple."

Anthony thought of Lessons's eulogy. Here it was being repeated. "What was she like, Mrs. Bailey?"

"Tall and slim. Just like a lovely flower to look at."

"Dark or fair?"

"Dark, sir. Lovely dark hair. Almost black. Like a great cloud of dark beauty, it was. And lovely eyes. Ted was ever so proud of her. And she was just as proud of him in return—I can tell you, sir."

"She had money, I suppose, to be in a position to go away as she did? What I mean is—she wasn't dependent on any job that she had down here, for instance?"

"Oh, no—she had an income of her own. A good deal. Her father and mother were dead, you see. They both died some years ago. Stella being the only child inherited some money from her father, and then when her mother died a year or two later, the rest of the family money came to her. Stella was a well-educated girl—far above the average—but you mustn't think that my Ted was after her because of that and the money she had. If she hadn't had a farthing to bless herself with she'd have been his girl just the same." The mother spoke proudly.

"I have no doubt about that," said Anthony, "from what you have told me, I am convinced that they were genuinely attached to each other." He rose from his chair and faced her. "Well, Mrs. Bailey, I don't think that I need detain you any longer. It has been very kind of you to put up with me as you have, and to tell me so much. And those thanks, of course, include you, Miss Bailey, as well."

The girl flushed at Anthony's remark. Mrs. Bailey, however, was composure itself.

"That's all right, sir," she answered. "I'm only too pleased to help. But now I want you to tell me something. Will you?"

Anthony smiled at her. "I think my answer must depend on what it is, Mrs. Bailey."

She came across to him and eyed him steadily.

"You think that my son was murdered, don't you, sir?"

"Yes, Mrs. Bailey, I do."

"Would it be by a gang of roughs who set about him?"

Anthony thought for a moment or so before he answered her. "I don't know about that—yet. But—if you must have an answer—I *don't* think so."

Her eyes looked fearlessly into his.

"Do you mean, then, that you think he was murdered by one person?"

"I am not sure."

She still eyed him steadily. Her manner was unwavering. "Do you think it likely for a moment that *one* man could have knocked Ted out like he was supposed to have been?"

Anthony shook his head at her. "At the moment I cannot say, Mrs. Bailey. With any certainty, that is. I am sorry if I disappoint you."

She gave a little gesture of impatience.

"Tell me this, then. *Why* was my son murdered? What was the reason for it? There must have *been* a reason! People aren't murdered for the fun of the thing."

Anthony shook his head again.

"I don't know. I wish I did. I am as completely in the dark as you yourself are. But I *shall* know, Mrs. Bailey. All in good time. And then your son may be avenged. I assure you it won't be my fault if he's not."

Mrs. Bailey repeated her previous statement as though she had not heard what Anthony had said.

"There must have been a reason. People do not murder others unless they have a reason. And yet I cannot think, try as I will, why *anybody* could have wanted Ted dead. That's why I can't sleep at night. Why I worry all the day long, why the whole thing is on my mind always. There was no reason in the world why my son should have been got rid of. And until I know the truth I shall never be able to rest. Not if I live to be over a hundred. You may think it foolish of me—but I shall never change." She shook her head with a resigned sorrow.

Anthony shook hands with her, and then with her daughter.

"Mrs. Bailey," he said, "I entirely agree with you, and I see no reason why you *should* change. Hold fast to your beliefs. Good-bye, and once again many thanks for your valuable help. By the way—there's one more thing I should like to ask you. When your son's body was found—were the hands or wrists injured or lacerated?"

She shook her head. "No, sir. The scratches were on the face, neck, and shoulders."

"Thank you, Mrs. Bailey."

Miss Bailey accompanied him to the door. Outside the house in Tresadern Street, Mr. Bathurst came to a quick decision. He thought over what he had just heard, and felt more than content with it. He would *not* go to the police headquarters at Northampton. For the time being he had heard enough! And enough on this occasion had been better than a feast!

CHAPTER XI
GODFREY SLADE

ANTHONY Lotherington Bathurst sat in his flat and awaited two visitors. By name—Star Merrilees and Godfrey Slade. Emily had been at her scintillating best from the sheer standpoint of her culinary art, and the table that had been prepared for the guests bore ample testimony to her taste and ability. Anthony looked at his watch. His guests should be here, according to arrangement, within a few minutes. Miss Merrilees had 'phoned him two days previously, much to his satisfaction, and had made the appointment as he had suggested she might when they had been together in the Diadem room at Murillo's. Anthony rose, looked at the table, put in one or two extra deft touches and sat down again. As he did so, he heard the sound of car-wheels drawing up outside. A moment or so later, Emily having seen to the preliminaries, Star Merrilees, as delightful as ever, was introducing him with a certain proud shyness to Godfrey Slade.

Anthony was at once most favourably impressed by the latter's appearance. In height, five feet eleven inches as near as made no odds, weight round about twelve stone, Godfrey Slade had blue eyes, black hair and a length of arm with a breadth of shoulder which made him the admiration and the envy of most men, to say nothing of the women. Anthony dispensed drinks, had his own Clover Club, his guests took the seats to which he directed them and Emily, on time to the tick, brought in the oysters.

Gradually Anthony directed the conversation to the business of the evening. Up to that moment, Star Merrilees had almost monopolized the conversation. Her qualities of radiance and flame-like attractiveness were fully in evidence. She had begun by rallying Anthony upon the fact that she had accepted his invitation to this dinner at his flat. Slade had laughed at her remarks good-temperedly. Anthony saw quickly that Slade attracted her intensely. Every time she spoke, her eyes went to Slade to see the effect that her remarks had made upon him. Slade was quiet and reserved, extremely self-contained and all the time well poised and entirely at his ease. He said little but all that he did say was relevant and to the point. Anthony listened to the flood of small talk with tactful patience and then with skilful direction achieved his object.

"Well, Mr. Slade, and what is the latest position with regard to the fight? Is it coming off after all or has Sir Cloudesley accepted the inevitable?"

Slade laughed again. "What do you mean exactly by that, Mr. Bathurst? That he's already pushed his hand into his pocket and taken out his cheque-book to pay old Secretan?"

"Not quite."

"Well—that's what it would come to, I'm afraid. And it's none too pleasant a prospect for the old man, I can assure you."

"I don't suppose it is. Especially in times like the present. What's he really doing about it?"

Slade looked towards Star Merrilees rather apprehensively. Anthony wondered why. She gave Slade no help, however, but went on eating with the utmost deliberation. Slade, therefore, took it upon himself to answer Mr. Bathurst's question.

"Well, Mr. Bathurst—there's nothing really fixed yet . . . which can be regarded as anything like a certainty . . . but so long as the Guv'nor can put a man in the ring at the appointed time on the appointed day, he's within his rights, and can put up a scrap."

Anthony nodded. "I understand that. I understood it on the morning I met your father and mentioned it to him ultimately. It may be a way out for him."

Slade laughed and looked again at the lady.

"Well . . . there you are then . . . that's how it is."

Miss Merrilees flashed a look of antipathy round the table that was all embracing. Anthony knew that she was merely biding her time. He kept, however, to the main issue as regards his conversation with Slade.

"Has he anybody in mind?"

By now Slade had become acutely uneasy. "Well," he replied, "not exactly. He has one or two ideas in view, but I wouldn't say that there was anything definite . . . yet."

Slade's uneasiness increased. Anthony was determined to be relentless.

"What are these ideas? I'm really tremendously interested."

Slade took out his handkerchief and mopped the perspiration from his brow. Star Merrilees gave Anthony a look of gratitude. Things were beginning to go her way at last. Anthony looked at Slade as he awaited his answer. Slade realized that there was no escape for him. Anthony was smiling at him guilelessly. Slade then fidgeted in his chair.

"Well," he said, still supremely uncomfortable, "the Guv'nor at the moment has two ideas with which he's toying . . . two strings to his bow, I suppose, would be the better description."

He paused and drank. When he replaced his glass, he saw that four eyes were gazing at him expectantly. He knew that he had to go on; for two of the watching eyes belonged to Star Merrilees. He wiped his lips. Anthony clinched the issue.

"And what are these two strings, Mr. Slade? What are their names? Pardon my curiosity."

Slade at last realized that capitulation was inevitable and gave up the ghost. "Number one string—Mike Jago of Bath in the county of Somerset. Number two string—a comparatively unknown man—actually an amateur. He'll do his best, but in all probability that best won't be nearly good enough. However, we shall see about that. Time will tell."

Slade showed his white teeth as he laughed. The secret was out and he felt decidedly better and easier in his mind. But Mr. Bathurst hadn't finished with him yet and he was at once brought back again to the point which Anthony and Star Merrilees had at issue.

"Really," said Anthony, "that's more interesting. And what's the name of this amateur?"

Slade laughed again. "It's pretty evident, Bathurst, that you mean to pin me down. Every time I try to wriggle away from you, you bring me back without any mercy. I feel something like a human butterfly at the mercy of an ardent entomologist. The name of this amateur who may come to the attempted rescue of my father, is Slade, Godfrey Slade. I fancy that you may have met him. Not a bad bloke!"

Star Merrilees intervened indignantly.

"Not if *I* have anything to do with it. Still you've told Mr. Bathurst now—before I say any more, let's hear what he has to say about it."

Anthony played up to her attitude and expressed considerable surprise at Slade's statement.

"You yourself? I really had no idea."

"It's true enough," nodded Slade.

"I don't know that I can reasonably contribute any opinion; worth anything, that is. At first glance, the proposition seems an extremely plucky one on your part—but is it wise? Are you in Blood's class?"

"No," returned Slade—"but I'm what they call 'useful' and I might bustle him up with a bit of luck. You never know. I shall want a lot, of course. I might slip in a lucky one or Blood might stumble and fall at a critical moment—as I said—you never know in boxing."

Anthony shook his head. "Yes—but all that's distinctly unlikely I should say. And another thing—there's the public to be considered as well."

"I'm glad to hear you talk like that, Mr. Bathurst," said Miss Merrilees severely as she fingered the stem of her wineglass, "because I've been telling Godfrey much the same thing for days. But he won't listen to me. He simply will *not* listen. He *may* listen to you. And for a solid packing of sheer unadulterated obstinacy in his make-up, he'd be hard to beat. You can take him so far—but if he's made up his mind not to move any farther than that, no argument or persuasion from anybody in the world will make him. He's a Slade! I know him, you see."

Godfrey Slade grinned at the criticism and pressed her arm affectionately.

"Now, Star, there's no need to get on your hind legs. I listen to you with regard to all matters where your advice may be valuable. You know that as well as I do. When it comes to my taking on Phil Blood, it's my own funeral and I have to make my own decision. In Life one has to do things like that—and what's more—one has to take one's risks. Sorry and all that."

The lady answered him with a trace of bitterness. "Your own funeral! I congratulate you on your choice of words. You couldn't have described it better. I only hope you'll be recognizable when the fight's over and they lower you into your coffin."

"Good Lord, Star! Have a heart. To hear you talk one would think that I was a novice. Actually speaking—I'm pretty useful when it comes to putting the cards on the table."

"Blood's Blood," she replied—"and nothing you say can alter the fact—he's not Ben Barnes of the X Division of the Metropolitan Police or Claude Walters of the Midland Bank. Why on earth don't you listen to me and see reason?"

Anthony however was listening intently.

"I can take care of myself—don't you fret. And if the redoubtable Phil gives me a bashing, my natural beauty will stand the strain and be restored to me within a week."

"I know. That's what you think. Blinded in an eye—for life perhaps—*you* who are such a grand man—all for a wretched fight for beastly money. I hate it all. It's horrible."

Godfrey Slade winked at Anthony. "Devotion, my dear Bathurst. Have a good look at it while you've got the chance—because you don't meet it every day of the week. Not love, my boy—that's too mild a word. This is worship pure and simple."

"And yet," said Anthony continuing in the same vein, "we are led to believe that the female of the species is more deadly than the male."

The lines round Star's mouth grew harder as she responded. "It might be," she said, "that devotion could be very . . . deadly . . . I can imagine it being so."

Slade laughed outright. "Good old Star! You stick to your guns to the last round, don't you? Well, I can't find it in my heart to blame you."

She shook her head at him with a half-smile. Anthony found an interest in watching them. They were a distinguished pair. There was no gainsaying that. His thoughts reverted to Bailey, the fighter from Northampton and the girl who had been within an ace of marrying him . . . until "they met Murder on his way with his seven bloodhounds following him." Bailey and his lady had been a grand pair likewise! But Miss Merrilees was talking again.

"Why don't you promise me, Godfrey, what I ask you? What I've asked you so many times. To give up this crazy idea of taking 'Lefty' Donovan's place against Blood. I can't understand your refusing as you do. It isn't a *lot* to do for me."

For the first time since the dinner started, Slade began to show signs of impatience.

"It's not a question of what I'm prepared to do for you. What you are asking me to promise isn't a fair proposition at all. It's just like a silly twerp of a girl who says to a man she's hitched up with 'I want you to give up smoking . . . it's not asking much of you—if you love me, you can easily do a little thing like that.' The particular sacrifice is always referred to as 'a little thing' and when the bloke refuses . . . absolutely justifiably . . . the idiot of a girl sets up a moan—'you don't love me. You *can't* love me' and there's one hell of a damned row. Whereas what she really needs to bring her to her senses is a jolly good caning on the seat of her trousers." He leant over to Miss Merrilees. "And I *mean* that, my girl—every word of it."

Miss Merrilees made no reply. The banners of annoyance were unfurled in her cheeks. Anthony, realizing more than ever that the onlooker sees most of the game, waited for her further contribution.

But none came. Beyond the gesture of shrugging her shoulders. At that moment Emily entered with the sweets.

"Ice pudding," announced Mr. Bathurst. "I hope you both like it."

"We do," returned Slade, "and I for one will do justice to it."

Again Miss Merrilees said nothing.

"Put the pudding just there, Emily, will you, please?"

Anthony indicated a portion of the table just in front of him. Emily obeyed his instructions. Anthony served his guests liberally. Star spoke to him as she passed her plate.

"How is that poor Mrs. Donovan these days? Have you seen her recently?"

"No, Miss Merrilees. I feel rather ashamed of myself in that direction. Some people might even accuse me of neglecting her. The point was that I had no good news for her. So I stayed away. The look in her eyes hurts and haunts me."

"Poor thing," said Star; "she's lost a man she loved and it's possible that the sun may never shine for her again. I think that I know exactly how she feels. She has all my sympathy."

Slade winked gracelessly at Anthony. "Star's sympathy to-night is almost overpowering. I don't know where she gets it all from. She'd adore having it burnt at the stake. She ought to have been a nurse. She'd have made a topping nurse. I'd be willing to have beri-beri for a period of six months if I could be certain that Star would be there to nurse me."

Star Merrilees replied doggedly. "You can tease me as much as you like, Godfrey! I don't mind. All I know is that what I've said to-night is *true*. And some day, Godfrey, both you and Mr. Bathurst will realize that I am right. I shouldn't be surprised too, if that day comes much sooner than either of you expects."

Star Merrilees closed her lips with firm determination. Slade looked at his watch. "Just on nine o'clock," he announced.

Anthony nodded towards the radiogram in the corner of the room. "Would you care to hear the nine o'clock news?"

"That's an idea," returned Slade. "Switch on, will you, Bathurst?"

Anthony rose from his chair and switched on the set. After a short interval the news began to come through. For a long time it was ordinary, and devoid of any distinctive feature or flavour.

"Nothing much to-night," said Godfrey Slade, "news lately seems conspicuous by its absence. And the extraordinary part of it is that nearly all the evenings are the same. There's never anything to give us a jolt."

"Just as well, perhaps," replied Anthony Bathurst.

Suddenly Star Merrilees sat bolt upright in her chair,

"Listen," she said with upraised finger. Anthony and Slade concentrated on the announcer's voice. They had missed the opening words which Star had heard . . . "has been missing from his home at Bath in Somerset since last Tuesday, the fourth day of December. The following description of the missing man may be of assistance to listeners. Height 5 feet 11 inches. Weight 12 stone 10 lbs. Fair hair. Blue eyes. Teeth excellent. Age 22 years. If any person has any news of the missing man will he or she please communicate with . . . telephone number . . ."

Anthony looked at Slade with anxiety in his eyes and then swung round towards Star Merrilees.

"Tell me," he said almost peremptorily, "who was that? The missing man, I mean."

"That," replied Star, "was a reference to Mike Jago of Bath in the county of Somerset."

Slade gasped. "Bailey . . . Donovan . . . and now Jago. What's it all mean?"

"I wish I could tell you," replied Anthony gravely. There came a long silence. Anthony and his two guests sat and looked at each other.

CHAPTER XII
THE END OF MIKE JAGO

"SIT down, Mr. Bathurst," said Chief Inspector MacMorran. Anthony took what was his favourite seat in the Inspector's room at the 'Yard'—on the corner of MacMorran's table. Anthony smoked a cigarette and swung his legs.

"I have something to tell you," said the Inspector, "something of the greatest importance."

"Re the Donovan affair?"

"Yes."

"In relation to the missing Bath boxer, Mike Jago?"

"Yes."

"Dead?"

MacMorran nodded gravely. "Dead. The news has just come through. Getting a little *too* hot, isn't it?"

"Where—this time?"

"Same territory. Lancing. Or near Lancing, to be exact."

"On the beach?"

"Ay. The same technique all over again. Face in ribbons. Chest, shoulders and ears tom and cut in the same way. Hands and wrists untouched." MacMorran leant over to him. "What was the name of that bird you were telling Lilley and me about down at Littlehampton? I've forgotten it."

"The Pteranodon. But I thought from your remarks that you were the confirmed sceptic?"

"So I was," growled MacMorran, "and still am."

"Good old Andrew," murmured Anthony, "unswervin' devotion to a cause. Any details through yet from Lancing?"

"No," returned the Inspector, "beyond what I've already told you. We heard those about an hour ago. From Sussex. They got through to us first of all and then were getting through to the police at Bath."

Anthony clasped his hands across one knee. "Pity we don't know all. At this stage I could bear to hear all the details. Might feel more certain of my ground, if I did."

MacMorran stared at him wonderingly. "What are you thinking of . . . particularly?"

Anthony unclasped his hands and rubbed his cheek contemplatively. "Footprints . . . shall we say . . . on the sands of Time? Not altogether *unlikely*, I should think. What do you think about it yourself, Andrew?"

MacMorran scratched on his blotting pad with a pen. "The same. I adore consistency."

"Bailey, Donovan and now Jago," said Mr. Bathurst almost to himself. "And all killed the same way. What's the answer to it, Andrew? Is there one? Have *you* got one for me?"

MacMorran shook his head gloomily. "Can't think of anything. My mind's a blank."

"Fighting youth," said Anthony, still half meditative, "all of 'em as fit as fiddles. Grand specimens. The rich red wine of youth was there all right. Poured out as waste. Why? Motive Andrew, motive, What is it? Where is it?"

"Search me. Don't get it at all. Sorry I can't help you—but that's how it is."

Anthony went on from there. "If the idea were to remove Donovan from the point of view of the Blood scrap with which he was concerned, how on earth does that idea team up with the elimination of Bailey and now Jago? And Bailey came first—remember!"

"Went first," corrected MacMorran.

Anthony ignored the sinister amendment. "Why the three, Andrew? What have they got in common—these three—beyond the fact that they're 'scrappers' in the first flight?"

"To get to the bottom of this problem," responded MacMorran, "we shall have to do what they were taught to do. Box clever."

But Anthony still pursued his own line of thought. "And think of this, Andrew—all about the same age. All about the same height. All about the same weight. What else can you tell me, Andrew?"

MacMorran made no reply.

"Huh! So you won't talk—eh, Andrew? What do *I* do, then, if *you* won't talk?"

"That's easy. Wait for somebody else to talk. One voice is as good as another. Sometimes better."

"Who else is going to talk? Whom we can feel certain about."

MacMorran shrugged his shoulders. "The Sussex Police authorities for one. I'm expecting them to come through any moment now."

"Why didn't you tell me that before?"

MacMorran grinned. For the first time during the encounter. "Why didn't I? If I had told you you'd have known as much as I do."

Anthony grinned back at him. "Or even more, Andrew. It's possible. Have you thought of that?"

"I've thought of everything and I fear that I'm no nearer the truth than when I started."

MacMorran relapsed again into gloomy pessimism.

Anthony, from his seat on the table, leant over towards him.

"Look here—if you think—"

The telephone rang before he could complete his sentence. MacMorran rather ungraciously removed the receiver. "MacMorran speaking . . ." He clapped his hand over the mouthpiece and spoke to Anthony. "From Lancing," he murmured. "More information coming through . . . hallo . . . yes?"

Anthony waited patiently for the news. He could obtain no sound clue from MacMorran's interjections as to what was being said at the other end of the line. MacMorran, however, was frowning and Anthony knew what that sign portended.

"I'm much obliged," Anthony heard him say eventually, "and you may rely on our complete co-operation at this end." MacMorran replaced the receiver.

"Well," said Anthony, "out with it."

MacMorran raised his head slowly and looked at him. "The claw print's there. Close to the body. Two of 'em this time. Between the body and the sea. Just as with Donovan. I don't like it, Mr. Bathurst. It's makin' me shiver—and I don't mind admittin' it."

Anthony's eyes mocked him. "And if a confirmed sceptic gets cold feet and his knees can be heard knocking together—how can ordinarily credulous mortals face the acid test?"

"This is no time for joking. It's out of place."

"Still less for shivering, Andrew. If you'll allow me to say so."

Anthony Bathurst walked to the window and looked out across the river. "This third time may prove lucky for us, Andrew. Let's hope so in case not. Jago's wife or Jago's mother may have kept the letter or the envelope of the decoy message. Like Mrs. Donovan did. And that's *more* hoping by our side."

"I'll make a note of that point and put it to Bath when I hear from them. As you say, we might have the luck on our side for once. It's time it broke our way. But this 'bird' idea of yours, Mr. Bathurst—I can't help thinking about it. It kind of worries me. If such a thing *had* happened—as you described to Lilley and me—"

Anthony cut in unmercifully. "How is it that it always carefully selects boxers? Clever bird! Is that your question, Andrew? Because if it is, I'll admit at once that the same point puzzles me and that I can't answer it."

MacMorran saw that Anthony was pulling his leg. "Of course, if you put it like that—" he started.

Anthony broke in on him. "Get a copy of that claw-print, Andrew. From Lancing. We must have a careful look at it. Compare it with the other. And ask for as many details as you can get when you enquire about the letter and the envelope from Bath. I don't want delay on either of those points. I hate delay at any time and I shall positively writhe under it here."

"I've an idea," said MacMorran suddenly.

"No!" replied Anthony incredulously.

"Yes," said Andrew MacMorran—"and I'm serious about it. Listen! Secretan—the man that old Slade's up against—Marcus Secretan, isn't it?"

"That's right, Andrew."

"It would be to his advantage to put 'Lefty' Donovan out of mess, wouldn't it?"

"Of course it would. From a money point of view. But you heard what I just said regarding Bailey and Jago, didn't you?"

"A blind—very likely. Secretan may be a man that sticks at nothing. Supposing for a moment that he decides on a certain plan of campaign—"

Anthony interrupted him. "Nothing doing, Andrew. I can't take it. Sorry—but you're down the wrong street. It's a *cul-de-sac* that one!—you'll never be able to get out of it."

MacMorran looked annoyed at the interruption.

"We're up against something much bigger than I think you imagine, Andrew. Something more horribly *evil*. Something, I fear, which kills for the mere sake of killing. That's a terrible thing for me to say, I know—but I feel that it's true. We've fought sadists before, you and I .... but I don't think we've encountered one of this particular calibre. There's something very much like a monster in this background and it may be that he will get us before we can get him."

"If it's flesh and blood I'm facing, I don't mind, Mr. Bathurst. I know what to prepare for. What I can't tackle is ... er ... ."

"Feathers and claws—eh, Andrew? Is that the idea?" Anthony grinned. MacMorran caught the mood and grinned back at him.

"All right, Mr. Bathurst. Have it your own way. You win."

Anthony thumped him on the back. "Good for you, Andrew."

MacMorran at once became severely practical. "What are you going to do?"

Anthony swung his legs. "Don't quite know. Puzzled. Wait for more from the Jago end, I think. If we're lucky, it may put us on to something. And then—after that—" he stopped. The Inspector waited for him. He went on. "Well—there's the fight. *If* it takes place. Assuming that there's dirty work about that there scrap—giving you the bare bones of your own theory, Andrew—we may well be on the verge of further developments."

"When is it due?"

"In a few days' time. On the twelfth. At the Belfairs Stadium, Not such a terrific time to wait, is it?"

"One of the most remarkable features of the affair," tangented MacMorran, "as I see it—is the complete disappearance of Bellamy. We've had a thorough comb-out for him all over the country and haven't made a touch anywhere. Not the hint of one. That worries me."

"On the other hand, I rather like it."

"What on earth makes you think like that?"

"It fits in with an idea that I have. That Bellamy, my dear friend 'Banjo' Bellamy, with whom I have a pressing appointment in the near future, has a hide-out all set where be can flit at any time when it suits his book. It can be found, Andrew, this place where the Bellamy goes to in the winter time. In other words, if he can find the way, so can we."

"I don't share your optimism."

"Never mind, Andrew. Pack it all up for the time being—and come and share some beer."

MacMorran rose immediately.

Chapter XIII
ASATER

ANTHONY Lotherington Bathurst sat on a high stool in a snack-bar. To be precise in the snack-bar of the establishment which bore the sign 'The Bishop Latimer,' and which is not over-far from New Scotland Yard. It was a place which Mr. Bathurst strongly favoured. For in the snack-bar of the 'Bishop' he always found both quality and quantity. Warmth in the winter and in the summer grateful coolness in the heat. On the present occasion he was enjoying a plate of cold Scotch beef with a garnish of pickled walnuts.

Suddenly Anthony became aware of a most extraordinary sensation. From immediately behind him it came and it seemed directed towards the nape of his neck. It was as though a huge door had been opened behind him and a great torrent of chill air were rushing at him to engulf him. Anthony gave his shoulders a shrug in an effort to throw off this feeling of intense coldness. But the effort was of no avail to him. Almost against his will, Anthony turned his head round. To his utter amazement he saw behind him the figure of a man. Of the biggest man by far he had ever seen in his life. The giant, who must have stood several inches over six feet, with abnormally long arms and terrific shoulders, was standing there staring fixedly, it appeared, at the back of Mr. Bathurst's neck. He was dressed in a long black overcoat, wore startlingly light brown shoes with gloves to match, and had a black felt hat pressed firmly on his head. On the whole, and taking everything into consideration, his face in repose was not ill-favoured although the ears were large and the nose flattened. Directly Anthony saw him, and it must be remembered that he was seeing him for the first time, he felt that in some way this man was concerned with him.

Coincidentally as Anthony's mind registered this thought, the giant stepped forward and slipped with surprising agility on to the stool on Anthony's immediate left. His legs sprawled round the stool. Everything that was a constituent part of Anthony's make-up warned him to be on his guard against this unusual neighbour. Every nerve of his being hammered the truth of it into his brain. His jaw closed and he set his teeth. All that he could think of at the moment was that menace and deadly peril were close to him.

"Morning, carver," said the stranger to the white-capped chef who came to take his order. "Just give me a large plate of 'am and tongue, will you, carver, and cut it liberal?"

"Anything with it?" asked the chef curtly.

"What ya got?"

"Beetroot, tomatoes, most kind of pickles. What do you fancy?"

"Just what pickles?"

"Any kind. Tell me what you fancy and I'll serve you."

"Give us some mustard pickles. Hot and strong. And jump to it, Claude, will ya? I'm sure in a hurry."

The chef eyed him viciously but recognizing discretion as the better part of valour, said nothing more. A few minutes later he handed over the giant's requirements. At that moment, the latter turned and looked at Anthony. As he did so, he smiled and a most remarkable transformation came over his face. The chin dropped, the lips curled away from the mouth in a sinister grin, the teeth obtruded disgustingly and the whole face seemed to be peeled back as it were from the upper lip and became completely transformed in character. Anthony ignored the smiling overture and went on with his cold beef. The stranger, however, persisted in his overtures.

"Morning. Bit squeezed for room—eh? So close—almost touching. Just hope I don't intrude." He leaned over further towards Anthony. "You'll tell me if I do, I guess—yes?"

Anthony understood that he would be compelled to answer. It was futile to anticipate that he could go on ignoring the man till further notice. "This is a public bar," he said, "and you have as much right here as I have. But I should have imagined that you knew that as well as I do."

Huge fingers broke bread near him. Anthony noticed their length, strength and suppleness.

"Still," said the fingers' owner, "an intruder's just trash—you can't deny. Sure, he's not wanted . . . by anybody. For why? He's just poking in his nose, I figure. And nose-poking's a sure dirty trick. You think along them lines I don't doubt, same as I do. Yes?"

Anthony smiled. "Excellent," he said.

The giant showed signs of being puzzled. "How d'ya mean?" he asked with a frown.

"What you said."

"What I said?"

"Yes. Rules for living. Potted philosophy. My dear sir, you have your fingers on a great truth as well as on that roll. You must keep them there—you really must."

His companion sought security in further understanding. "I take it you just feel you agree with me—eh?"

"My dear sir," said Anthony, his eyes simulating amazement, "how could you possibly think otherwise?"

"Huh. That's all right then. Nose-poking's a fair dirty game. Yes, sir! There's no two opinions about that. Can't be. With you and me. That's good. Just how things ought to be between gentlemen."

Anthony nodded reassuringly. But the next remark jolted him severely and showed him that things were worse than he had thought them to be.

"Now supposing you and me had an acquaintance. A mutual acquaintance. Name? Well—the 'moniker' don't exactly matter. It sort of don't signify. He's just a third party as you might say. You know him. I know him. We both know him. Let's suppose for the sake of argument we call him 'Bathurst.' *Mister* Bathurst. That name would do as well as any other, wouldn't it? Seems to me that's so."

"It's certainly a good name," returned Anthony nonchalantly, "and I must congratulate you on your circle of friends. Pardon me—I should have said acquaintances."

His companion nodded with a sinister hint at dark designs and profound perplexities. "Yes. You've said it. I do mix with them what count, don't I?"

"You sure do," drawled Anthony.

The giant smiled again and Anthony once more felt sickened at the sight of the dropped chin and the *risus sardonicus* which took complete possession of the entire face.

"You feel mighty pleased with yourself, I guess."

"I hope not. I should hate to think that any self-confidence I may possess could in any way exude from me and come to be regarded as offensive."

"I don't know nothing about that. What I said was that you've got a great liking for yourself."

Anthony ignored the persistence of the challenge. The unabashed stranger went on.

"And folks with a great liking for themselves often get what is called a rude awakening. I should just hate to think that that was going to happen to you."

The threat and the menace in the man's voice were no longer veiled. He was coming more into the open. Which, from Anthony's personal point of view, was all to the good. If this fellow had the idea that he could be cowed by mere threatenings of personal violence, the man must soon be called upon to readjust his opinions.

"That's most considerate of you," he rejoined—"because on the contrary I'm afraid I'm not at all concerned as to what may or may not happen to you."

But his fellow-diner threw off the implication and continued in the same strain as previously, quite unperturbed by Anthony's last remark. "Nose-poking's a dirty game as I calculated just now. But dirt ain't its only feature. No, sir. It's sure unhealthy as well. So unhealthy that before you've got shot of it, it brings on a disease. That disease is usually fatal. To the nose-poker. D'ya get me in that?"

The unpleasant voice had taken on a silky veneer of cold and calculated cruelty. Its owner pushed away his plate, sucked vindictively at a back tooth and called loudly to the chef. "Buddy—a nice little bit o' cheese. And make it Stilton, will ya? Only the best is good enough for me."

Anthony crumbled bread and turned away from him. The chef saw to the order in silence. The giant took his plate of cheese and cut into the Stilton. Anthony was smiling and it seemed that his general reception of this unconventional encounter was at last beginning to get under the stranger's skin. There were signs of frayed temper. The gloves then came off with a vengeance.

"So you won't understand that the medicine's good for you—eh? You know too much—eh? You want to go your own sweet way—eh?" He bent over and whispered the concluding words. "Just listen carefully and get this, Mr. Bathurst, will ya? Watch your step. Every one you take . . . the step after and the step before . . . or maybe . . . you won't find yourself talking any more. Which would sure be a terrible misfortune . . . for ya."

Anthony brushed a crumb from his coat, turned away for a moment or so and handed a ten-shilling note to the chef. "Take what I owe you, will you chef?"

The chef nodded. Then Anthony swung quickly round in his seat and almost faced his companion. The latter drew back a little at the suddenness of the movement. "So you know my name. We can dispense, therefore, with that mystical third party who figured so prominently in your conversation. You've been doing a lot of talking. Now it's my turn. Listen to this. You can convey my compliments to those who sent you here and tell them that there's one crime the English law never forgets. If you don't happen to know what the name of that crime is—I'll tell you. Here and now! It's 'murder.' You're taken out of your cell one morning. As a matter of fact, it's a morning you've been rather looking forward to, for about three weeks as a rule, and they stand you on a sliding board. I'll explain the idea to you more fully if you'd care to listen to me. They put a black cap over your head and a noose round your neck . . . and you're pinioned. . . ."

The giant looked sheer ugliness at him and cut in "Sure they do. Sure they do all them things you've just described. But I'll tell *you* something. Something ya seem to have forgotten. They got to catch ya first. Got the idea, mister?"

Anthony countered. "Don't you worry your hard head about that. You'll be caught all right . . . never fear. Sooner or later which will probably be sooner . . . if I'm any judge."

Anthony stepped down from the sitting position on the stool. His unwelcome companion did the same. As they faced each other Anthony decided that his *vis-à-vis* was five inches or so the taller.

"Look here . . ." commenced that gentleman.

"Don't raise your voice," said Anthony, "you'll call even more attention to yourself. I feel sure that you have no real desire to do that."

The huge man looked round the saloon a trifle uncertainly. The chef brought Anthony the change that was due to him. Anthony counted it. He handed the chef his usual *pourboire*.

"That's all right, sir. Thank you very much."

The giant was still standing a few feet away. Anthony turned to him again. "You were about to say when I interrupted you. . . ."

The giant made a threatening gesture but was silent. Anthony simulated surprise. At that moment the swing doors of the apartment opened and there entered the dour figure of Chief Inspector Andrew MacMorran. He walked straight up to Anthony Bathurst.

"Good afternoon, Mr. Bathurst. And the compliments of Scotland Yard. Now what was it you wanted to . . ." Anthony indicated the presence of the giant. "This is the man, Inspector. Perhaps you might like to take a good look at him while you can. It may be a help to you from the point of view of the future."

MacMorran looked the colossus up and down. The other occupants of the saloon seemed to stir with a subdued interest. Many curious eyes were turned towards the three figures by the counter of the snack-bar. The largest of the three glared malevolently at MacMorran.

"It's a free country and you ain't got nothing on me, so I'll advise ya to keep your distance."

The Inspector turned to Anthony. "Do you wish to charge him, Mr. Bathurst?"

"No," said Anthony, "oh no! I merely thought it was too good an opportunity for you to miss. Thank you for coming along, Inspector. Very sporting of you."

MacMorran spoke severely to the other. "Get off out of it, d'ye hear? You're not wanted here. Understand?"

The giant sniggered loudly, shrugged his massive shoulders, turned on his heel and deliberately walked to the door. When he reached the door, he turned again and with his hand extended, made an offensive gesture towards MacMorran. Before the latter could move, however, the offender had gone. Anthony intervened.

"Well, there you are, Inspector, you've seen him. I'm sure you aren't likely to forget him in a hurry. I should regard that as an almost impossible task."

MacMorran looked grave. "I don't like the look of things. He's new to me."

Anthony went to a side table and took the inspector with him. He ordered drinks. MacMorran asked a question.

"How did you get the message through to me? I'm puzzled."

"Via the chef here. I managed to scribble a note to him, with your 'phone number, while I was crumbling a roll. I reckoned that there was a two to one chance that you'd be in. I gave the message to the chef wrapped up in a ten-shilling note. The old boy turned up aces. I shall have to reward him with an extra tip next time I have lunch here. All the same I'm as disappointed as you are. I hoped you'd be able to place the man."

"It's the Donovan affair, I suppose? There's no doubt about it, is there?"

"Not a flicker of doubt, Andrew—as I see it. We're forcing them into the open at last. All to the good. From that particular point of view we've scored."

MacMorran sighed and drank beer. Anthony waited in patience until the Inspector had replaced his tankard on the table.

"It's outrageous," said MacMorran with slow emphasis. "Tell me exactly what that villain said to you."

"Oh—it was highly picturesque—all of it. Boiled down—it amounted to this. That if I went any deeper into the circumstances of the Bailey-Donovan-Jago murder chain, I was to be either politely or impolitely—probably the latter—'bumped off.' The process of investigation was described by our recent acquaintance as 'nose-poking'."

MacMorran nodded. "I see. 'The Gypsy's warning' so far as you were concerned. All friendly and take my advice—eh?"

"I don't know about that. Not too friendly—believe me. Of course—you know what he is, don't you, Andrew?"

"He's a boxer."

"Yes—look at his beautiful build—arms and legs. I don't know that I should care to offend him."

"I agree with you entirely. A decidedly dangerous customer."

"You'll put a man on him at once, I take it, Andrew? There must be no delay."

"That was arranged before I left the 'Yard,' Mr. Bathurst," replied the Inspector with a twinkle in his eye. "Evershed came along with me. When I came in, he stayed outside. To follow the chap when he came out. His orders were of the strictest."

"Good. With any luck we may get a line on the man."

"I'll be getting back," announced MacMorran.

Anthony stood up. As he did so, a barmaid beckoned to him. He walked over to her.

"If you and your friend have had any trouble with that man, perhaps I can help you. For one thing—I can tell you his name. He was in here before you arrived. He was with another bloke who went when you came in. I *think* that they were waiting for you. I heard them talking together. His friend called him 'Asater.' I'm telling you this in case you don't know."

"Thank you," said Anthony Bathurst, "I'm obliged for the information. Asater! Thank you again."

He returned to MacMorran. "I've just been informed, Andrew, that the gentleman's name is Asater. That sharp-eared barmaid overheard it. He had somebody with him when I came in here. The girl heard them talking."

MacMorran whistled softly. "Asater! Never heard of him. But all the same I wonder what I can find out."

"Asater," repeated Anthony Bathurst. "Asater! I have a feeling that you and I will meet again, Mr. Asater."

"Don't leave me out," complained Chief Inspector MacMorran with righteous indignation.

CHAPTER XIV
PANIC AVERTED

MACMORRAN'S usually quiet room at the 'Yard' was both full and disturbed. Besides himself it held the persons of Sir Cloudesley Slade, Lambert, Sam Whitfield, and Anthony Lotherington Bathurst. The Inspector looked worried and anxious, but Sir Cloudesley's face showed that in both these respects he was suffering far more than the Inspector. Sir Cloudesley was on his feet talking. The others were listening. In the cases of Lambert and Whitfield, they were punctuating Sir Cloudesley's remarks with sharp nods of approval. With this approval, one could easily detect signs of indignation. Sir Cloudesley brought his remarks to a conclusion.

"Well—that's how it is, Inspector. I've passed on to you the full dope. We've all three had one. That's why we've come straight to you. I always say and I always have said it—when you want prompt action there's nothing like going straight to the fountain head."

MacMorran said nothing in reply to him. He was busily engaged in examining three notes. The first was addressed to 'Sir Cloudesley Slade, Regium House, Mayfair.' It read as follows: *"Where is 'Lefty' Donovan? You know! The whole world knows. If your son fights at the Belfairs Stadium, he will go where Donovan has gone. That is as certain as night follows day. So take this advice, call the fight off without delay. For your own sake and the sake of your son. A Friend."*

"H'm," said MacMorran, "pretty definite, I must say." He passed the note over to Anthony Bathurst. "Read it for yourself, Mr. Bathurst." Then he busied himself with the second of the notes in front of him. This, he saw, had been addressed to 'Mr. J. Lambert, Conway Chambers, Fleet St.' MacMorran proceeded to read it: *"So 'Lefty' Donovan has persisted and been removed! Well—it was his own fault—he asked for it. Call it the penalty of disobedience. That will do as well as anything else. The same fate will come to young Slade if he fights at Belfairs. You must warn and advise his father at once. If young Slade disregards this advice and goes on with his mad idea, they will get him as they got Donovan. For God's sake don't disregard this warning. You will not receive another. A well-wisher."*

MacMorran handed over the second communication to Anthony. "Here's number two for you, sir." He picked up the third of the papers. In this case, the address was 'Mr. Sam Whitfield, 11 St. Eanswyth Walk, Mitcham.' MacMorran read this also. It was worded thus: *"Tell Godfrey Slade to give up the foolish idea of fighting on the 12th. If he does this—he will be all right. If he persists, however, in this crazy scheme to help his father, it will be the worse for him. He will just be wiped out in the same way as Donovan was—make no mistake about that. One who knows."*

MacMorran grunted at these vague vapourings and passed over the third note. Anthony took it, smoothed it out and placed it in a line with its two predecessors. There came a silence. It appeared that they were all content to wait for Anthony to conclude his inspection and then make his comments. He looked up and formed this idea himself.

"There's at least one thing evident from these three effusions that we have just looked at. And that's this. They've all emanated from the same person. The handwriting of both the letters themselves and the envelopes they came in seems to differ, but that effect may well have been faked. A handwriting expert would be able, in all probability, to give a valuable opinion on that point from a merely superficial examination of the three notes. But the similarities in the phrasing and in the general expressions used, convince me that one person is responsible for all three efforts."

"I entirely agree with you, Mr. Bathurst," contributed Inspector MacMorran. "I formed the same idea myself directly I had read the three of them."

Sir Cloudesley Slade also acquiesced. "I agree with you, too. One blackguard sent all the three."

"The envelopes are different. All white in colour. But all of a different style and quality of paper." Mr. Bathurst held them up as he spoke. "Let's have a look at the postmarks. We'll take yours first, Sir Cloudesley. What's the postmark here? It looks to me like Basingstoke."

"It *is* Basingstoke," said Sir Cloudesley curtly, "no doubt about that."

"What about yours, Mr. Lambert?"

"Maidenhead," replied Lambert curtly.

Anthony nodded his agreement. "Now yours, Mr. Whitfield. What has your envelope got to tell us?"

"It looks like Windsor," returned Sam Whitfield slowly, "that's as near as I could make it."

Anthony examined the postmark on the envelope that bore the Mitcham address. "Yes," he said, "I agree with you. This is Windsor all right. When did you receive this letter?"

"By the first post yesterday morning."

Anthony turned to Lambert. "And yours, Mr. Lambert. When did you receive your letter?"

"Same as Sam here. First post yesterday morning."

"That fits in then with my theory. The letters could have been posted on the same *journey*, as it were. Now you, Sir Cloudesley.. When did you get your letter?"

"By the same post as the others. First post yesterday morning. Peculiar—eh?"

"Now then—let's have a look at the post office time stamp on the three envelopes. Whitfield's is 12.30 p.m. Dec. 1st. Lambert's is 1.45 p.m., Dec. 1st. Sir Cloudesley's is 12.30 p.m., Dec. 1st. Now that's a somewhat remarkable thing."

"Hold hard a minute," put in Slade, "doesn't that prove that my letter and Sam's *couldn't* have been posted by the same person? It seems to me that it does."

"Wait," said Anthony, "before we rush to premature and perhaps rash conclusions. We must be careful and remember this! This time that's shown on the envelope is not necessarily the time the letter was actually posted. It's the Post-Office clearing stamp after the letter has been collected. It is usually some few minutes after the collection time. Now the problem which we are called upon to face is *this*. What is the time of the next previous post to the midday post at both Basingstoke and Windsor? Supposing there was a next previous post at Basingstoke—and I mean by that a *collection*—as early as 9.30. That gives us a margin of three hours between the two collections. You'll admit, gentlemen, that that's a most liberal margin, and if it errs it errs unmistakably on the generous side. Sir Cloudesley's letter is slipped into the post-box—say at 9.35. A mere five minutes after the postman has picked up his previous collection. Could the person who posted that letter, be at Windsor with the other letter for Whitfield by about 12.15 noon? It could be done I suppose—but I doubt if it was."

He shook his head slowly. MacMorran turned and reached for the telephone. "We'll soon settle that for you, Mr. Bathurst. I'll put an enquiry through to Basingstoke G.P.O. at once."

"Don't forget the complementary possibility—Inspector. While you're doing that—enquire at Windsor as well, as to their posts."

MacMorran nodded. "O.K. I'll do that too."

They waited while the Inspector worded the two enquiries. He asked for Kingsley, his 'blitzkreig' enquiry clerk, the man who seldom failed him in affairs of this kind. MacMorran made it quite clear to Kingsley what he wanted to know. The others who listened heard him come to his conclusion.

"Let me have that information as soon as possible, Kingsley. It's important. Yes . . . if you will. Thank you, Kingsley."

Sir Cloudesley Slade pushed his hands into his pockets and thrust out a jutting chin. "Congratulations, Inspector. It's a pleasure to run up against an official somewhere in this lazy sit-on-your-rump country who can step on it. Who doesn't pick at his top lip, murmur about 'the old man' and then wait three weeks for his superior officer to give him permission to do something—by sticking his initials in the corner of a piece of paper."

MacMorran grunted unintelligibly. He was of the type that preferred censure to praise. Anthony found it difficult to resist a smile. He knew that MacMorran was both embarrassed and uncomfortable at what Sir Cloudesley Slade had said. The Inspector fidgeted with the edge of his blotting paper. Anthony turned away and studied Lambert and Whitfield. They seemed to have placed themselves almost unreservedly in Sir Cloudesley Slade's hands, Had the writer of the anonymous notes which had brought both them and Sir Cloudesley to the 'Yard' been in a position to watch their faces, he would have assessed their power of influencing Godfrey Slade in any way, at an extremely low standard. Anthony had resolved to say no more with regard to the problem until he had heard what Kingsley had to report concerning the post times. Kingsley came back to them within five minutes. He put a slip of paper in MacMorran's hands.

"What you wanted, sir."

MacMorran looked at it keenly for a moment or so. Then he looked up and spoke to them. "Sir Cloudesley Slade's idea is the right one. There are posts at Basingstoke at 11.35 a.m. and 12.15 p.m., at Windsor we have 11 a.m. and 12.15 p.m., which proves that the same person couldn't have posted both of them—as Sir Cloudesley has pointed out."

"There's one point we haven't considered," contributed Anthony, "and that's the possibility of an aeroplane having been used . . . I rule it out myself . . . there are no airports handy that I know of, and there's the condition of landing to be thought of—"

"You can eliminate it," cut in MacMorran. "I feel sure it is not practicable. Sir Cloudesley's letter and Mr. Whitfield's letter must have been posted by two different people."

"Although the same person wrote them." This interpolation came from Anthony Bathurst.

Lambert grunted. The grunt exuded dissatisfaction, and perhaps criticism. His eyes, so much like blackcurrants, as Anthony had thought before, looked ominous in the extreme. "Meanwhile," he said with flat and heavy sarcasm, "what do we do? Still go on talking?"

Slade snapped at him as per invoice. "How do you mean, Jack? Explain yourself. And if you've got anything tucked away snug at the back of your mind, out with it, because we can do with it! This is time for pooling ideas."

"I mean about young Mr. Godfrey," said Lambert sullenly.

This touched Slade on the raw. His affection for his only son was almost household knowledge. "Go on," he said quietly.

"Well," continued Lambert, "do we sit still twiddling our bloody thumbs while these thugs carry on their dirty work and get him?"

Slade's jaws were set. "We do *not*," he said.

"Well then," said Lambert, "that brings me to my point. What steps *do* we take to stop their little game? Because to my mind, prevention's a bloody sight better than cure."

Whitfield nodded his approval of Lambert's outspoken opinion. "Some things *can't* be cured. It's often too late to cure them."

"*Which* is why we've come here," barked Sir Cloudesley. "For help and protection! Where better could we go? If Scotland Yard can't give it to us—who can?"

MacMorran rubbed his nose with his forefinger and looked at Anthony Bathurst. It seemed that he desired Anthony to give him a lead. Anthony took the hint.

"Sir Cloudesley—you may or may not remember our previous conversation. Concerning the coming fight and the *conditions* of that fight. I was presumptuous enough to make one or two suggestions to you. Can you recall those suggestions?"

Sir Cloudesley's hard-hewn face lit up with satisfaction. "I remember all your conversation with me. You're quite right. If I didn't thank you then, I'll do so now."

Anthony grinned at him. "That's all right, sir. But tell me this, so that I may have a clear understanding of things. Is Godfrey Slade fighting for you at Belfairs on the 12th of this month?"

Slade caressed his chin as though he had been asked an awkward question. He looked at Lambert and Whitfield. It was some seconds before he gave Anthony an answer. "Look here—I didn't want this known at all . . . beyond my own personal circle, that is . . . but in all probability, he *is*. It's not absolutely certain—and it won't be for a few days longer—but, well—I've given you an answer—you must make the most of it."

Anthony leant over and spoke one word. That word was in the form of a question. "Jago?"

"You mean—?" Sir Cloudesley paused.

"Had you thought that Jago might fill your bill, Sir Cloudesley?"

Sir Cloudesley Slade brought his right fist into his left hand. "Of course! That's where the hellishness of it all gets me. Jago was fit and well and quite prepared to put the gloves on for me. And a nice boy, too. Lambert here and I had seen him twice in the matter. Things were pretty well fixed up between us. Godfrey had offered to fight before . . . when Donovan was taken . . . but was ready and willing to stand down for Jago. Even now, Godfrey's only doing what he is doing for my sake. For some unearthly reason he thinks the world of his crusty, bad-tempered, old dad."

But Anthony was thinking hard. "This Jago business— did *you* approach *him* in the first place?"

"In the first place—how do you mean?"

"I put it badly perhaps. What I mean is this. When you realized that Donovan was gone and couldn't fight for you—did *you* make an offer to Jago? Or did Jago make overtures to you?"

Sir Cloudesley's face cleared. "Oh—I get you! I misunderstood your remark. *We* contacted Jago. That is to say, I did. Through Lambert here, of course. Lambert sees to all that sort of business for me. That's what I pay him for."

"You looked on Jago as a good man from your own point of view of the scrap with Blood?"

"Naturally." Sir Cloudesley nodded and went on. "I told you on the occasion of our first meeting that I held a high opinion of Mike Jago. That was the reason I picked on him."

"He accepted your terms without demur?"

Slade grinned. "Not exactly. No—I couldn't say 'yes' to that. But we soon *came* to terms. There were no difficulties that were insuperable. As I said, we weren't long in getting matters fixed up. From the financial standpoint I was treating him just as well as I was going to treat Donovan. Looks as though somebody hates my guts, doesn't it? Got a pretty hefty grudge against me."

Anthony shook his head again. "But for Bailey and the death of Bailey I should agree with you. As it is, I'm more than puzzled."

MacMorran nodded. "And that goes for me, too."

Anthony came to Slade again with a further question. "Who knew that Jago was fighting Blood for you?"

"I can only answer for my end," replied Sir Cloudesley, "as you can see for yourself. Lambert, Whitfield, Godfrey and I were the only people who were aware of the arrangement so far as I know. That means, 'to the best of my knowledge and belief.' It was to be a surprise for Secretan. I kept my own counsel. I am sure my son has, and I'd go bail on Jack Lambert and Sam Whitfield. I trust 'em as I trust myself. If there's been any leakage, it must have come from Jago's end in Somerset. You know what country people are. The villages hum with scandal and gossip."

"Bath," continued Anthony judicially, "is not a village by any stretch of imagination. And when Bath races are being run on the Lansdown—"

Sir Cloudesley cut him short unceremoniously. "Bath itself may not be—I know that as well as you do, but there are many villages close at hand in that quarter of Somerset, and Jago was actually training in one of them before Sam was able to fix him up with special quarters at Epping. So you can readjust your ideas in that particular direction, Mr. Bathurst."

Lambert took up the cudgels on his own behalf. "I was as mum as an oyster all the time we were fixing things with Jago. Never breathed a word to a soul. I had placed a nice bet, too. In addition to my original stake. More than I want to lose, I can tell you. I liked Jago's style immensely."

Whitfield nodded his approval of these statements with enthusiasm. "He was the goods—and no mistake. Got a lovely left on him. Like a horse kicking. And he would have come along a lot, too, if

I could have slipped a good fortnight's stiff work into him. And I kept *my* counsel about him—you can bet your life on it. Wouldn't have suited my book to do otherwise." As he concluded the projection of his opinion, Whitfield assumed an air of profound sagacity.

Anthony rubbed his chin very much as Sir Cloudesley had some little time previously. He felt that he was making but little progress with the main problem. Sir Cloudesley rose to make his departure. Lambert and Whitfield took their cues and followed suit. For a few moments they stood awkwardly in the background, hats in restless hands. Sam Whitfield's uneasy fingers played with the brim of his—unceasingly.

"Well," said Slade, "we've brought our troubles to you. Help us if you can. That's all I'm asking of you. We know you can't perform impossibilities so we shan't expect them. We neither ask nor demand you to—but—well—as I said—do what you can for us. I assure you, gentlemen, that you won't find me ungrateful."

"I am quite sure of that, Sir Cloudesley," answered Anthony.

MacMorran held up his hand. "Just a minute. Before you go. Something I'd like to ask you. You three gentlemen are well acquainted with the boxing world and have been for years now—I expect. N.S.C. and all that."

Sam Whitfield burst in. "I should say so, Inspector. You've come to the right shop and no mistake. Why—I remember the 'Fighting Five' and the night when 'Tucker' Woodman fought 'Sacky' Baggs in the Stepney Wash Hall and knocked him right out of the ring. Little Bertie Higgins was referee. When 'Sacky' came to, he said to little Bertie—'Who hit me?' and later when he went home that night his mother said 'you ain't my "Sacky"!' The betting was—"

MacMorran cut short Whitfield's flood of reminiscence. "Well then, answer me this. Any one of you. Do any of you know the name of 'Asater,' in the game? Has any one of you ever run across it?"

The three men looked at him blankly and began to move their heads. "Asater?" said Sir Cloudesley Slade, "it's a new one on me."

"Never heard it," said Lambert.

Whitfield shook his head. "No—nothing doing as far as I'm concerned. It's nobody of any reputation—I can tell you that for certain."

"Why do you ask," said Sir Cloudesley, "have you got on to some-thing worthwhile?"

"We're not sure," said MacMorran in reply, "*yet*. So you don't know the name? Well—thank you very much, gentlemen. I thought I'd ask you. I won't keep you any longer."

The three men waved their adieux. Whitfield was the last to leave. He closed the door. Anthony sat on MacMorran's table—his chin in his hand.

"I don't like it, Andrew! I don't like any of it a little bit. I'm still groping. Groping in the dark and pretty hopelessly at that. Which is a condition I utterly and completely loathe, as you know."

MacMorran leant forward and reached for an official-looking document. "I waited until they had gone, to tell you about this. It came this morning. It's from Bath in answer to my general enquir-ies. They're co-operating very well—the Bath people. Better, in fact, than I expected."

"I was very much afraid," murmured Anthony, "that you were about to say 'the Bath chaps.' I doubt whether, at the present moment, my constitution would have survived the substitution."

MacMorran frowned at the levity. Then he coughed. The cough held censure. "As I said—this came through from Bath. From the police. To me. I'll read to you what they say. First—the reply to your question about Mike Jago's letter. You remember the point you wanted information about?"

Anthony nodded approvingly. "There is no trace," continued the Inspector in his best official manner, "of either the letter or the envelope in which the letter was sent. When he went out, ostensibly to keep the appointment which the letter had presumably made for him, the letter was in Jago's pocket. That's according to the evidence of his mother. He was unmarried, you see—just as Ted Bailey was—and lived at home with his parents. That satisfies you on that score, Mr. Bathurst."

"I wish it did," murmured Anthony, "but I know what you mean."

Again MacMorran frowned.

"Go on, Andrew," said Anthony—"don't let it put you off—read-ing, I mean, not frowning."

"I am now going to surprise you. At least, I think that I shall. In Jago's jacket-pocket when he was picked up off Lancing beach, was found a photograph. Or better—a snapshot. The Bath police have sent it on to me for report. I have it here—I'll show it to you. I rather fancy you'd like to look at it."

MacMorran put his hand down and pulled open a drawer. From the drawer he took out a small photograph. He handed it over to Anthony Bathurst. "Well—do you know the lady?" he enquired; "ever happen to meet her?"

Anthony paled a little when he saw who it was. For him there was no mistaking it. "This, Andrew," he said gravely, "is a photo of Flora Donovan."

"You're tellin' me," returned MacMorran; "rather bewildering, isn't it?"

But Mr. Bathurst was staring straight in front of him. Mac-Morran waited for him to speak. Eventually Anthony emerged from his brown study.

"Something you can do for me, Andrew." Anthony spoke very quietly. MacMorran was impressed by his unusual earnestness.

"What's that?"

"Try to trace the whereabouts of a Miss Stella Molyneux—will you—who left the town of Northampton suddenly somewhere about ten months ago."

MacMorran looked up quickly. "Did you say ten months ago? Left Northampton?"

"I did. Somewhere about the end of February. To the consternation of all her friends and acquaintances in that district."

"Who told you all this?"

"Didn't I say I'd been and seen the Baileys?"

"Yes—but I can't recall that you mentioned this Miss—er—what was the name?"

"Molyneux. Stella Molyneux. One-time fiancée of Ted Bailey—the first link in the murder chain of dead boxers."

"Ten months ago," said MacMorran reflectively, "would bring us back to February, as you said."

"Quite right, Andrew. Accurate as ever—both of us."

"Bailey was killed in February."

"Keep on, Andrew. I think our Police Inspectors are wonderful."

MacMorran took no notice of the banter. He found a piece of paper and wrote down the name of the missing girl. "So she cleared out when Bailey died?"

"Soon after, I fear."

"H'm." MacMorran grunted.

"See what you can do for me about it, Andrew—will you?"

"I will that. You've given me an idea."

"You must endeavour," said Mr. Bathurst, edging towards the door, "to accustom yourself to new sensations."

Chapter XV
THE FIGHT AT BELFAIRS

THE night of the twelfth day of December came cold and clear. The roads and ruts were hard with frost. The air was crystal in its rare and intense purity. The stars winked and twinkled like tiny glass stones hanging from the ebony canopy of High Heaven. Some thousands of vehicles of all kinds made their way to the famous Belfairs Stadium. The challenge that had passed between the popular Sir Cloudesley Slade and Marcus Secretan had thrilled the entire boxing world and the Press had given it their universal support and catholic publicity and advertisement. The somewhat unusual and peculiar conditions underlying the challenge had fanned the flame of excitement and this flame had reached the dimensions of a tremendous blaze by reason of the deaths in such bizarre circumstances of, first, 'Lefty' Donovan and then, Mike Jago. And the fact that Sir Cloudesley Slade was still able to fulfil the conditions of his acceptance by producing a man to fight Blood, who was as yet unnamed, and might even be unknown into the bargain, only added attractive fuel to the raging fire.

The contest was timed to commence at half-past nine. At ten minutes past nine, with twenty minutes to go, the Stadium was well packed. Despite all the slings and arrows of outrageous Fortune which had assailed Sir Cloudesley Slade, the fight had *not* been declared off. That was more than good enough for the crowd. They told each other that they had known as one man that Sir Cloudesley

Slade was far too good a sportsman to let them down. Sir Cloudesley would produce an opponent for Blood and moreover, one who would make something like a fight of it for their delectation. Phil Blood was immensely popular with the ring generally, but it seemed that on this occasion the romantic halo that was poised over his unknown antagonist's head by reason of the abnormal circumstances, would inevitably mean that Sir Cloudesley's nominee would hold and carry the affections of the crowd within the vast Stadium.

Anthony Bathurst, starting out comparatively early, drove Mac-Morran down in his car. Slade had secured ring-seats for them. As he entered the Stadium it must be admitted that Anthony's uppermost thoughts were of the widowed Flora Donovan. The skein of murder was winding in a mysterious way its menaces to perform. The indoor Winter Hall of the famous Belfairs Stadium was crammed to the pitch of personal discomfort and the great centre arc light directed on to the raised ring platform with its roped square, looked eerie and almost unreal when Anthony, from his seat, turned his eyes towards it for the first time. The betting was three to one against 'Sir Cloudesley's nomination' and few could be found ready to take the odds. The weighing in during the afternoon had been conducted with no Press men present.

When Anthony and MacMorran took their seats, Anthony looked round for Sir Cloudesley but failed to see him. The atmosphere hummed with that suppressed excitement so common just before the start of great sporting encounters. MacMorran spoke.

"If young Slade fights, as I shouldn't be surprised, knowing what I do know, what's his height?"

"About 5 ft. 10 in. I should say. Perhaps an inch taller. The old ring 'experts' used to say that was big enough for anything on two legs. I don't think they were far wrong, Andrew. They knew what they were talking about."

"What's Slade's weight?"

"Round about twelve stone. Very nice, too. Got a good reach as well. But Blood's ringcraft and experience will prove too much for him, I'm afraid."

MacMorran nodded. "No doubt about that I should say."

Anthony looked at his watch. "Just on the half-hour, Andrew. Not long to wait now. We should hear the preliminaries in a few minutes from now."

As he spoke, a tremendous cheer burst out spontaneously and rang through the Winter Hall and, turning, Anthony was able to see the form of Sir Cloudesley Slade, immaculate in evening dress and pushing its way towards his favoured seat close to the roped square. At the spontaneity of the cheer, he took the cigar he was smoking from his mouth and waved a gay hand to the applauding crowd. Sir Cloudesley was nothing if not a good showman. Simultaneously with his wave, another roar of cheers rang to the roof of the hall. Phil Blood, in a scarlet dressing-gown, with white seams on the pockets, had slipped into the ring, waved to the crowd and taken his corner. As he did so, Anthony saw him put a finger to his temple to a cadaverous looking man with a high bald forehead and keen piercing eyes under bristling eyebrows, who was seated close to the roped square. 'Marcus Secretan' thought Anthony to himself, 'for an even "fiver".' In this conjecture it may be stated, Mr. Bathurst was right.

Blood's seconds then busied themselves with their charge's hands. Blood himself leant back in his seat—his hands extended—the picture of supremely easy confidence. Anthony was straining his eyes to catch the full expression of Blood's face, when another salvo of cheering rent the air. A tall, lithe figure was entering the ring and as it straightened itself, Anthony saw with something like a thrill that it was Godfrey Slade.

"You're right in your prognostication, Andrew," he whispered to his companion, "it's young Slade right enough. Have a good look at him. He's worth looking at."

Godfrey Slade was in an orange-coloured dressing-gown and like his father had done before him, he waved a hand to the cheering crowds in the great hall. His seconds were soon at work on him and as he stretched out his hands to them, Anthony noticed again what he had noticed in his own flat on that evening when Godfrey Slade and Star Merrilees had dined with him—the unusual length of Slade's arms.

MacMorran bent over and spoke. "Well—I've accomplished one thing. The murdering gang who got Bailey, Donovan and Jago didn't get Godfrey Slade—did they? Despite all their threats and anonymous letters I I've had eight of my best men watching Slade ever since Sir Cloudesley and the others came to the 'Yard'." He finished with a triumphant chuckle.

"Good for you, Andrew. Not long now—before the balloon goes up. Here's the referee."

MacMorran looked up to where Anthony had indicated.

"And here's Adrian Manning—he's going to announce the conditions of the fight. Listen—he's good."

A tall, imperious-looking man had climbed into the square. He advanced somewhat nonchalantly to the middle of the ring and held up his two hands to the crowd. "Ladies and—gentlemen!" he shouted. There immediately followed a terrific uproar. Manning was cynical and unperturbed. When the din had died down he tried again. The result was the same. Adrian Manning thrust his hands into his pockets and grinned comfortably. He was far too old a hand at the game to be unduly worried by the actions of any crowd such as he had in front of him now. He scratched his cheek and came up for the third time. "Ladies—and gentlemen!" The noise was now beginning to subside. It gradually died away to a murmur. A smiling Manning waved his hands almost pontifically. Bedlam, now showing signs of accepting discipline, gradually became less than a murmur and no more than a subdued hum. Manning, seizing his opportunity, was immediately into his stride.

"Ladies and gentlemen," he bellowed, "the fight tonight is between the nomination of Mr. Marcus Secretan and the nomination of Sir Cloudesley Slade. The stakes and side-bets are private. The winner takes £2,000. On my right—Phil Blood of Burgess Green, fighting in Mr. Secretan's colours—on my left—Godfrey Slade, formerly of the Bellenden Club and the 'Nightjars,' fighting in his father's colours and hereby forfeiting his amateur status. The match is to be under 12 stone 7 lbs. When the two contestants weighed this afternoon in the presence of the referee and myself, Blood went 12 stone 6½ lbs. and Slade 12 stone 2 lbs. The contest will be the best of 15 two-minute rounds with the normal intervals. If the fight run the full distance, the winner will, as usual in matches of this kind, be declared on points. The referee will be Mr. Douglas Bradfield, the well-known referee from the N.S.C. I may say that he has been agreed upon by the two backers and also by the two contestants themselves which is *most* satisfactory. Mr. Bradfield!"

To the accompaniment of a thunderous uproar, Bradfield went into the ring and waved to the crowd. Adrian Manning turned from one combatant to the other and made the usual gesture of introduction: "Blood—Slade." The coverings slipped from the shoulders of the two principals. They advanced from their corners and delicately touched gloves. The referee made certain inspections. He smiled. Phil Blood and Godfrey Slade smiled at him and with him. Anthony made a quick assessment of the two men when he saw them stripped for the first time. Godfrey Slade was certainly in magnificent condition. His skin shone with health and his supple muscles rippled like silk in their folds. Slade was tall, lithe and spare. Anthony likened him to a panther. His muscular development was finely hard perhaps, and his power would probably come from his vast resources of nervous energy. Anthony summed him up as a trifle fine-drawn, running a little light on the loins, but as hard as a bag of nails and fit to fight for a kingdom.

The professional, however, looked by far the more formidable figure. Much more so than the weight advantage of approximately 5 lbs. would have suggested. His skin was not as clear or as shining as Slade's but he looked harder and tougher altogether and in every way stronger than his opponent. Anthony dissected his appearance as he stood there and faced Slade. His shoulders were broader, his fists were browner and his head much bigger. In height, too, Blood had a slight advantage. Anthony tried to measure the length of his arms. Here, Anthony thought, whatever advantage there was, lay most definitely with Godfrey Slade. As he formed this conclusion, Anthony heard a voice behind him. It was Sir Cloudesley Slade's.

"It was all I could do," he whispered, "to accept Godfrey's offer. In the circumstances it was better than disappointing the public. There was nobody else. With all the breaks, he's got just a dog's chance." Sir Cloudesley waved his hand and slipped back to his own seat by the ring side.

The men were now facing each other. As they advanced to the scrap, Anthony found it difficult to imagine that the elegant Slade could ever deliver anything like a K.O. to the stalwart Blood. Sheer strength seemed to be antagonized with merely alert activity. Blood looked heavily resolute, and minatory. Godfrey Slade looked eager and enthusiastic. There lay the essential differences. Slade came to closer quarters and faced his man with curiously dancing footwork. His skin gleamed like silk and every muscle rippled down his shapely shoulders and along his beautifully moulded arms. They bunched into hard knobs of ivory or rippled into long sinuous curves according to the manner in which he moved his hands. Then Anthony looked away and could see the hard abdominal muscles of Blood. Muscles steeled and trained to perfection, and ready to take and withstand blows under which the ordinary man would wilt and collapse in sheer agony of pain.

Phil Blood stood and faced the dancing Slade with a grim smile, his left arm partly extended, his right held fairly low. He was determined, it appeared, to allow Slade in the early stages to carry the fight to him. Slade tapped Blood twice with quickish left leads but for all the effect they had they were as flicks from a butterfly's wing. Slade danced in again and then, at once swayed from Blood's first real counter-blow. Blood then, with beautiful timing, crossed with his right, but Slade, ducking like lightning, avoided serious trouble. Again Blood came at him with his left and again Slade reeled under the furious force of it. Blood flashed in again as the bell went. Blood's round beyond the shadow of a doubt but a decidedly good opener in the opinion of everybody. The crowd in the Stadium fairly hummed with ardent approbation.

The second round was quiet. Blood's ring-craft was manifestly superior to Slade's and never was this fact more evident to the expert spectator than in this second round. Blood, grim and watchful was serenely content to let Slade waste much of his strength. Every one of the latter's eagerly attempted blows was either skilfully parried by Blood or deftly avoided. Suddenly Blood unleashed himself as it were, and wading in with the speed of a darting dagger, caught Slade a staggering rib-binder. Slade sagged unsteadily and Blood scorched in again—but as before the sound of the bell barriered him. Blood's round again without a doubt.

MacMorran leant over from his seat and whispered to Anthony. "Slade's outclassed—as I see it—the fight won't go half a dozen rounds."

Anthony who had been watching carefully the seconds in Blood's corner shook his head. "I'm not so sure, Andrew. Wait and see. There's plenty of time yet."

MacMorran clicked his tongue in disagreement as the men came out from their corners into the ring again. Slade this time leapt in without a fragment of hesitation and landed home a juicy right smack on to Blood's chin. He then adroitly dodged the inevitable return blow and scored beautifully with his long searching left. Blood tossed his head, spat out a tooth and smiled but Anthony saw the smile and had his own opinion about it. Blood easily held off Slade for the remainder of the round, but it was Slade's round when the bell went.

"Listen," said Anthony, "listen to the bookmakers." MacMorran obeyed. "Five to two against Slade. The odds are shortening, Andrew. Hear that?"

The Inspector shook his head contemptuously. For in the fourth round Blood, with superb ring-craft, manoeuvred Slade into his corner, and then, when he had him where he wanted him, fell upon him like a tiger. Slade tried to turn to evade the onslaught, but he had gone too far and it was too late. Blood drove in a terrific right uppercut which Godfrey Slade only partly parried. Blood followed up the blow with another, delivered in exactly similar fashion. Slade ducked frantically and Anthony looked to see Blood administering the *coup de grâce* with his left. But for some reason he refrained and Slade pluckily closed with him. Blood pushed him away again hard and as Slade danced away, Blood clipped hard at his left ear. Easily Blood's round.

Anthony, however, saw two significant things as he watched the work in the two corners after the bell had gone. Slade was tired—that was evident. But Blood's seconds were again crowding round him and when one of them half turned towards the onlookers, Anthony saw that his face held anxiety. Rounds five, six and seven were quiet, uneventful and tame. Slade was more tired. Blood was content to pile up the points by consummate ring-craft allied to superb judgment. In the eighth round, Slade seemed to take a new lease of life. He appeared to realize that he was well behind on points and must force the running to the finish if he wished to be successful. Slade held his own in this and also in the ninth and tenth rounds. In the eleventh, Slade went to work right from the start. He sprang right into Blood and shook him up with a beautiful long raking left. It appeared to Anthony, as he watched keenly, that the professional replied to the blow somewhat half-heartedly. Anthony glanced at Secretan to see with some surprise that he was smiling cynically towards Slade and the efforts which Slade was making. Secretan, evidently harboured no doubts as to the ultimate outcome of the contest.

Again Slade peppered Blood with his stinging left and again he found the mark—more than once at that. Suddenly he feinted, changed his feet and cross-jabbed at his opponent with his right. But Blood was wary this time and countered it skilfully. Slade seemed now to have cast away all his jaded weariness and to be in remarkably high feather. Blood had a big lead on points it was true, but there were five rounds yet to go—and in any one of those rounds anything might happen. Slade danced in again almost on tiptoe and drove another lashing left to Blood's jaw. Blood's return was feeble and Slade was out of danger again when the bell rang. Slade's round undoubtedly. Anthony whispered to MacMorran. "All is not right with Phil Blood. I can't quite make it out. There's something the matter with him. Hark at the betting now. Two to one against Slade. The odds have come down a full point since the start."

MacMorran shook his head in what was evidently meant to be utter disagreement with Mr. Bathurst's opinion. Full of confidence now Slade came from his corner for the twelfth round in similar mood to that he had exhibited in the round immediately previous. Blood seemed to be moving slowly and Slade darted in to use his left. He sprang forward and at the psychological second Blood lunged and struck. The next instant Godfrey Slade lay in the middle of the ring. Foolishly and over-confidently, he had exposed himself to the professional's right. With a tautened and tensely rigid arm, Blood had driven home a crashing uppercut to the point of the jaw. Anthony saw Slade twist round helplessly before he fell. The vast crowd rose to its feet in a roar. Blood crouched over Slade's prone figure but Douglas Bradfield waved him back peremptorily. "Stand back, Blood . . . d'ye hear?" The fateful seconds were being called. "One . . . two . . . three . . . four . . . five . . . six"—Slade came to his knees . . . mechanically . . . like an automaton . . . "seven . . . eight." He was up . . . his hands were again automatically guarding his body against Blood's smashing onslaught. Four times Blood hit him with the right hand and at the fourth blow Slade reeled blindly and hopelessly and slid like a sack to the floor.

"That's the bundle," said Anthony, "he'll never get up after that pasting."

The voice of the timekeeper could be heard again. "One. . . two . . . three . . . four. . . five. . . six . . . seven . . ." and then the bell rang!

A torrent of cheering burst from the crowd and Anthony could hear the voice of Sir Cloudesley Slade at the height of the din. "Saved by God . . . saved! And the scrap's not all over yet."

Slade's seconds were working on him frantically. His head lolled upon his shoulders but Anthony knew from personal experience what the rest would mean to him. The cold sponges and douches were already doing their work. Slade was round again but he looked appallingly weak and helpless. Anthony doubted if he could last anything like another round. If the fight ran to its full length, there were still three more rounds to go. Once more there came the usual warning, "Seconds out of the ring," and Slade tottered out to meet his opponent. For a time, he knew, he must go slow in the hope that some of his strength at least, would come back to him before it was too late. Blood, still using his right, came at him with a will. Slade's jaw and neck were excruciatingly stiff and painful from the fierce force of the uppercut, but although he lurched and rocked from time to time, he managed to fend his opponent off and towards the end of the round, thanks mainly to his youth and superb physical condition, was actually giving blow for blow.

This brought the fight to the last round but one and it opened brightly with Slade whipping in a fast left to the mark. Blood parried it with his usual nonchalant skill and then Anthony saw him wince with pain and suddenly throw his right hand above his shoulder. Slade stood back . . . surprised and a little suspicious of the movement. But he need not have felt the latter . . . it was indicative of neither trick nor artifice . . . for a towel came flying into the ring from Phil Blood's corner. For some mad moments the uproar that followed the tossed towel prevented any explanation from being heard by the spectators. Bradfield beckoned to Manning. Manning went up and then Bradfield, with both hands upraised, made the following sensational announcement. "I regret to inform you that Phil Blood has broken a bone in his left hand and retires from the fight. I award the fight, therefore, to Slade. Slade wins."

He raised Slade's right hand to the crowd . . . and pandemonium was let loose again. The crowd shouted in indescribable confusion. Bradfield yelled himself hoarse and all that Godfrey Slade could hear was his own name taken up and tossed high in a swelling chorus. He seemed to be passing through an excitement such as a dream might bring.

Sir Cloudesley, almost beside himself with joy, dashed between Anthony and Inspector MacMorran. He caught Anthony by the lapel of his coat and swung him round. "What did I tell you. What did I tell you? What a fight! What a scrap! The boy was Goddam lucky I know, to get the verdict as he did . . . but could any other amateur in the country stand fourteen rounds against a pro of Blood's class as young Godfrey did? No, sir! I'm tellin' you. There isn't one who could do it."

He seized their hands and pump-handled them vigorously. Anthony contributed congratulations. "A grand show, Sir Cloudesley, I wouldn't have missed it for worlds. You must be proud of him."

"Proud! I'll say I am. And blast the money. What's money any way? Don't care a rap for that. Murder would they? And threaten to kidnap my boy? Even now I've dished 'em—the murderin' blackguards. Thanks to you, Inspector."

His eyes gleamed with triumph and delight and he caught MacMorran's hand again and shook it at least a dozen times. . Then he caught sight of somebody else in the cheering multitude who was waving and calling to him and dashed away as suddenly and as precipitately as he had come to them. Anthony tried to find Marcus Secretan but in the chaotic conditions that were prevailing, the task was impossible. He looked round for him everywhere, towards the middle of the Winter Hall, round the ringside and towards the many exits that studded the building. There was no sign of Secretan. Suddenly he saw something that caused him to catch his breath and then look again. He turned and grabbed MacMorran by the arm.

"Look, Andrew. Quick. Over there. Going towards that side-door on the left there! Just by that placard marked 'K Block.' See him?"

MacMorran followed Anthony's indications. "You're right," he said laconically, "Asater. It's him right enough. Well—I can't say that I'm altogether surprised. I expected him to be somewhere about. He's got a woman with him. A big powerful hulking woman. I'd have said it was his mother. See her? To his right. A shade or two in front of him."

This time Anthony looked as MacMorran had directed. He saw a big, heavy-shouldered woman walking a few paces ahead of Asater and evidently on the way out. Her head was close-cropped and her two arms moved loosely as she walked. Suddenly as he looked towards her and her companion, Anthony let go a whoop of amazement and satisfaction. For on the side of the woman's neck he could see a large wen!

"Andrew," he cried, "our luck's in. That's no woman with friend Asater. Do you know who it is? That's 'Banjo' Bellamy whom you've been trying to find for nearly a month now. Bellamy in woman's clothes. Andrew—it's up to you—get busy."

Without further ado, MacMorran accepted the statement and dashed for the exit. But unfortunately for him there were hundreds of people between Asater and himself and Anthony harboured grave doubts, as he watched, as to whether the Inspector would be able to make it. The last he saw of MacMorran that evening was of a figure pushing an authoritative way through the crowd like a man possessed.

CHAPTER XVI
WHO LAUGHS LAST

As HE turned his head from the contemplation of MacMorran pushing his way through the crowd in the wake of Bellamy and Asater,

Anthony Bathurst felt somebody pulling his arm. Turning, he saw that it was Sir Cloudesley Slade at his side again.

"Look here," the Baronet was saying, "You must join my party at the Turin Grill this evening. For a bite of supper. You know—a bird and a bottle! Several bottles. I won't hear of a refusal. You and that policeman pal of yours. What's his name? MacGillicuddy? I DON'T CARE WHAT HIS BLASTED NAME IS! Jove I'm excited! What a night! There'll be a hot time in the old town to-night. Red? I'll say! We'll paint it Crimson Bloody Lake—not red, my boy."

He swung Anthony round in his elation and yelled again with excitement. Anthony was just able to murmur a conventionally polite acceptance.

"You'll know 'em all—that are comin' along," went on the elated Sir Cloudesley, "so you won't feel out in the cold. There'll be you and your 'busy' pal, myself, Godfrey and his girl friend whom you've met, Whitfield and Jack Lambert, Adrian Manning who announced the scrap and Doug. Bradfield himself, the referee. Nice little family party—what—Bathurst? The bubbly's on the ice in the buckets already. Meet me in the vestibule at the Turin just before midnight. You'll be going up by car, I suppose? Yes? Right. That's on, then. Don't forget to tell MacClutterbuck. See you there."

Sir Cloudesley pranced off, the picture of wild delight. Anthony grinned at his retreating figure. "On such a night," he whispered to himself, "did Thisbe" . . . and then fell to wondering how Inspector MacMorran was faring in the chase. If the Inspector didn't come back pretty quickly how was he going to pass Sir Cloudesley's invitation on to him? Bit of a problem—that. Anthony looked at his watch. Time was getting on. He had little of it to waste if he were going to keep a punctual appointment with Sir Cloudesley Slade at the Turin Grill. He decided that he would wait a quarter of an hour for MacMorran . . . not a minute longer. If the Inspector didn't turn up by that time he would go. He kept to his decision. At the end of the quarter hour, there was still no sign of MacMorran's return. Anthony made his way out, found his car, drove quietly back to town, changed at his flat and was waiting in the vestibule at the Turin with eight minutes to spare.

Sir Cloudesley Slade arrived with most of his party at two minutes to the hour. He bustled up to Anthony—the crevices of his face creased and crinkled with cordiality. Anthony explained the unavoidable absence of MacMorran. Sir Cloudesley waved the excuses aside. "Don't worry about that, my boy. If you haven't seen him, you couldn't ask him—and that's that. So what's the odds? All the same, I should have liked him here. Decent fellow—Macconnachie."

He introduced Anthony to Manning and Bradfield. "Godfrey and his girl friend are coming along separately," he continued. "He just *had* to go and make his peace with her." Sir Cloudesley winked at Anthony. "You know how these things are, Bathurst—I expect you've been through the mill yourself—so you must make allowances for Love's Young Dream! I do. Old as I am. I'm not done with yet. There's still some life in the old dog. Very likely they've arrived by now and have gone up to the supper-room and are waiting there for us. We'd best go up and find out for ourselves. Come on, you chaps."

He beckoned to the others. They followed Sir Cloudesley up a flight of heavily-carpeted stairs to the room he had engaged. Anthony arranged matters so that he brought up the rear. When he entered the supper-room, Sir Cloudesley was shepherding his guests to their seats. But his prognostication that Godfrey and Miss Merrilees would have arrived in advance of the general party was ill-founded because Anthony could see no sign of either of them. He noticed, too, that despite his assurances, Sir Cloudesley was obviously worried by the fact of the absences inasmuch as he continually consulted his watch. Manning and Bradfield were talking 'fight.' Anthony could hear them plainly. Whitfield and Lambert were comparatively silent but every now and then they would lean over towards each other and solemnly shake hands with each other. Anthony found the action so irresistibly comical, that he smiled every time he saw it happen.

Sir Cloudesley began to fuss about with the waiters. But the watch-checking activity of his still went on. At last he gave the signal for the supper to start. Anthony took the seat which he saw had been assigned to him. Waiters with two eyes on the clock—for it was getting late—appeared from all parts of the room. Sir Cloudesley made a general announcement. "We'll start without the lion of the evening. It's not our fault—it's his own. When he does come, he'll commence with a handicap." Sir Cloudesley laughed. "Not that he'll be put off by that. So get to it, boys."

The party set to. But Anthony had scarcely disposed of his oysters when there came an interruption. A girl came quickly into the room and walked straight to Sir Cloudesley Slade seated at the head of the table. With a catch of surprise, Anthony saw that the girl was none other than Star Merrilees. She spoke rapidly to Sir Cloudesley who half-rose from his seat to hear what she was saying. A grey look took possession of his face and his eyes grew haunted by fear and foreboding. Anthony saw him move his head several times. Star Merrilees shook her head. It seemed to Anthony that in some way which he couldn't understand, they were in disagreement. Suddenly, Bradfield spoke to him across the table.

"There's trouble at the top table, Bathurst. I didn't hear what the girl said when she first sailed up to the old man but I've managed to catch one or two snatches of the conversation since. In fact, from what I can gather, I rather fancy that you'll be pressed into service before many minutes have passed. There you are! What did I tell you? Call that acutely intelligent anticipation."

Bradfield's last remark was in reference to Sir Cloudesley Slade's beckoning finger in the direction of Anthony. For Sir Cloudesley was beckoning to Anthony in a manner concerning which there could be no mistake. The latter pushed back his chair and at once made his way towards his host.

"Bathurst," said Sir Cloudesley in a lowered voice, "you've met Miss Merrilees, I think. She's in a terrible way. She's brought me damn bad news, boy. Damn bad news. It's fairly knocked the guts out of me. Don't mind admittin' it. She wants me to tell you at once. But Godfrey's gone. Disappeared!"

Anthony turned and looked at Star. "Tell me," he said simply. "Tell me all you can."

Star Merrilees sank into the chair next to Sir Cloudesley. Her fingers moved nervously and convulsively. "I did not go to Belfairs this evening. You know why—perfectly well. I explained my views as to Godfrey fighting, before, and nothing has occurred since then to make me change my opinion. But I had arranged to meet him after it was all over at Charing Cross underground station at eleven o'clock. *Whatever* the result of the fight. At a quarter to eleven, Godfrey 'phoned me at my flat in Little Stanwick Street a few moments before I was coming out. He was lucky to catch me. He told me the result of the fight—which was very natural, I suppose, and especially considering all I had said about it—and then told me that he was on the way to meeting me as we had arranged. I went straight to the rendezvous. I waited there for him in vain. Godfrey has never come. I at last decided to come here hoping against hope in a vague sort of way that he had missed me by some mischance and gone straight on. I'm sorry but that's all I can tell you, Mr. Bathurst."

Anthony looked grave at the news. "When he 'phoned to you at Little Stanwick Street at a quarter to eleven—have you any idea from where he 'phoned? Did he say anything?"

"No. But it was from a call-box, I feel sure. He didn't tell me where he was and I didn't trouble to ask. I was too excited, I suppose—and again—the need didn't arise."

Sir Cloudesley had crumpled into his seat. His fingers plucked at the edge of the table-cloth. His face was ashen and the blue eyes had dulled. Coming so precipitately upon his mood of triumphant exultation, the shock of Godfrey's disappearance had been in the nature of a terrific reaction and had shaken him to the depths. Anthony wished that MacMorran were with him. The resources of the "Yard" are vast especially when the vital need of the moment is the quickest of quick action backed by authority and force. But MacMorran was *not* there, so mere wishing was vain and empty. Anthony went to Star Merrilees again.

"So your point is. Miss Merrilees, that Godfrey Slade was intercepted somewhere between the call-box he used to 'phone to you and Charing Cross underground station?"

She nodded in agreement. "It seems to me that he must have been. What else is there for me to think?" Waiters hovered and bustled near at hand. The mockery of the supper-party was still going on around them.

"Stay here a moment," said Anthony to Star. "I'll see if the 'Yard' are able to trace that call. What's your number, Miss Merrilees?"

"Maxwell 1922," she answered.

"Thanks. I'll cut along now. You hang on here for a minute or two."

Anthony found a telephone and got through to the 'Yard.' He asked for MacMorran's junior colleague. Supt. Hemingway. Hemingway heard what Anthony had to say.

"Right you are, Mr. Bathurst. I'll do that for you with pleasure. Where are you speaking from?" Anthony gave him the information. "All right. I'll 'phone you back as soon as I can. Leave word with somebody that you're expecting a return call, will you? That'll be all right."

Anthony said he would and hung up. Then he returned quietly and thoughtfully to the Slade supper-room. Whitfield and Lambert were now standing round Sir Cloudesley Slade. The meal, with its courses, had evidently broken up. Bradfield and Manning having sensed the trouble that had descended upon their host seemed in the depths of despondency. Sir Cloudesley was talking.

"They threatened to do it. They warned us all. Before the scrap took place. And now they've carried out their threat. Serves me right for takin' it lightly. Serves us all right. We were too confident. It never pays to under-rate your adversary." He shook his head despairingly and then sat staring straight in front of him.

Anthony went across to the group at the head of the table. "Look here," he said to the old man, "things are better this time than they've been in the other instances. We're red hot this time. There's been no appreciable interval to mean delay. They haven't much more than an hour's start of us. Also—we know roughly the district where they got their man. Things are bad, I agree, but don't imagine the worst immediately. I'm already through to the 'Yard' and I shall be hearing from them within a few minutes at the most. You don't mind if I smoke a cigarette, do you?"

Sir Cloudesley shook his head aimlessly. Anthony smoked and thought of MacMorran. If MacMorran had managed to get on the trail of Asater and Bellamy, things might even be better than he had foreshadowed to Sir Cloudesley. In a way the luck had been on their side and it might well be that it would continue to run for them. As he sat and mused, he saw a waiter coming towards him.

Anthony anticipated the message and was up before the waiter reached him.

"Your call, sir," announced the waiter, "you asked to be informed as soon as it came through."

Anthony thanked him with a nod and went straight to take the message. Hemingway had been as good as his word. "I've traced that call for you, Mr. Bathurst. It came from a call-box on the Kenriston road and was timed at 10.47. Kenriston is about three miles from the Belfairs Stadium, if that's any use to you."

"Thank you, Super. That's good of you. Smart work on your part. Now I want to ask you something else. Is Inspector MacMorran at the 'Yard'?"

"No, Mr. Bathurst. You'll pardon me remarkin' on it but I had the idea that the Chief was along with you. Been to the fight together, haven't you?"

"Yes, that's right—but the Inspector had another appointment afterwards. I wondered if he had got back to the 'Yard' by now— that was all."

"Not expectin' him . . . till the morning. He told me not to—when he left this evening. Anything I can do for you, Mr. Bathurst?"

"Yes, I think there is, Super. I'll tell you what I know." Anthony recapitulated the story he had just had from Star Merrilees. "Now that call that was put through by Slade, as you've just told me, came from Kenriston. Which means that something must have happened to him between Kenriston and Charing Cross underground station where he was due to meet Miss Merrilees. Remembering Bailey, Donovan and Jago, you had better get busy. Super. Tell the Chief that I'll be along to the 'Yard' first thing in the morning. I don't think I can do any more now."

Hemingway acquiesced in the suggestion. "I'll tell the Chief what you say, Mr. Bathurst. And I'll get the other job in hand for you at once. Rely on me."

"Good. And you might take a special message from me for the Commissioner himself. Will you take it, please? I'll give it to you now." Anthony gave a message to Sir Austin Kemble of which Hemingway took full note. Hemingway called it back.

"Very good, sir. I'll see that that's delivered directly Sir Austin comes in."

"Thank you again, Super," returned Anthony, "as I said just now, I don't think we can reasonably expect to do any more at the moment."

Anthony hung up and walked thoughtfully away from the telephone. Certain ideas were flooding his brain—thick and fast. Why was Bellamy masquerading as a woman to attend the fight between Blood and Godfrey Slade? In the company, be it noted, of the man Asater. He comforted himself with the assurance that MacMorran was on their track and would doubtless return with much valuable information. Mr. Bathurst came to the supper-room again and to the head of the table. By this time, all the guests had gathered round their host in a rough circle. Anthony spoke directly to Star Merrilees.

"I've established the fact that Godfrey Slade 'phoned you from Kenriston at thirteen minutes to eleven. Kenriston isn't much more than three miles from the Belfairs Stadium."

"I know that," she said, almost absent-mindedly.

"What are you doing, Bathurst," croaked Sir Cloudesley from the depths of his chair.

"Well—so far, sir, I've given the 'Yard' full particulars of everything that we know. They've already got to work. The 'Yard' don't let the grass grow under their feet, believe me, Sir Cloudesley."

The old man nodded half to himself and half to Anthony. To the latter's eye he had aged considerably since Star Merrilees had entered with her ill tidings. Anthony began to talk again.

"I've been wondering, sir," he said, "as to why the 'technique' has been varied on this occasion. I'll explain to you what I mean. Bailey was decoyed by letter. In Donovan's case, the letter sign was repeated. Ink monkey ink. And we find that the same methods were used again in the case of Mike Jago . . . he had the fatal letter delivered to him on the morning he disappeared. But your son has had *no* letter. Even on the occasion of the warnings that were received with regard to him, they didn't go to *him*—they went to you, to Lambert and to Whitfield."

"Just a minute. How do you know he hasn't had a letter?" countered Star Merrilees, "how do you know, for instance, that a letter wasn't delivered to his dressing-room at the Belfairs Stadium? It might have been sent after the fight was over."

Sir Cloudesley Slade gave her a quick glance of interest. "That's certainly an idea, Bathurst," he said—"you've got to admit it."

Lambert and Whitfield were emphatic in their denials. Neither had seen Slade receive any communication.

"Who was with him on the way home?" demanded Sir Cloudesley, "after the fight? Anybody?"

"Nobody," retorted Lambert, "he was in his own car. Driving himself. Insisted on doing so. He told us he had a date. With an angel he said it was—begging this young lady's pardon for the allusion."

Star Merrilees coloured deliciously. Sir Cloudesley came to life again and bristled fiercely at Anthony. "Where were MacMorran's men then? If Godfrey went off on his own? That's what gets me. Where were they as I arranged at the 'Yard' with the Inspector? They ought to have been red hot on his heels all the time." He glared round at everybody with more than a touch of his old fire.

Anthony defended MacMorran. "If Inspector MacMorran made any promises, I have no doubt that he carried them out. I know the Inspector too well to think otherwise. Until we know for certain what has happened, don't let us start apportioning blame."

Sir Cloudesley grunted at the implied censure. "All I know is that this murdering gang have got Godfrey. I can't think of anything else."

All his cocksureness had departed from him. Star Merrilees also found reproaches. "If he hadn't fought, nothing of this kind would have happened. If only he had listened to me! Why *won't* people ever listen to those who their welfare at heart?" She twisted her handkerchief in her hands.

"Stuff and nonsense," came back Sir Cloudesley, "you women interfere a damn sight too much. All the world over. You get far too much rope these times—it was different in my young days."

Anthony felt suddenly that he must sleep. "Have you your car with you, Miss Merrilees?"

She shook her head. "No—I came by taxi. To do so was the first thing that came into my head. I thought it would be quicker."

"Then unless you particularly want to stop on here, I'll give you a lift as far as Little Stanwick Street. I'm going on. I've had enough for one day."

Star looked at him doubtfully. "I suppose I can't do much if I do stay here."

"You can do nothing whatever. I'm afraid, that so far as that goes, we're all in the same boat."

"All right then—I'll come along with you." She turned to the others. "Good-bye, Sir Cloudesley. Good-bye everybody. The bird of ill-omen that spoiled your supper-party will go back again to her own place."

The bitterness in her voice was there for all to hear. Anthony waved his good-bye to the others. To Sir Cloudesley he went and said: "if you want me in the morning, Sir Cloudesley, give me a tinkle. Make it early. And if you can, sir—keep smiling—while there's life there's hope." Star walked along with him. "My car's parked just round the corner. Wait in the foyer and I'll run it round in a couple of shakes."

She gestured her understanding. When he had Star seated beside him in the car, Anthony talked more or less commonplaces. But Star was adamant and would have none of them. She persistently brought him back to his horses. "Well," she urged, "was I right? *Has* it all turned out badly?"

"*Must* you be feminine and chuckle 'I told you so.' You—of all people." He turned and glanced at her face and saw that it was hard and set. She suddenly shivered and pulled her evening cloak closer to her neck.

"It's bitterly cold," she answered irrelevantly.

Anthony said no more. The car came to Little Stanwick Street. Before she alighted, Anthony opened the door and then looked straight at her. "Miss Merrilees," he said gravely, "perhaps you may be able to help me. I'm rather hoping that you will. In any of your wanderings through the Bright Lights of this gay city, have you ever run across a girl named Stella Molyneux? A girl with black hair?"

His companion shook her head. A few seconds elapsed. She spoke slowly. "No, I don't think so. The name is not familiar to me. She had black hair—you say? How perfectly lovely."

Anthony pressed her hand sympathetically. "Thank you, Miss Merrilees. I'm sorry you can't help me. Good night—or rather good morning. Let's hope things will be better next time I see you."

His car slid away as Star Merrilees walked to the front door of her flat.

CHAPTER XVII
AT THE 'DOUBLE-TOP'

MACMORRAN spoke curtly to Supt. Hemingway. It was evident that he was far from being in the best of tempers.

"Bring Mr. Bathurst up directly he comes along. It's more than important—so don't forget."

"Very good, Inspector. I've already made the arrangements."

As MacMorran turned away to another task, Hemingway dropped his jaw in mock solemnity. As he had just remarked to one of his own subordinates, he thought again to himself, 'The Chief's got a touch of liver this morning. He can keep himself next week. Every day of it.' MacMorran scrawled savagely at the foot of several documents. He jabbed the point of his nib into the texture of the paper and swore audibly. Hemingway gave a rather too realistic start of surprise. MacMorran looked up truculently and scowled at him. Hemingway coughed discreetly behind his hand. MacMorran for the nth time looked at his watch. Hemingway watched him and fidgeted uneasily in his chair.

"Fine scrap last night, Chief," he ventured, "or so I'm told."

"Scrap's right," grunted MacMorran laconically.

"I suppose you were well to the front."

"What do you mean exactly by that?"

"Well—in a good position."

"Depends."

"How d'ye mean? If you were sitting close to the—"

MacMorran's patience snapped abruptly. "Oh—shut up for God's sake. Your blasted mouth-opening makes my feet ache. Pipe down. You're enough to make a monkey bite his grandfather."

"Sorry, Chief. No offence. Didn't know you felt like that about it. I expect Mr. Bathurst'll be here in a moment or so."

MacMorran turned on him swiftly. "Look here, Superintendent. You seem to forget that up to the moment we haven't the vestige of a clue with regard to the disappearance of Godfrey Slade. It may suit *you* and your ideas—but I tell you candidly it certainly doesn't suit me."

He brought his fist down heavily on the table in emphatic accompaniment. Hemingway scratched at his top lip. He felt that he must defend himself.

"Well—Chief—it's early days yet. Have a heart. I've got five men at work on it. Got 'em going directly Mr. Bathurst asked me to—early this morning. Because nothing's come through yet that isn't to say we *shan't* get something later on. Must be patient, Chief."

MacMorran murmured trenchant criticisms. Hemingway shrugged his shoulders and tapped his front teeth with the butt of his pencil. On the point of making a further remark, he was interrupted by a tap on the door. Hemingway rose to attend to it but before he could reach the door to open it, Anthony Bathurst had entered the room. He made his way to the corner of MacMorran's table.

"My seat, I think, Andrew, if you don't mind—and er—good morning to both of you. Quite a treat to see so many cheerful faces."

The relief had at once shown on MacMorran's face. "Glad you've come. Sit down—of course."

Anthony sat on the table. "Glad I've come—eh? Why? What's the news?"

"None," returned the Inspector. "Not a sausage."

Anthony whistled. "Bad as that—eh? That's no good at all. I was hoping something might have come through by now."

MacMorran shook his head. "Nothing. Hemingway's been at work ever since you communicated with him but up to the moment his men have picked up nothing."

"Bad luck," commented Anthony, "still—there's plenty of time yet. We'll go on hoping. Now—tell me about last night. What happened?"

MacMorran looked glum. "The answer's the same." He called Hemingway over and gave him certain instructions. "See that it's all done before you return," he concluded. "I'm concerned about it." Hemingway took himself and a look of extreme annoyance out of the room. "I haven't told Hemingway," volunteered MacMorran, "and I don't intend to—so if you don't mind—"

"Of course," returned Anthony—"I understand perfectly—but tell me, my dear chap—what was doing?"

"You saw me go after Asater and the woman directly you told me you had spotted them—didn't you? I knew that I ought to lose no time over the job. I pushed my way through the crowd and take it from me—it wasn't too easy by any means."

"I know. I saw you going hell for leather through the mob. Andrew—you were a bonnie sight—you were an' all. I felt proud of you. You moved so fast you might have been going off duty. Did you catch up with our two friends?"

"Listen and don't be in such a damned hurry. When they got outside the Stadium—some good few seconds before I did—they must have made straight for a car—because when *I* got outside and started to look round for them, I saw them about fifty yards ahead, just on the point of getting into a biggish car."

Anthony smiled. "Go on, Andrew."

"Well—I realized that to have any chance of getting to grips with them I must have a car as well. So I looked round for one. It's no good being a Chief Inspector of Police unless you put your foot down sometimes. I couldn't see where your 'bus was parked—I had come out on the other side of the Stadium to where you and I had gone in—otherwise I should have 'half-inched' that. I knew you wouldn't mind as the cause was so close to your heart. As it was, I had to do a quick bit of thinking."

Anthony looked at him sympathetically and grinned. "I was afraid so. I thought you weren't looking too fit." MacMorran ignored the cynicism and proceeded with his story. "Standing near to me was one of our fellows. I beckoned to him and told him who I was and what I wanted. He turned out to be a smartish chap. Within another few seconds he had found me a police-car and pushed me into it. The fellow who was driving took his orders well and we went after Mr. Asater and Company like the wind. The bloke in the police-car drove as fast as you—only a good deal better."

Anthony's grin expanded. "Andrew—you're a blighter. You wait till you're in my car again. I'll remember that remark—to your cost."

MacMorran continued his story. "But that pace only lasted a little while. There were thousands of cars on the road. As you can well guess. Neither Asater's nor mine could get a clear run for anything like a good spell. Stoppage followed stoppage and jam was close on jam. We went from one traffic jam to another—very often in a matter of a few seconds. But we managed to keep Asater's car in sight. That was held up likewise. Once or twice, perhaps, my driver lost it—but never for long so that it was of no consequence. By stepping on it he managed to catch up with our birds again. We reached as far as Kenriston."

Anthony nodded.

"Yes, Mr. Bathurst, I know what you're thinking of—but of course when I arrived there last night it meant less than nothing to me. In Kenriston, Asater's car showed signs of stopping. It slowed down. My bloke in the rear of them did likewise. I told him to maintain a reasonable distance between the cars and he did. I must say that all through the piece, he did his job remarkably well. It was quite a pleasure to have an intelligent companion for once. Suddenly the Asater car stopped."

"A monkey to a macaroon that I'll tell you where."

MacMorran took up Anthony's challenge. "All right. Where?"

"At the 'Double Top', on the left of the road there. The roadhouse."

"You're right—but you'll have to wait for the macaroon. I don't keep any on the premises. Well—we couldn't see what was happening but we felt pretty certain, my driver and I, that Asater and his supposed lady friend were going to make an early morning call at the place. So I told my driver to pull up as inconspicuously as possible, so that I could hop out and do a bit more sleuthing. This he did and I got out. Told him to wait till I returned. I walked up to the roadhouse and then marched in. As I expected, the place was packed. Crammed to the ceiling. Nine-tenths of 'em, of course, had been to the fight. Still, I barged my way in and ordered a drink. I wanted to see if either Asater or his companion teamed up with anybody. Associations of that kind I've found from experience usually assist the course of justice."

"Don't be pontifical, Andrew. It doesn't suit you. Be your own noble self."

"It wasn't one of my times for nobility. I was just human and besides that—a policeman."

"Don't contradict yourself—it spoils the story."

"Don't interrupt—it spoils everything."

Anthony grinned at the aptness of MacMorran's comeback. "Go on. What happened after you ordered the drink?"

"I laid low for a bit. Reckoned it would be my best policy. Did some useful 'eye' work round the place. Suddenly I noticed that Asater was alone. He and the 'woman' had previously been drinking together at a table in a sort of alcove with lights stuck on the wall. I hadn't seen the 'woman' *move*—let alone go—and she must have slipped off like a flash. I happened to look at the time just about then. It was almost exactly a quarter to eleven. As long as Asater was staying there, I didn't worry overmuch as I reckoned the woman would be sure to rejoin him. Every now and then the band would strike up and there'd be dancing. And while I could see Asater at his table I didn't mind. I felt I was on safe ground. More and more couples took the floor and all of a sudden I realized with a certain amount of misgiving that there were at least half a dozen of them between me and Asater and that he had been completely blotted out. I jumped up from my seat, circumvented a swaying pair of dancers, and lo and behold Asater had gone!"

Anthony nodded. "He had recognized you. He'd seen you before—remember. With me. That was all worked with deliberation and malice aforethought. I haven't a doubt of it, Andrew."

"Very likely. I'm inclined to agree with you now. But it's easy to be wise after the event."

"I won't argue about that. Well—what came next?"

"Well—what do you think? I shot out of the 'Double Top' like greased lightning. There was no sense in staying put. But of course the start they had of me was too big. The Asater car had gone and I hadn't the slightest idea as to which direction it had taken. I was snookered."

"Bad luck, Andrew. And so you gracefully accepted the inevitable and—"

MacMorran shook his head lugubriously. "Hold on a moment. You haven't heard the sequel. I don't mind admitting that I hate telling you. That was why I sent Hemingway out just now. I went back to my police-car. My intention, late as the time was, was to come on here to the ' Yard.' I gave orders to my driver and opened the door of the car. What do you think I found on the seat at the back?"

Anthony rubbed the top of his nose. There was a humorous glint in his eye as he spoke. "I'll take a chance on that, Andrew. I was always attracted by a long shot. A parcel of feminine clothing?"

"You win. A black silk dress. It was the dress which had been worn by Asater's companion."

"Rubbing it in rather, wasn't it, Andrew? Salting the tail of the 'Yard'—eh?"

MacMorran nodded ruefully. "It was that! I'd be the last to deny it. In fact, I was so fed to the teeth with the whole business and so dispirited generally with my own performance that instead of coming back here to the 'Yard,' I went home to the missus. And that's that."

Anthony put his head back and clasped his fingers across a raised knee. "Tell me, Andrew—all the time you were round about Kenriston and in the 'Double Top'—did you catch any glimpse of Godfrey Slade?"

"No. As far as I know, Slade wasn't inside the 'Double Top.' As a matter of fact, I looked for him."

"That's bad. I was hoping for a line there. As I see things, Slade must have been in Kenriston about the time you were there. We have Miss Merrilees's word on that. He 'phoned to her flat just about the time that you lost sight of 'Banjo' Bellamy. A quarter to eleven. I wish you had seen him—Slade, I mean."

"Not more than I do. If I'd have known last night what I know now—I might have acted differently."

"What were you doing at that time with regard to Slade's body-guard?"

"I had relaxed it. After the fight. I mean as soon as the fight was over. I was a fool. I thought that the *danger* was over. The threat had been to nobble him before the fight. As it turned out I was wrong—of course."

"It looks now as though you were. Still—I don't know that I can justifiably blame you. Sir Cloudesley is inclined to be critical. But that's human nature. Most of us would be, I suppose, were we in similar circumstances." As he spoke, Anthony came off the table and began to pace the room. He thrust his hands deeply into his pockets. "I'm worried, Andrew. About young Slade. I'm worried to hell."

"No more than I am. The great big British public will be asking unpleasant questions soon. Godfrey Slade's a popular figure. And he'll be more popular than ever after last night's fight with Blood."

Anthony continued to pace the room. His mind was questing in a multitude of directions. "How did they entice him, Andrew? With Bailey and the others it has obviously been with promise of things to come. A lucrative offer of some kind. The kindly fruits of the earth and so on. That bait wouldn't have worked with Slade. It was no temptation to him. Unless he were attacked and removed by force, which fact might explain things. Point is what *would* have been a temptation to him? That was likely to draw him into danger? What are the blandishments that draw a man, Andrew?"

"Money, power, women—that's about the lot, isn't it?"

"I don't suppose you're far out. Those three will certainly do to be going on with."

"Looks like the last-named, then, doesn't it?"

"We're in the dark so. What happened to Slade between the end of the fight and his disappearance? All we know for certain is that he got to Kenriston and 'phoned from there to Star Merrilees. What other contacts did he make? If we knew that, we should know a hell of a lot." Anthony turned suddenly in MacMorran's direction. "That dress you had presented to you, Andrew, under such romantic conditions—anything striking about it?"

The Inspector shook his head. "No. Nothing. Just an ordinary black silk dress. Not a mark of any kind on it. You can see it if you want to."

"No. Doesn't matter. If you're satisfied. I know the man who wore it and where he used to live. That's good enough for me. And I never forget that I have an account to settle with him."

Anthony rubbed the point of his chin reminiscently. For the first time that morning, MacMorran grinned. "Optimistic—aren't you?"

Before Anthony could answer, there came an interruption. The telephone on MacMorran's table rang insistently. "Hallo," came from the Inspector. "Hemingway? . . . Yes . . . what is it, Super? . . .

what . . . is that so . . . eh . . . bring it up to me at once, will you? Yes. That's all right—Mr. Bathurst is still with me."

MacMorran looked up from the telephone and his eyes met the gaze of Anthony Bathurst. "That was Hemingway. And there's a fresh piece of ominous news. Godfrey Slade's dinner-jacket has been picked up on a piece of waste ground between Kenriston and Hadow. There is blood on it. A working-man found it."

Anthony went white at the news. "Where is it now?"

"Hemingway's bringing it up. Hadow, I might point out, is between Kenriston and London."

Anthony nodded. His face was grave and set. These were deeper waters than had hitherto been encountered.

CHAPTER XVIII
ASATER SHOWS HIS TEETH
(METAPHORICALLY)

HEMINGWAY brought in the dinner-jacket and hung it over the back of one of MacMorran's chairs. There were dark stains on the left lapel. Also three or four mudstains on the back and sleeves.

"How do you know it's Godfrey Slade's?" asked Anthony.

"From two letters in it. Both addressed to him. Ordinary letters, Mr. Bathurst. Nothing much in 'em. One dated six months ago *re* a dinner-dance and the other enclosing a receipt for a subscription. Also old." Hemingway's face showed that he was confident of the truth of his statement. He handed the envelopes over.

"H'm," said Anthony, "nothing of any importance here. It might be a good idea to check up on it for certain. Who's the tailor?"

He gave the letters back. Hemingway examined the tab.

"Kempster, Cross and Hawes, Hallam House, Savile Row."

"Give 'em a ring," said MacMorran—"at once. There you are. Use my 'phone."

Hemingway, with rather ill grace, picked up the receiver. The operator did the necessary. Anthony and the Inspector waited for Hemingway's information to come through. They heard him ask questions and saw him nod to the replies he received. He replaced the receiver and turned to his superior officer.

"O.K.," he said. "All confirmed. Slade was their customer."

"Seems satisfactory," commented MacMorran.

"I agree," said Anthony.

"I must get into touch with Sir Cloudesley Slade at once," went on MacMorran.

"Yes. I should do that first of all if I were in your place. He ought to know what we know."

MacMorran issued further instructions. "Get through again, Hemingway. To Sir Cloudesley. The number's on my pad there. Right at the top. In pencil."

Hemingway went again to his task. Anthony sat deep in thought while the Superintendent was telephoning. There were so many entanglements about the case that his worry and anxiety were increasing almost daily. Nothing, at the moment, was emerging clearly and definitely, and as the days came and went, confusion and disorder were gathering round his feet. Try as he might, he was unable to get his fingers on to the all-important threads. The threads *must* be there, though, somewhere in the general entanglement and he must strain every nerve to recognize them and grasp them. Hemingway came again with relevant information. He spoke to Inspector MacMorran.

"Sir Cloudesley's at the Ludorum Club, sir, in Piccadilly. Just arrived there I should say from what he's just told me. He would like you to go straight there, if you wouldn't mind—by car, he suggested. What shall I tell him. Inspector?"

MacMorran looked across at Anthony Bathurst. The look held enquiry. Anthony nodded. "I think we might both go, Inspector. In the special circumstances. And then if we want him to come along here, we can bring him back with us."

"That's not a bad idea," replied MacMorran, "although I don't know that you—" He turned again to Hemingway. "Tell Sir Cloudesley we'll fall in with his idea, Hemingway. We'll come along there at once. To the club in Piccadilly. He certainly ought to be told this latest news immediately."

"As you haven't your other chauffeur available, come along in my car, Inspector, then we may get there before this evening."

MacMorran ignored the thrust. "Suits me," he said tersely.

Anthony followed him out and Hemingway was left alone. His face showed disapproval and true to tradition he immediately rang the bell to pass on the condition more acutely to an unfortunate subordinate. Anthony and MacMorran found but few people in the Ludorum Club. The Inspector's credentials were honoured directly he presented them and he and Anthony were quickly in the presence of Sir Cloudesley Slade who was seated in the smoke-room. He waved them into big brown leather arm-chairs.

"This is a quiet corner," he announced. "We can talk here. It would have taken me much longer to get to you than it has taken you to get to me. That's why I suggested you came along here. Now—is there any news?"

The suddenness of the question discomfited the Inspector. He had desired to come to that point in his own time. Sir Cloudesley's directness took him somewhat aback. He could find no evasion.

"Yes. We have had news. I'm sorry—it's bad news." Sir Cloudesley looked horrified. He swallowed hard twice before he could find words for his next question. "Not—not dead?"

Anthony was content to let MacMorran do the talking—or at least the preliminary talking. The Inspector shook his head at Sir Cloudesley's question.

"No, Sir Cloudesley—I'm glad to assure you that it's not as bad as that."

The colour came slowly back to Slade's cheek. "What is it then? Tell me, man. Don't prevaricate. I'm not a damned old woman. Tell me the truth."

"A dinner-jacket has been picked up. On a piece of waste ground between Kenriston and Hadow. The tailors are Kempster, Cross and Hawes, Hallam House, Savile Row. I believe that they are your son's tailors."

Sir Cloudesley moved his head anxiously. "Yes . . . yes . . . that's true. He did buy his clothes there. But how was it found? What are you hinting at, Inspector? Where is my son? Can't you tell me that?"

"Just a moment, sir. And please be patient. I can't answer all your questions. I want to tell you more about the dinner-jacket. There's blood on it. On the lapels."

Sir Cloudesley gasped. His face flinched as though it had been struck a heavy blow. There was no fierceness in the deep-set blue eyes now. They were quelled and dulled.

"Blood," continued MacMorran, "and also a certain amount of mud. I fear it's conclusive that your son has been the victim of a brutal attack. But I have no doubt either that he gave a good account of himself and that there is no reason to fear the worst . . . yet."

"I'll say he did! My boy Godfrey—that licked the great Phil Blood last night. He'd give any bloody murderer something to think about."

This showed a touch of the old Sir Cloudesley. The fire was still there—even though the flames were burning low. The old lion wasn't done with yet. He continued. His outburst seemed to have restored besides fire and courage some at least of his former confidence.

"Well—go on, Inspector! What else do you know? What are you hiding? Don't keep me waiting. Out with it man."

"Nothing, Sir Cloudesley—that's where we've come to a full stop."

Slade slumped again. "No more, Inspector? Really no more? You aren't hiding . . . anything from me . . . deliberately . . . because you think I can't take it?"

"No, sir. You know as much as we know."

"But what are you doing—man? Talking's no earthly use."

"Well, in the first place we'd like you to come back to the 'Yard' with us, Sir Cloudesley."

This remark came from Anthony Bathurst. It was his first contribution. "For one thing—there's that jacket of Godfrey's. It won't do any harm if you have a look at it—you may be able to help us even further."

A gleam of suspicion shot into Sir Cloudesley's eyes. He thrust out his jaw towards Anthony. "You *are* concealing something from me! I know it now. It's as plain as a pikestaff. Why the hell can't you be frank about things?"

Anthony denied the charge as MacMorran had before him. Slade seemed to believe him and to accept the situation. He surrendered. "All right. I'll come with you. The sooner the better. I believe you.

I'm rattled this morning, I can't help it. This business has got me right down. You must forgive an old man showing his tantrums. I'm ready. Take me to your car now."

The three men left the premises of the Ludorum Club.

As they passed through the entrance of the club by means of the big revolving door and commanded a view of the street outside, Anthony turned suddenly and caught MacMorran by the arm.

"Look, Andrew—quick. Coming this way. About a hundred yards off."

The Inspector's eyes followed Anthony's indication. He saw the man whom Anthony had seen. He whistled. "Well, now! What a surprise! Would you believe it! Asater—eh?"

"Pity it's not Bellamy. You could hold *him* on a charge of assault and battery against me. But you've got nothing on this fellow—beyond mere suspicion you're helpless."

Sir Cloudesley, who had left the Ludorum Club a pace or so in front of Anthony and MacMorran, heard them talking and turned back to them. "What's the matter now? What are you jabbering about?"

Before Anthony had time to reply, Asater with telling strides had come up to them. To their complete and utter amazement, the giant walked straight up to Sir Cloudesley Slade and faced him truculently. The latter drew back a pace but thrust out his jaw menacingly. It was clear that he had been quick to resent the action. His silk hat went even further to the back of his head.

"What the devil do you mean—shoving your ugly face into mine? Get away—you trash or I'll give you in charge for insulting behaviour."

Asater, however, like ambition, was made of sterner stuff. He refused to be intimidated by Slade's courageous reception of his breach of manners. "You keep unpleasant company, sir. Yes. When the time comes it will be remembered against you. See here. I have been sent by the High One to give you that message."

MacMorran's hands itched for action. His right hand went to his pocket instinctively. But he realized that Anthony's statement of a few moments since was substantially correct. It was too unpleasantly true, from his point of view, that he had nothing on Asater. But—at the first false step that Asater made—

"What the hell do you mean?" demanded Sir Cloudesley.

"I give you the message," said Asater—"no more than that. I hope you will profit by it. Good morning."

His eyes blazed hate as he turned on his heel. Slade was white. Grey almost—with shock and anxiety.

"I like that," he declared, "and on the King's highway, too. What's it all mean, Inspector?"

"I wish I knew. But just a minute. Wait here for me." MacMorran dashed away.

"Where's he gone?" demanded Slade.

"To deal with our over-large acquaintance. He'll have him shadowed from now on. He put a man on him before—but Asater gave him the slip."

Suddenly Sir Cloudesley clutched Anthony by the shoulder. "Bathurst! It's just occurred to me. Do you think that scoundrel has anything to do with Godfrey's disappearance. Or even with Donovan's death? If so—why don't you—"

"I think it's extremely likely, sir. That's why the Inspector's making arrangements with regard to him. But at the moment, you see, we can't do much more than that. We have no proof of anything against him. Nothing beyond mere suspicion. Besides—"

"Besides what? It seems to me that it's a suicidal policy to—"

Anthony shook his head. "Remember this, Sir Cloudesley. Because the point's vitally important to all of us. While this man's at liberty, he can be watched. If necessary, he can be kept under close observation and as a result of these activities prove to be of immense value to us as a means towards the getting of information. If we manufacture a charge against him, clap him into quod and keep him under lock and key, we negative his possibilities completely. He becomes no more than a dead cipher."

"I see. I suppose you're right. I admit that I hadn't thought of it in that way."

MacMorran came running back to them. "I've seen to that," he uttered between breaths, "there'll be two men on to Master Asater from now onwards. He won't slip them like he slipped Evershed the other day."

"My car's round here, Sir Cloudesley. Will you come along? We'll get back to the 'Yard.' I've been thinking," continued Anthony, as he took the driving-seat and started the car, "what did Asater mean by his somewhat dramatic reference to the 'High One'? Also why pick on you, Sir Cloudesley, for the delivery of this menacing message? How do you and your son follow in the succession? They're points that are puzzling me."

"The succession?" queried Sir Cloudesley Slade.

"A—ha! Why, for example, Bailey to begin with—and then Godfrey Slade at the end of the chain? And then having got their claws into your son—why show their teeth at you? I don't get it."

He spoke to MacMorran—"any idea in what direction the Asater hide-out may be, Andrew?"

"That's what I'm going to find out," returned MacMorran with grim resolution.

"And where Asater is, there also will be Bellamy. For me—that's a sacred and pious hope."

"Who's Bellamy?" queried Sir Cloudesley.

"Asater's stable-companion. They run in double harness. And another lewd fellow of the baser sort. As a matter of fact, sir, I'm particularly anxious to have a few poignant words with Bellamy. But that is another story. Here we are, sir. Do you mind getting out this side? You'll find it easier."

They went straight up to MacMorran's room. Hemingway was covering it. MacMorran produced the dinner-jacket which Slade had come to see. "There you are, Sir Cloudesley. There's the jacket. Is it your son's—for a certainty—we want to feel sure about it before we move any further?" The fierce face that looked down at the jacket was ravaged with emotion. Slade picked up the dinner-jacket and examined it carefully. He pointed to the dullish stains and smears on the lapel. "Blood?" he demanded curtly.

MacMorran nodded. "Ay, there's no doubt about it. Still—that may not mean a lot."

"It's ominous, though," retorted Slade, "say what you like about it," but the retort lacked fire. He looked inside the jacket and then inspected the tailor's tab. Anthony saw him nod when he read the name. Slade handed the dinner-jacket back to the Inspector.

"As far as one can judge over a thing like an ordinary dinner-jacket, I should say this is Godfrey's all right."

He sank into a chair. MacMorran told him of the two letters which had been found in the jacket. He then motioned to Hemingway and the Superintendent made notes. Slade said nothing. After a moment or so's silence, he buried his face in his hands. Eventually he looked up at them.

"It doesn't do to have one child, gentlemen. That's what I've been thinking. It's a fatal mistake. Parents should have either a bundle or none at all. You don't miss what you never had. They're the truest words which have ever been spoken. But in my case one taken away from one leaves none and it hits me hard—whereas one from four leaves three. Which isn't so devastating." Slade shook his head wearily. "If I don't get Godfrey back I'm going to be a lonely old man. My dear wife died many years ago. Sorry, gentlemen, to inflict my personal troubles on you. All I can hope is that you understand."

Anthony nodded in silent sympathy. MacMorran was engaged on official business with Hemingway. "You say that there is no further report whatever."

"No, Chief. Nothing's come through while you've been out. So there's no worse news—that's one thing."

Sir Cloudesley caught the end of the last remark. "Don't forget another thing, Inspector. Donovan's body wasn't found until some days after he disappeared. It was the same with Jago too. If we're going to strike, we mustn't delay on any account. We must strike at once."

"I'll strike all right—when I know who and when and where. But I can't strike in the dark. I should probably hit the wrong man."

MacMorran's tone bordered on curtness. Slade subsided again. Hemingway went on with the relation of certain details. MacMorran, it seemed, was checking up on them. Suddenly Sir Cloudesley was galvanized into life.

"How would it do," he suggested, "if I offered a substantial reward? I'm willing to. Almost to my last penny. Would it be of any use, do you think? He eyed MacMorran eagerly.

"Wouldn't do any harm, Although—"

"Although what?" demanded Slade suspiciously.

"Well," replied MacMorran a trifle desperately, "the point as I see it is this—we don't know why these things are happening. We're still in the dark as to the question of motive. That's why I'm doubtful as to this reward idea of yours being successful."

Slade blazed at him. "Look here—get this into your head, Inspector, here and now. I want my boy back! At the moment nothing else matters. Get that—will you?"

Anthony sought to pour oil on troubled waters. "Yes, Sir Cloudesley, of course. We both understand that, first and foremost. And Inspector MacMorran will do his damnedest to bring your son back. Upon that you may rely absolutely. Personally, I think your idea of publishing a reward an excellent one. History teaches us that the lure of filthy lucre will often find a chink in an enemy's armour."

"Good," returned Sir Cloudesley, distinctly mollified, "I am glad you think like that about my idea. I'll do it then."

"Make it as big as you can, I suggest," added MacMorran—"it's no good sending a boy to do a man's-work."

He turned and noticed a look that had suddenly taken possession of Anthony's face.

"What's the point now, Mr. Bathurst? What are you on to?"

Anthony smiled. "I've just thought of something, Andrew. And directly I thought of it I wondered why I hadn't thought of it before."

MacMorran pressed home his curiosity. "What is it?" Anthony smiled at him again. "Boxing-gloves, Andrew. Just boxing-gloves and nothing more than boxing-gloves." MacMorran stared at him without understanding and then shook his head. "Boxing-gloves," he repeated questionably.

Anthony nodded. "Yes, Andrew. Just what you said. No more, no less. Boxing-gloves."

He took a cigarette from his case and saw that Sir Cloudesley Slade, tired and worn out, had sunk into a chair again and was staring almost blankly into the heart of the fire.

CHAPTER XIX
A LINK WITH LIFE

"ANDREW," said Anthony quietly but with decided emphasis, "if you cherish any overwhelming desire to kick me, you may indulge that desire to your heart's content."

Sir Cloudesley looked up at the words—puzzled. Besides the banter there was an ominous note in Anthony's voice.

"Why?" asked the Inspector—"why the sudden access of humility?"

"I'll tell you, Andrew. My recent reference to boxing-gloves has reminded me of an almost criminal piece of forgetfulness on my part. I'm not even sure that negligence wouldn't be the better word."

"And what may that be?"

"Champagne-corks," replied Anthony laconically.

"What about them? Do you mean Donovan's—"

"I refer to those two champagne-corks that were found in Donovan's trouser pockets."

"Well—how have you been forgetful with regard to them?"

"Why—I intended to have a word with Mrs. Donovan concerning them. And I forgot to translate that intention into actual effect. I suppose that events have crowded upon us, so thick and fast that the idea got pushed out of my mind. That will have to serve as my excuse. That ejection was, however, but temporary. Like a temporary clerk in a municipal office—gone to-day and here tomorrow. In this instance to-morrow's to-day."

"What the heck are you talking about? Do you know?"

"Primarily, my dear Andrew, champagne-corks. Now I wonder—" He broke off abruptly.

"You wonder what?"

Anthony's eyes had strayed towards the Inspector's telephone. "I was wondering if I could get into touch with her by telephone from here. There's a woman who lives close to her who'll take a call for her. Mrs. Donovan made that arrangement with me. I rang there once before. Her name was Cannon and she's an obliging neighbour. Shove me over that directory, will you, Andrew? A to K?"

MacMorran pushed the book towards Anthony and the latter flicked the pages and found the number that he required. The others heard him ask for Mrs. Cannon and then subsequently for Mrs. Donovan.

"It hurts me speaking to this girl," he said softly as he waited for the response with his hand over the mouthpiece. "I feel almost as though I've struck her across the mouth and then laughed at her pain."

He waited patiently and then . . . "is that you, Mrs. Donovan? It's Anthony Bathurst this end. Oh yes . . . yes . . . thank you . . . I hope you're not too bad. Good. That proves what I've always thought of you. You've got heaps of pluck."

Sir Cloudesley and the Inspector saw him nod several times as he spoke. "Yes . . . yes . . . of course . . . certainly I understand. I knew if I rang you up I should find you as you are. Now I want to ask you a question. You remember those two champagne-corks which were found in 'Lefty's' pockets? Yes . . . I know . . . now tell me this. Did he ever . . . what? Oh—he *always* carried them—you say? For luck? He was superstitious? Yes . . . I know . . . most prominent sportsmen are. What? He didn't always carry the *same* two corks? Oh . . . I see. Those were the two he had most recently acquired? I understand. They came from a dinner he had attended at Evenino's Restaurant? When? Last January—eh? He was a guest at this dinner, you say . . . many sporting celebrities were present. Well, I can understand that. So he carried them just for luck—well, I'm extremely obliged to you, Mrs. Donovan. The police and I wanted to get the rights of it. It's as well to know as much of things of this sort as possible. Your information will help us considerably. Good-bye."

Anthony hung up. He turned to the Inspector and Sir Cloudesley Slade. "Well—you heard best part of that conversation. Donovan always carried champagne-corks in his pockets. Piece of personal superstition on his part. He had the idea that they were 'luck'-bringers. Mascots! Which proves that the corks belonged to Donovan himself and not to the circumstances of his murder. *Not* so good. Just a minute though. Supposing he had—"

Anthony stopped and seemed to be lost in thought. Sir Cloudesley spoke in a dull, lifeless voice.

"I went to that dinner you mentioned. At Evenino's. Can remember it well. A big gathering of celebrities. Everybody who was anybody in the sporting world was there."

Anthony stared at him. "Tell me, Sir Cloudesley," he said, "was Ted Bailey there by any chance?"

"I couldn't answer that. There were over four hundred sat down to dinner. But I should say very probably."

"Was Jago there?"

Slade nodded. "He was. I can answer that. I remember seeing him. *And* Godfrey."

"In whose party was Donovan?"

"I couldn't even tell you that. There were so many tables. Some private—some to do with clubs. I was at the top table. So was Godfrey."

Anthony nodded. "I see."

"What's your point behind all this, Bathurst?"

"The corks, Sir Cloudesley. Carried by Donovan. I was wondering who paid for the wine he drank."

"Does it matter?"

Anthony spoke bitterly. "It seems to have mattered to Donovan."

Slade shrugged his shoulders. "I don't see that you can assert that with any degree of certainty."

"Perhaps not. Call it a flight of fancy on my part. I suffer from 'em sometimes. Time will tell."

Anthony went back to MacMorran. "Check up on Marcus Secretan, Andrew—will you? As soon as you possibly can. Put Chatterton or somebody on it for me. I find myself harbouring an inordinate curiosity concerning Mr. Secretan."

"I told you all about him," put in Sir Cloudesley, "on the first occasion I spoke to you. Money, rings, tie-pins. *Rolling* in money. Otherwise—quite a decent chap. If there is any otherwise. Which I strongly take leave to doubt. Still—after all—"

Slade stopped. Anthony took him up.

"After all—what, sir?"

Slade smiled for the first time for many hours. "I like him better—much better—since I relieved him of that 'bees and honey'—thanks to Godfrey."

The mention of his son's name, however, and the returning realization of its present implication, sent him back to the slough of despondency. He crouched in his chair, his hands clasped tightly in front of him. MacMorran asked questions of Anthony Bathurst.

"Why this sudden curiosity concerning Secretan?"

"He's in the forefront of the picture, Andrew. Very much so. Men in the forefront of a problem picture usually attract my attention. Haven't you noticed that peculiarity of mine? As I said—put Chatterton on to him."

There came a tap at the door and Supt. Hemingway entered the room. He spoke quietly to MacMorran. The latter looked up with startled interest. "Really? Where is he, Super?"

"He's here now."

"Bring him up to me at once. This is a stroke of luck. He couldn't have arrived at a more opportune moment." Hemingway nodded approving acquiescence and made his departure. MacMorran imparted the information that had just been brought to him.

"There's a bloke in Hemingway's room who's supposed to have brought something in to do with Godfrey Slade."

Sir Cloudesley looked up eagerly the moment he heard the name. "Who is it? What is it?"

"Tell you more, Sir Cloudesley, when I've had a word with him. And I'm going to have that word right now. He's something to do with a Library—but we'll find out more in a few moments. Hemingway's gone to get him. Here they are. I can hear them coming."

Hemingway brought in a man whose facial expression reminded Anthony of nothing so much as an empty tureen. It was vacuous and vague. "Chief Inspector MacMorran," announced Hemingway, "Mr. Roland Croker from the St. Crispin Free Library."

"Sit down, Mr. Croker," said the Inspector genially—"I understand that you have brought some valuable information with regard to the missing man—Mr. Godfrey Slade. I may as well tell you that this gentleman is Mr. Slade's father."

MacMorran indicated Sir Cloudesley with a gesture of his hand. Croker, the librarian, looked uncomfortably nervous. Anthony saw that he was clasping a book in his hands, very much as a fishmonger might handle a cold cod. He bobbed his head forward in MacMorran's direction and sat down in a chair which Hemingway had placed for him. His voice was thin and reedy.

"I am the Senior Librarian at the St. Crispin Free Library. I have come here this morning because I think that I have information which should be passed on to you." As his eyes showed a certain semblance of emotion, his face began to resemble that of a large owl.

"And that information is?" urged MacMorran.

Croker held up the book which he had been clasping in his hand. "This book was returned to the Library—I mean the library under my charge—at about a quarter-past ten this morning. The young lady assistant who took it in and dealt with the card index in relation to it, accidentally knocked the book off the shelf where she had previously placed it. When she stooped to pick it up, she noticed that a slip of paper had evidently fallen from it. She brought this slip to me. I make a point of the young ladies confiding their troubles to me. I like to regard myself as a sort of Father Confessor." He giggled and simpered as he spoke.

"I know," said Anthony, "shall we say a kind of Mother Inferior."

Croker continued to gurgle in hollow, semi-sepulchral mirth. It was entirely a solo effort. When his noise had died down he looked at the circle of unsympathetic faces and decided that it was his best policy to go on with his story.

"I have that slip of paper here. Perhaps you gentlemen would care to have a glance at it." Croker handed a piece of paper to the Inspector. MacMorran took it and beckoned to the others to come round him. It was a slip of thin, plain, white paper.

Anthony, Hemingway and Sir Cloudesley Slade accepted the invitation. Anthony looked over MacMorran's shoulders and saw a message scrawled in pencil. It was short and to the point. The lines were wavering and the letters curiously formed. Indeed, the message could have scarcely been shorter. "Help! Godfrey Slade." Sir Cloudesley's eyes bulged with mingled fear and astonishment at what he saw. Anthony came at once to the practical issue.

"Is this your son's writing, Sir Cloudesley? As you know it?"

Slade looked at the flimsy paper with a strange anxiety "Yes," he said . . . "I think it is. Yes. But I'm not absolutely positive. It's . . . it's . . . strange . . . unusual."

"You are *not* sure then?" demanded Anthony.

"I am almost—but not quite. Damn it all—I want to help, not to hinder. I can't say more or less than I feel to be the truth."

"Of course, Sir Cloudesley. We understand your doubt and your difficulty. But we must deal with exactitudes. Don't worry—please."

Anthony turned to MacMorran. "It's been written under extraordinary conditions, Andrew—that's the explanation. And I fancy that this is some kind of cigarette paper. Get the other dope from Croker, will you?"

MacMorran nodded and came back to Croker. "This book that you mentioned. Where's it been in circulation recently and who returned it to your library?"

Croker licked his lips before replying. He was intensely gratified to be back again on centre stage under the spotlight. "It was issued ten days ago by one of my staff to the householder at 22, Gilbey Road. That's in the St. Crispin area. The name of the householder is Richard Butcher. But that's all I know about him." As he tendered the information, Croker looked more smug and more self-satisfied than ever.

"Who returned the book? The man Butcher himself?"

Croker shook his head at the Inspector's question. "No. That was the unfortunate part about it. Had the man himself brought the book back I might have been able to take immediate action. The book was returned to my library by a small child. To be precise—a little girl! Not the butcher-boy ah ha—but in this instance the butcher-girl." More simpering and giggling followed. MacMorran frowned.

"Did you detain her?"

"How could I? I'm not in your position, you know. I am not a policeman with a warrant in my pocket. I'm just a man who loves good literature and my work in the library." Croker spread out his hands in deprecation of the Inspector's question.

"Did you question her?"

"No—I didn't even do that. I thought matters over and came to the conclusion that my best course was to report the entire circumstances here. You see—I read of young Slade's disappearance in the morning paper. I'm sorry if I did wrong, Inspector."

Croker's regrets were accompanied by a bland smile of self-satisfaction.

"How far's the house from here?"

"Gilbey Road? Oh—a fairish distance. Half an hour by car. Not more than that. It's a poorish district, I'm afraid. Not slummy exactly—you couldn't call it that—but a definitely working-class neighbourhood. I trust that I make myself clear."

"Oh, quite," returned MacMorran curtly. He looked across at Anthony. Anthony seemed to understand that the look was an unspoken question.

"I think so, Inspector," he said in reply, "it's worth a visit and what's more—*at once!* Mr. Croker here will no doubt be good enough to direct us."

"May I come with you?" put in Sir Cloudesley Slade. "I should like to." His voice was flat and dull and lifeless.

"Certainly, Sir Cloudesley. I was on the point of asking you."

"Thank you, Inspector. I'd hate to remain behind and I might even be able to help."

After MacMorran had given Hemingway certain instructions, the four men made their way to the car. Anthony put his foot down and made Gilbey Road in considerably less time than the half-hour of Croker's estimate. Croker directed him. He called it the 'shortest way.' On the Inspector's advice, Anthony parked the car in a side-turning.

They walked to the house of Richard Butcher, borrower and returner of library-books. MacMorran knocked. A child answered the knock.

"That's the girl who brought the book back," whispered Croker.

"Is your father in?" demanded MacMorran of her.

She nodded brightly.

"Then ask him to come to the door, will you?"

"Yes, sir." She turned like an eel to call out shrilly. "Daddy! Some men want you."

Anthony could distinguish several words that came from the interior of the house. Mr. Richard Butcher evidently was giving tongue. A tall bony man came to the door with the evident intention of establishing the fact that an Englishman's home was his castle.

He was in his shirt-sleeves and had a small pipe in the corner of his mouth.

"What is it? Whadya want?"

MacMorran spoke to him quietly. His words had the desired effect. Mr. Richard Butcher, it seemed, was not entirely devoid of sense and intelligence.

"Well," he said with a certain grudging sullenness, "I don't quite know what you're talkin' about—but you'd better come in. Can't all stand on the doorstep. Don't look right. Not manners! Don't like it. Come in, will you—and you, young Marlene, you 'op orf for a bit—d'ye 'ear."

Mr. Butcher conducted his visitors into what he would have called his front parlour. "Sit down." He waved them to various uncomfortable chairs of hard and forbidding aspect. MacMorran was quick to state his case.

"A book? To the Free Lib'ry? Quite right. I sent it back this morning, Told my kid to take it. That's right—I won't deny it. Why should I? What's the odds about it?"

"Is this the book?" enquired MacMorran, producing the book of Croker's clasp.

Butcher nodded an affirmative. "That's it. My missus had it out. She likes that sort of yarn. *You know I Love!* Funny the muck what women lap up—ain't it?"

MacMorran produced the appeal that purported to come from Godfrey Slade. "Can you tell me anything about this?" he asked.

Butcher took the piece of paper with gingerly approach. He looked at it blankly. Anthony watched him keenly. Unless the man were a consummately skilful actor, this blank reception of Slade's message was honest and authentic. Anthony continued to watch him as he handled the slip of paper. Butcher shook his head.

"Never seen it before, Guv'nor. Never clapped eyes on it in my life."

"How then did it come to be between the pages of this book that you returned to the St. Crispin Library this morning?"

Again Butcher shook his head. "Search me. Don't ask me—you'll have to ask the bloke what put it there."

Anthony looked at the Inspector. MacMorran nodded. Anthony questioned Mr. Richard Butcher. "Mr. Butcher—will you kindly tell me this? How long has Mrs. Butcher had the book in the house here?"

"Since last Friday. I know that—because my nipper brought it in—along with my copy of the local rag. I'm daft enough to take it every week. Comes out on Fridays. Does to wrap things up in."

"And the book's been here ever since?"

"It has. Till this morning—when young Marlene fetched it back for her mother. But why—what's the idea behind these questions?"

"A man is missing. The man who wrote those words on that slip of paper that was shown you. It's almost certain that he has been the victim of foul play. *And* that missing man has made contact with that book! Since last night! Contact with that book which your child returned to the St. Crispin Free Library this morning! That's why you're being asked these questions. Do you get the idea now?"

Butcher whistled between his teeth. "You don't say! Well, I can't explain it. So it's up to you."

MacMorran took over the interrogation from Anthony. "You've had nobody here to see you since Friday? No friends or relations, for instance, have dropped in?"

Butcher smiled sweetly. "No—it ain't my week for a 'ouse party. I don't draw the Christmas Club money till next Saturday."

"What about your wife? Has she had anybody in here?"

Butcher screwed up his face. "If she 'ad—and I'd known about it—she'd be still lickin' 'er wounds and not on view at the moment. Still, you want to know about things—why not ask ''er 'erself. Be more satisfactory—wouldn't it? I'll call 'er in." He walked to the door. "Mavis!"

Anthony shuddered. In a few moments Mrs. Butcher arrived, chiefly bosom and dirt.

"'Ere you are, Inspector, 'ere's the missus—'ast 'er yourself."

MacMorran reiterated his question.

"No, sir," replied Mrs. Butcher with a decisive shake of the head—"not a soul's been in the 'ouse since I took that book out from the lib'ry except the members of the family. That's my 'usband, myself, young Marlene and my boy Warwick. Not a livin' soul, sir. That's the truth—if I never speak another word."

MacMorran, without further ado, accepted Mrs. Butcher's story. The lady, flushed with triumph, returned to the rear of the establishment. MacMorran—a trifle nonplussed—began to rub his chin. "Just a minute," said Anthony—he went and spoke to MacMorran who appeared to understand and nodded.

"Mr. Butcher," continued the Inspector, "bring your little girl in here—will you?"

Butcher looked ugly at the request. "Now look 'ere, Guv'nor, there ain't goin' to be no third degree put on my young Marlene. Not if I know it! I ain't standing for that."

"Shouldn't dream of such a thing," countered MacMorran. "Besides, you'll be here to hear what I ask her."

Butcher accepted the situation and assented grudgingly. "All right—but I shan't 'esitate to protest if I think the occasion demands it—I'm tellin' yer that. I don't 'old with draggin' kids through any dirt. With us old stagers it don't matter. Marlene! Come in 'ere—will yer?"

The child proved to be not unintelligent. Anthony questioned her at MacMorran's request. She glanced uneasily at Croker before she replied to the questions. Doubtless she connected him with officialdom, its inevitable officiousness, dire discipline and possible punishment. Sir Cloudesley Slade leant forward and listened intently to her answers. Anthony was simple and direct with her.

"Now—Marlene—when you were on your way to the library this morning with your daddy's book—did you call anywhere else?"

To his intense pleasure, Marlene answered immediately and without the slightest hesitation. "Yes, sir. Daddy sent me somewhere."

"Where was that, Marlene?"

"To the Post-Office, sir, at the corner of St. Crispin Street. Nowhere else. I went to buy him a postal order for his 'Littlewood's.' I buy him one at the Post-Office every week."

Anthony nodded. "There's a good girl, You're helping me a lot. Now—when you went into the Post-Office, what did you do with your daddy's library book? Can you remember?"

Marlene Butcher put a finger into the corner of her mouth as a remembrance incentive. "Yes, sir. I put it on the counter at the side of me when I asked the young lady for the postal order."

Anthony nodded again. "I see. Do you know I thought you might have done that. Now tell me again, Marlene, were there any people near you when you were buying the postal order? Think carefully."

The little girl nodded vehemently. "Oh, yes, sir. A lot of people."

"Can you remember any of them? What any of them looked like, for instance?"

Marlene looked reasonably doubtful. Anthony tried again. "Well—were they men? Or ladies? Or were they children—little boys and girls like yourself?"

Marlene essayed an answer. "All kinds."

Anthony tried again. "Any gentlemen?"

Marlene nodded. "Yes, sir, a good many."

"Any of them near you?"

"I don't know, sir. I didn't notice."

Anthony decided to try a longer shot. "Now think carefully, Marlene, and don't answer me unless you're absolutely certain of what you say. Did you see a very, very large man, like a giant, in the Post-Office when you were there?"

But this time Marlene had no doubts to assail her. "No, sir. I'm sure that there was no man like that there."

"Thank you, Marlene," said Anthony—"that's all I want to ask you. And there's something for yourself to buy some sweets with."

He beckoned to Inspector MacMorran. "We'll get her to take us to that Post-Office, Andrew. We may be able to pick up something. Some of the assistants may have noticed something. It's ten to one Godfrey Slade was in there when Marlene was buying that now-famous postal order. Get rid of this appalling apology for a librarian and you and I and Sir Cloudesley will go along to the Post-Office with Marlene and her dad. I'll leave the arrangements to you. I'll be in the car waiting for you. Don't be too long."

MacMorran assented to Anthony's suggestions. He walked over to Butcher and began talking. Anthony slipped out and made his way to where he had parked the car. The trail was getting warmer.

CHAPTER XX

THE TELEGRAM

ANTHONY waited in the car for the others to join him.

When they came into sight, he saw to his infinite satisfaction that MacMorran had taken his advice and shed Croker by the way. He opened the door of the car for the others to enter. They sorted themselves over the different seats.

"Come in the front, Mr. Butcher—do you mind? Next to me. You can direct me to your daughter's Post-Office."

Butcher climbed into the seat indicated. "Straight up," he blurted, "into St. Crispin Street, then first right—second left. The Post-Office is on a corner. You can't miss it."

"Is it a general shop that runs a Post-Office or a G.P.O.?"

"G.P.O.," replied Butcher, "none of your twopenny half-penny grocer's shops for me. I don't risk nothing with my sporting investments. Only the best is good enough for me. I'm used to it. My uncle was on the local council some years ago and lived like a fighting cock."

"That makes a difference, I agree," assented Anthony—"do I turn here?"

"You do," returned Butcher—"now watch out for second left. That's your next."

Anthony made the proper turning and a few minutes later Butcher announced the proximity of the Post-Office of their destination. MacMorran issued certain instructions to the various members of the party. Sir Cloudesley seemed to be disconcerted by what the Inspector said but eventually he accepted with good grace.

"If I'm under orders, I must obey orders, I suppose. Carry on, Inspector."

Anthony, Inspector MacMorran and Marlene Butcher made their way into the Post-Office. "Show me where you stood, Marlene," said the Inspector, "when you bought the postal order."

Marlene did so.

"And now show me where you put the library book."

Marlene pointed to a counter-ledge. MacMorran noted the positions. Anthony listened. MacMorran had already agreed that

Anthony should interrogate the Post-Office assistant who stood nearest to the two points of Marlene's contact. Anthony whispered to Marlene:

"Is that the young lady from whom you bought the postal order?"

Marlene nodded. "Yes. That's her."

"Good. Then I'll speak to her. We must ask her some questions to find out what happened."

Within a few minutes Anthony and his party were in the supervisor's room together with the postal assistant who had attended to Marlene Butcher. The supervisor accepted the position and Anthony commenced his questioning.

"The police are interested in certain people whom they suspect to have been on your premises this morning. That's why I want to ask this young lady assistant of yours one or two important questions."

"Answer please, Miss Spencer—to the best of your memory and ability." The supervisor was quick and business-like.

The girl addressed nodded in promise. Anthony could see that she was likely to prove bright and intelligent.

"First of all I want to test your memory," said Anthony. "Do you remember this little girl buying a postal order from you this morning? Stand up, Marlene, will you, and let this young lady take a good look at you."

Marlene stood up as directed and showed herself. Miss Spencer looked at her and gave a quick nod of understanding and recognition. "Yes, I remember her quite well. It was a shilling postal order you bought, wasn't it?"

"Yes," returned Marlene, "that's right. It's nearly always a shilling one."

"Good," contributed Anthony, "that proves we're on the right lines at least. Now, Miss Spencer—I'm afraid that my next question isn't going to be so simple for you to answer."

"I can try at any rate," fluttered Miss Spencer eagerly.

"Can you remember any of the people who stood close to—or even moderately near to this little girl when you were attending to her? Don't answer quickly or without thinking. I want you to take your time and, if you reasonably *can*, be sure of your answer when you give it to me."

Miss Spencer smiled. "I see what you mean. I'll think carefully." There was a silence. MacMorran was watching her intently. Suddenly she smiled at Anthony again and moved her head quickly. "I can answer the question all right. I could have done directly you put it to me—but in view of what you said I visualized the whole scene all over again—in order to feel certain of myself and the answer I was about to give. Three men came into the Post-Office just about the time I was getting this little girl's postal order. Round about ten o'clock, I should say it was. They were all of them complete strangers to me. As a matter of fact, it wasn't too much of an effort for me to remember because I served them immediately following Marlene. No—I must correct myself there—I served *one* of them."

"Oh—excellent, Miss Spencer," declared Anthony. "Now will you please describe them and tell us also exactly what took place."

The supervisor showed approval of the proceedings as far as they had gone. "Yes, Miss Spencer—do so, will you, please?"

Miss Spencer crinkled her mouth. It was not an unattractive mouth. Anthony suspected that she was enjoying rather, this position of centre-stage. "First of all, I'll tell you of the man who came up to the counter and gave me the order to attend to. He was a tall thin man. Middle-aged, say between forty and fifty. His name was Chandler."

"How on earth do you know that?" cut in MacMorran.

"Because he sent a telegram in that name," replied Miss Spencer almost triumphantly. "Quite simple."

"H'm," returned the Inspector—"doesn't follow—but good enough. Go on, please. We'll come back to that telegram later."

"The other two men stood by themselves—a bit away from the counter. One was stout—burly—and foreign-looking—what I should call 'distinctly coarse,' and the other was altogether different. A gentleman without a doubt. You know what I mean," she added archly—"old school tie. Tall—nearly as tall as you, sir," she indicated Anthony—"dark hair—and er . . . well set up altogether. Besides being nice-looking."

"That's Slade all right," announced MacMorran—"now show us a copy of the telegram."

The latter part of the sentence was addressed to the supervisor. The lady looked a trifle taken aback.

"Well—it's like this—the Postmaster himself isn't here—I don't know that I ought to—"

"Don't worry. I'm an officer of Scotland Yard as I told you. I'll cover you in the matter of all responsibility."

The supervisor seemed reassured at MacMorran's statement. "In that case—I'll let you have what you want. Bring the book in, Miss Spencer, will you, please?"

Miss Spencer smiled brightly and slipped out of the room. To return in a matter of less than a minute. She handed the information that she brought to her superior. The supervisor passed it on to the Inspector. MacMorran read the words aloud.

"To Smith. 8, Florestan St., Deptford. Meet V.E. this evening 9 p.m. Third seat (W) from C.N. Chandler." Anthony leant over and spoke quietly to the Inspector. The latter nodded in acquiescence and rose from his chair. "We won't trouble you any more. And thank you for your assistance. You have been most helpful to us."

The supervisor responded suitably.

"Come along, Marlene." Anthony took Miss Butcher by the hand. They went back to the car. "It was all right," said Anthony as he took his seat. "It was Godfrey right enough," he remarked to Sir Cloudesley. "First of all we'll return Mr. Butcher and Miss Marlene to their home in Gilbey Road—then we'll talk things over again. That O.K. with you, sir?"

Sir Cloudesley, understanding, signified his assent to Anthony's proposal. The car dropped the two Butchers at the house in Gilbey Road. "Back to the 'Yard'," ordered MacMorran—"and we'll get down to this telegram business. If you're pinched for exceeding the speed limit, I'll allow you to put the blame on me. Step on it, Mr. Bathurst."

The car shot forward and simultaneously a heavy downfall of rain came and beat violently on the windscreen. Sir Cloudesley pulled his heavy coat closer to his body. He shivered more than once. "It's cold," he muttered . . . "and that boy of mine feels the cold. If he's still alive that is . . ."

"He was alive this morning, sir," said Anthony, "and if we move quickly, please God, he'll be alive tonight. Come."

Chapter XXI
THE RENDEZVOUS

"There you are, that's the lot." MacMorran wrote words on paper. They were the words of Chandler's telegram. "I'm looking up Smith at once," went on MacMorran, "at 8, Florestan St., Deptford. That's step Number One. The rest will follow." He noticed the look on Anthony's face. "Well—don't you agree with me? Say so—if you don't."

"Well, Andrew—it's your pigeon—and you must do as you think best—but since you ask me—I wouldn't."

"Why not?"

Anthony shrugged his shoulders. "I'd let him keep the appointment—*re* Monsieur Smith."

Sir Cloudesley, unasked, backed his opinion. "I agree with Bathurst."

Anthony followed up this temporary advantage. "We shall learn things, Andrew. If you raid Comrade Smith—you may scare the whole covey and then—'na-poo.' Gone away."

MacMorran rubbed his nose. "Something in that." He looked away from them. It was the MacMorran habit to do this when he was inwardly debating an important decision.

"A great deal, Andrew." Sir Cloudesley also nodded violently. Anthony followed up again. "Let him lie snug and warm, Andrew . . . and then when the time comes . . . keep his appointment. It presents us with a magnificent opportunity. Take it from me."

MacMorran temporized. "All right. I'll wait and see. Give my decision later. In the meantime, let's get down to the consideration of this telegram." He read out the words again. "Meet V.E. this evening 9 p.m. Third seat (W) from C.N. This is going to be damned difficult. Like looking for a caraway seed in the sand. There must be hundreds of people whose initials are V.E." He shook his head with gloomy foreboding at the task which lay in front of them.

Anthony cut in with a smile. "On the contrary, Andrew, I don't consider that it is going to be so difficult after all. Once again, you see, we must agree to differ."

MacMorran looked up at him with surprise. "Why? What's your point? Who's V.E. then, of all people?"

Anthony grinned at him. "More like a lady than a man. At least—that's my opinion."

"Well—giving you the sex—I'm prepared to do that for the moment—who's the woman V.E.? That you can be certain of, I mean?"

"Her Christian name's Victoria," returned Anthony.

MacMorran frowned. "Victoria?"

"A-ha. Dear old 'Vicky.' The way of a Neagle. You know—we are not amused."

MacMorran's frown deepened. "I still am unable—"

Anthony proceeded calmly. "And the 'E,' my dear Andrew, you will eventually find stands for 'Embankment.' Our whole, then, in solution becomes 'Victoria Embankment! *Voila!*"

"You're chancing your arm a bit, aren't you?"

"No-o. Don't think so. No! Very confident. My nap selection. A racing certainty. The best thing of the day."

"Why in the name of conscience? Why so positive about it?" Before Anthony could reply, MacMorran had gone on. "Another thing—after V.E.—what about C.N.?"

"Another lady, Andrew. Much more ancient though. Egypt!"

"Egypt?"

"That's it. A famous namesake of mine found her attractive. Far too attractive. So much so that she wrecked his career."

"Don't talk like the clue of a blasted cross-word! I tell you frankly, I don't get it."

Anthony was bland. "Cleopatra, Andrew. I am dying Egypt, dying. With N for needle. In other words 'Victoria Embankment—the third seat from Cleopatra's Needle going in a westerly direction. The inserted 'W,' Andrew, I take to be a point of the compass. Well, any criticism for me? If so—let's have it."

Hearing Anthony's solution, Sir Cloudesley Slade was bristling with excitement. "You're right, Bathurst. Damn it all, boy—you're right. I see it all. I'd stake a 'monkey' on it."

MacMorran took the solution and Sir Cloudesley's enthusiasm with steady composure. "I think you're right too. Accept my congratulations as well. I'll confess that it never presented itself to me in that light. This is excellent." MacMorran rose from his chair and went to warm his hands at the fire.

"Therefore, Andrew," demonstrated Anthony, "it is now very much up to you. You have the time and the place. Also one of the vital names—Chandler. The rest should follow in due season."

"Smith," chuckled MacMorran, "will keep the appointment. I have made that decision which I delayed making. And when Smith keeps the appointment—we will keep it with him. Oh—great."

"What's worrying me," contributed Anthony, "is the *reason* behind this rendezvous. What's their game?" MacMorran looked reasonably dubious. "Two camps—perhaps. Smith in one of them and Chandler in the other. We don't know."

"Yes—but why do they want—" Anthony broke off precipitately. "I'm at a loss—I don't mind admitting it. I can't get a clear line on it at all."

"Does it matter?" intervened Sir Cloudesley Slade. "As much as all that? Why should we be bothering our heads as to why these blackguards are doing things? Our job is to checkmate them. Circumvent them. That's the stuff they'll understand and probably the only stuff. When they find bracelets on their wrists and the scaffold staring them in the face."

Anthony shook his head. "Admirable sentiments, no doubt, Sir Cloudesley. But they only deal with the simple, direct issue. Before I move to attack I like to see into the criminal's brain as much as I possibly can—and understand what he's thinking, *why* he's thinking it and then—*what* he's likely to do next. It's that next step and the step after, which are so vitally important."

Sir Cloudesley grumbled almost inaudibly. "Catch 'em—that's what counts. Never mind the fancy stuff. Too much of it these days. Cut it out. It's only in the damned way. I may be old-fashioned—but that's how it appeals to me."

Anthony suddenly seemed to find sympathy for him. "I'm sorry, sir—but I've just remembered something. Perhaps I ought to have remembered and considered it before. Your personal feelings in the matter. You're terribly worried. Of course you are. If you feel that we're risking your son's life by our policy of waiting until this evening before we act—for God's sake say so. *I* don't! But I'm not infallible as you've probably noticed by now. I feel certain, though, in my own mind, that these people will take no drastic step until *after* this evening. If things were the other way round—my opinion might be reversed. I'll explain what I mean. This Smith person is *not* at Godfrey's end. Godfrey's at the other end—the Chandler end. I'd go for Chandler like smoke if I knew his hide-out but I don't feel disposed to swoop on Smith. I'm positive that we shall do better to wait. I felt that I had to tell you this."

Sir Cloudesley who had listened patiently stuck out his hand. Anthony grasped it. "You've said to me what I've been wanting to say to you. Ever since you and the Inspector here were discussing ways and means. You've put into words, moreover, the very doubts that have been passing through my mind." He paused.

"Well—what's the verdict, Sir Cloudesley?"

The old man smiled a little sadly. "I'll be content to rely on your judgment, Bathurst. Yours and the Inspector's. I'll leave my son's life in your hands. There. Now you know where you stand."

He held out his hand again to Anthony and to the Inspector. The three men shook hands. "Thank you, Sir Cloudesley," said Anthony Bathurst.

Chapter XXII
THE THIRD SEAT FROM CLEOPATRA'S NEEDLE

ONCE again Anthony sat on the corner of Inspector MacMorran's table in the room that overlooked the Thames.

"There's one thing," commented the Inspector—"we haven't far to go—very homely indeed. They're coming almost under our noses, so to speak. Very considerate of them."

Anthony made no reply. He looked at his wrist-watch.

"How does it go?" enquired MacMorran.

"Just turned half-past eight. We ought to be moving in a quarter of an hour. As far as I'm concerned the sooner the better."

"There's another thing," contributed MacMorran, "they can't have the slightest idea that we're on their tails. That's a point in our favour."

"They *shouldn't* have," said Anthony, "unless their 'espionage' work is better than I take it to be."

MacMorran shook his head at the suggestion. "Don't worry in that direction. I'm confident that they're going to get the surprise of their lives."

"What time do you expect Sir Cloudesley to show up?"

"He should be here by now. He went home this afternoon for a rest. I suggested that he should. He was pretty well 'all in'."

Anthony scratched his cheek. "I sincerely hope he's not going to be disappointed to-night. I'm as near nervousness as I've ever been in my life."

There came a knock at the door. Hemingway entered to Mac-Morran's invitation. "Sir Cloudesley Slade, Chief," announced the Superintendent, "asking for you."

"Good. Then we're all set. Bring him in, Hemingway, will you?"

Sir Cloudesley came in almost on Hemingway's heels. He glanced nervously at Anthony who smiled in return.

"I'm not late—am I? Time's been hanging on my hands all day, believe me. Well—are we all fixed? Shall we get along?"

MacMorran nodded. "Going on foot. I'm armed. So's Bathurst here. I'm not sure that I ought to allow you—"

"Don't concern yourself about me. To be on the safe side I've brought a little protector along with me." Slade patted his pocket as an indication of his meaning.

"Come along then," said the Inspector.

The three men made their way out. The night was dark and a wretchedly cold drizzle only served to accentuate the misery of the general conditions. Anthony thrust his hands deeply into the pockets of his 'Burberry' and buttoned the collar high to his chin. A few paces forward and MacMorran issued his instructions.

"When we get fairly close to the seat we're after—we'll split. Part company. I'll take the seat to its immediate left, Mr. Bathurst will take the seat to the immediate right. You, Sir Cloudesley, had better take up a position in the rear where you can easily cover all the three seats and also anything that may take place. You'll have to keep your eyes skinned and use your wits if necessary—and your discretion. That all right for you, Sir Cloudesley?"

Slade nodded. "No complaints here. I'm under your orders, Inspector. What you say goes. You may rely on me."

"Good. It's five to nine. We haven't far to go and we shouldn't have long to wait." They had now reached the Embankment parade itself. Few people occupied the seats. For one thing it was comparatively early and for another, the night was too cold and wet for all except the most wretched and squalid.

"This is where we part forces," said MacMorran. "Each man to his place."

Without a word and with almost silent tread, the three men slipped away in the different directions that had been assigned to them by the Inspector. Anthony went quickly towards the seat on the right which MacMorran had assigned to him. Spattering rain stung his cheeks whipped with a wind from the river. As far as he could see in the gloomy conditions there were but few people about. He managed to catch sight of a few flickering figures moving to and fro and hazy in the distance. They seemed, however, to belong to single individuals—not groups—and Anthony regarded them in no way as ominous or forbidding. Anthony reached the seat that was his objective. He thought that he could see MacMorran away to his left but he could get no glimpse of Sir Cloudesley.

Suddenly he had something in the nature of a surprise. For as far as he could trust his eyes in the conditions of rain and darkness he felt that the seat between MacMorran and him—the seat of their interest—was occupied. What looked suspiciously like the form of a huddled drunken woman was sprawled at one end. But drunken woman or not, Anthony decided to watch her and her movements, like a hawk. Every now and then a boat's horn hooted away on the river with a hint of mocking mystery and Anthony could hear the splash of rippling water as the boats of the River Police cut through it with their sharp and imperious insistence. The rain began to fall with increasing severity. To protect himself as well as he could, Anthony crouched against the natural shelter of the seat. Half-turning his head, he could now pick up the tall figure of Sir Cloudesley Slade hovering in the rear. Mr. Bathurst kept his eyes steadily trained on the seat of his interest and objective. He held his watch closely to his eyes to find out what the exact time was. Three minutes past nine! Any moment now and the figures in this callous conspiracy of murder and decoy might be but a few yards away from him and who knew what dreadful work they had in mind that night? His fingers closed on the butt of his revolver. He intended to be ready at the precise moment of being needed. But nothing transpired! Nobody approached the third seat going west from the Needle of Cleopatra! Sheets of rain billowed up in a blinding lashing stroke and Anthony huddled his body even further into the corner angle of the seat. The sooner this business was over and done with, the better! And the 'drunk' still lay in serene unconsciousness on the rendezvous seat! Minutes passed. Five minutes became ten, ten minutes grew to a quarter of an hour and a quarter of an hour dragged itself into half an hour. No wet bedraggled evening traveller or travellers came to the seat between Anthony and Inspector MacMorran.

Then—unexpectedly—Anthony heard footsteps behind him. On his guard as he was, his senses tautened preparatory to action. But he was destined for disappointment. It was MacMorran who had come up at the back of him. The rain glistened on his face and dropped from his hat.

"We're barking up the wrong tree. There hasn't been a soul go near that seat all the time we've been watching. I'll take my dying oath on it. Besides there's an old girl on it. Been there ever since we arrived. Drunk, I fancy. If not drunk—sound asleep. Dead to the world. I don't think our birds will fly this way to-night. Too wet, perhaps, for operations."

Anthony shook the rain from the shoulders of his mackintosh. "You certainly do pick the nights, Andrew. Out of the top drawer. This is a beauty—and no error. But I don't know that I altogether agree with you concerning our 'birds'. The weather may have *delayed* their operations. I think we ought to give them another half-hour. To be absolutely on the safe side."

MacMorran shook his head dubiously. "I don't know that we need. I'm convinced that we're on a wild-goose chase." He coughed.

"And there's just the chance too, that you *may* have misread that telegram. Homer's head wasn't always steady."

"There may be—but it's a hundred-to-one against your 'chance' for all that."

Anthony showed signs of impatience. It was a night when tempers were easily frayed and spirits ruffled. As he finished his sentence, Sir Cloudesley Slade, looking the picture of misery, came up from the rear and joined them.

"What's happened?" he asked tersely.

"Why—there's nothing doing," returned the Inspector testily, "we're all wasting our time—all three of us. I've just been telling Mr. Bathurst that we might as well accept the position and retreat gracefully. The people we've come after are conspicuous by their absence. They may even have called our bluff. They won't come to-night. That's all there is to it."

"H'm," said Sir Cloudesley, "doesn't sound too good to me. I've been wondering what had gone wrong. At the same time, I feel disposed to agree with you, Inspector. Also—it's a hell of a night. Doesn't Bathurst see eye to eye with you?"

"On the subject of the night—I'm in full agreement. With regard to the matter of our friends, Messrs. Chandler and Co.—I'm by no means so sure of things as Inspector MacMorran claims to be."

Anthony gazed ahead into the pelting rain and darkness. Slade's eyes followed his. Anthony spoke his thoughts. "There's a drunken woman on the seat we've been watching. But she was there when we came along. I haven't taken my attention off her since. Nobody's been near her—I can swear to that fact. Is it possible by any chance, do you think, that she's upset their plans at all? Just by accident?"

"No," responded the Inspector impatiently, "I don't think so. Not for a moment. They wouldn't have worried about her. They're not the kind. They'd have found ways and means to clear her out of it. No—you can take it from me—Annie doesn't live here any more—there'll be no meeting round here to-night. Well—I think we'll be getting back to the 'Yard.' And to a drop of something hot with lemon and sugar in it. That appeals to me more than anything."

He looked at Anthony as he spoke. He saw that Mr. Bathurst was still peering intently into the black curtain of rain in front of him.

"Just a minute, you two," whispered Mr. Bathurst—"I've an idea—stay here for a moment or so, will you? I think I'll go across to that seat there and have a closer look at things."

"What do you mean?" declared MacMorran. "What do you want to go to the seat for."

"Because something's just occurred to me, Andrew. Wait here as I said. If I want you for anything—I'll beckon you to come along. Watch out for me."

Without further ado, Anthony shook off the others and strode off into the darkness. Sir Cloudesley and MacMorran watched him from where they stood. The rain was now hitting the pavements and the puddles on the pavements with relentless persistence. The two men who watched saw that Anthony made straight for the third seat, travelling west from Cleopatra's Needle. Half an idea suddenly entered MacMorran's head and he cursed softly under his breath as he took in its entire significance. Slade was muttering inaudibilities. The waiting period through which he had recently passed had frayed his nerves and played havoc with his poise and balance. With the Inspector, he saw Anthony Bathurst approach and then go right up to the seat. They watched his subsequent actions with a strange, almost breath-catching fascination. Anthony stopped at the seat. He bent down towards the woman lying huddled on it. They saw him bend down closer and apparently touch the sleeping form. Then he seemed to start with surprise and back away a pace or two as though amazed at something he had seen. Turning with a quick movement of his body, he beckoned to them in what MacMorran thought was almost a frantic desperation. The Inspector began to run towards the seat where Anthony was standing. Sir Cloudesley seemed to understand what was expected of him and ran behind the Inspector. MacMorran had no real idea as to what they were about to find but that vague impression which had come to him when Anthony had started out towards the seat was taking shape in his mind and growing less nebulous and obscure. Doubts which had assailed him were now passing from him and the fact that he was now nearer to action than he had been, was assisting materially in the deletion of these doubts.

Within a few minutes he and Sir Cloudesley Slade had reached their objective. Anthony met them and pointed to the prone figure on the seat with a gesture of dramatic emphasis.

"Look here," he cried excitedly, "and understand why this woman occupied this seat!"

MacMorran stooped and gazed at the recumbent figure. "Good God," he cried—"it's Godfrey Slade!"

"What?" almost screamed Sir Cloudesley—"my son? It can't be. . . . Yes . . . it is . . . He's not dead, Inspector . . . tell me he's not dead."

Sir Cloudesley in his agony of apprehension propped up his son's body against his shoulder and stared hopelessly into the livid face.

"He's not dead," replied Anthony, "although he seems in a bad way. We must get him to the 'Yard' at once. Pray God we are not too late. Give me a hand with him, Andrew, will you?"

He and MacMorran stooped and raised Slade's body. "Thank goodness we haven't far to go."

As they reached the 'Yard' with their burden Anthony was frail in the presence of temptation. "He's rather heavy, Andrew, for a wild-goose! Don't you think so?"

MacMorran's reply was inaudible. But his face was eloquent.

CHAPTER XXIII
WHAT HAPPENED TO GODFREY SLADE

GODFREY Slade in his freakish costume was carried into MacMorran's room. The Inspector at once sent for Supt. Hemingway and telephoned for the Divisional Surgeon, Dr. Sugden.

"Give us a hand here, Hemingway," MacMorran ordered, "push some chairs together and lay this chap on them. Get these absurd clothes off him. And get some blankets and a couple of hot-water bottles. The Doctor'll be along in about ten minutes and then we shall know better 'what's what'." Hemingway stared with some surprise at his superior's use of the masculine gender. Anthony attempted to interpret his doubt to his advantage. "It's all right, Superintendent. You may shed your surprise. This is Godfrey Slade, the missing man. He's fallen among thieves, in all probability."

Hemingway's look of incredulity passed from his face. "He's not dead, is he?" he asked anxiously.

"No," replied Anthony, "but I don't know how far along that last road he has travelled. Sugden will tell us when he comes. I only hope he won't be too long." He looked with some anxiety at his watch.

MacMorran ventured an opinion. "In my view," he advanced doggedly, "young Slade's doped."

"I agree with you, Inspector," interposed Anthony, "the look in his eyes gave me that idea when I first saw him on the seat. That and the lividness."

Meanwhile Sir Cloudesley Slade paced the room, the victim of a battalion of taunting fears and mind-racking emotions. Repeatedly he stopped abruptly in his task of walking and came to the line of chairs where lay the body of his son. Here he would stop and his face register the full flush of his fear as he watched the prone figure. Then he would turn away suddenly, gesture mechanically, almost helplessly and resume his restless route round the room. Anthony also watched the younger Slade's face as he lay. He seemed now, he thought, to be breathing a little more easily than before and his face had taken on a trifle better colour. But the contraction of the pupils was still much in evidence and the eyes themselves were fixed and staring. As though the stricken man in his last moments of conscious-ness had been forced to behold something ghastly and intolerably horrible which, if he were destined to live, he would never forget. The minutes of waiting passed. MacMorran passed his hand across his forehead. Anthony consulted his watch again.

"The doctor's taking his—"

Before he could complete the sentence, the door opened and in came Doctor Sugden, the Divisional Surgeon. Obviously his temper was not of the best.

"Why *must* you, Inspector?" he said reproachfully, "and on a night like this too? You're fast becoming a public menace."

MacMorran's reply was to motion towards the blanketed body on the chairs. "This is Godfrey Slade, Doctor, the missing man. Been missing since the night he fought Blood at the Belfairs Stadium—and beat him. As you probably know, this gentleman is his father—Sir Cloudesley Slade."

The doctor bowed. "Good evening, Sir Cloudesley."

He went across to the prostrate figure and frowned. "Come, come . . . let's have a look at him . . . what's all this about?"

He gazed intently at the body and then gently pulled down the lower eyelid of the right eye with his forefinger. Anthony listened eagerly for anything that the professional Sugden might choose to say. The effort of listening was destined for speedy reward.

"H'm. Narcosis. Very definite."

He turned and beckoned to Anthony. "Come and look here. Profound insensibility. Condition closely resembling normal sleep. He should, however, not be entirely indifferent to sensory stimulus."

"What's the drug?" asked Anthony.

"Opium, I should say. He'll be all right. Notice the livid lips and face and the cold sweat? I don't think he's had enough to finish him off."

Sugden rapped out orders. "Get some coffee made, Inspector. At once. And I shall want brandy as well. In the meantime—"

MacMorran nodded to Hemingway. Hemingway went out. Sugden went to his bag. Anthony saw that the doctor was preparing to administer an injection.

"Antidote?" queried Anthony.

"A-ha. Sulphate of atropine and strychnine. Full doses." Then he seemed to think of something else. "Oh—and Inspector, see that I can have two or three wet towels to hand quickly—will you please?"

MacMorran looked up. "Now, sir?"

"At once—please. I must get to work. Mustn't leave him too long. That would only make matters worse. But he'll be all right. Hasn't taken too much. Feel pretty sure of that."

He completed the preparation of the injection, gave the patient an emetic and inserted the needle under the skin of Godfrey Slade's right arm. The Inspector slipped out for the towels as the Superintendent came in with a bottle of brandy and glasses.

"Coffee in a few minutes, sir," he announced "and here's the brandy for you now."

MacMorran stopped himself on the threshold. "Wet towels, Hemingway—three—at once. And give me that bottle."

"Very good, sir." Hemingway handed over the Martell's. Sugden took the brandy, poured some into a glass and forced some between Godfrey Slade's lips.

"Those towels," he muttered—"as soon as you like."

"They're coming, Doctor. I've given orders for them."

"Tell 'em to get a move on. What do they think I am? Can't wait all night."

Considering what Sugden had previously stated, Anthony was surprised to hear him talking like this. He wondered if the doctor had observed anything to make him change his opinion. A knock at the door which MacMorran answered, brought Hemingway with his wet towels and the coffee.

"Pour out a cup," ordered Sugden. "Quick."

Hemingway, still looking supremely uncomfortable, obeyed him. Sugden administered the coffee as he had done the brandy some few minutes previously. Then he took one of the wet towels, brandished it and flicked Slade on the forehead and cheeks. This procedure he repeated time after time—striking harder and harder. Sir Cloudesley and Anthony stood at his side and watched him. The former looked 'all in.' He seemed to have aged several years in a few days.

"He's all right," said Sugden again, holding up in his efforts for a while—"only a light dose as I said when I first clapped eyes on him. I felt pretty certain of my ground. More coffee and more brandy. Jump to it."

Hemingway saw to his requirements. Sugden poured more of each liquid down Godfrey Slade's throat.

"Perspiration," muttered Sugden between breaths, "sure sign of opium poisoning, that and the contraction of the pupils. And the livid colour. With alcoholic poisoning you get the reverse conditions—dilation. Give me that other towel you have there, MacMorran, will you?"

The Inspector passed over another wet towel to the doctor. Again he slapped and flicked the drugged man on the forehead and cheeks. He maintained this exercise at a steady pace for a good five minutes. Suddenly he bent down and shook Godfrey Slade forcibly by the shoulders.

"Wake up, man. Wake up. Snap out of it. D'ye hear me—wake up."

Slade seemed to respond and half moved his head.

"Can you get me a dressing-gown," cried Sugden—"quick. I'm on top now. We'll soon have this chap round now and out of danger."

Hemingway—muttering criticisms—dashed out again. The doctor shook Slade by the shoulders again and again.

"Come on man. Don't you hear what I'm saying to you? Pull yourself together. Make an effort . . . make an effort, I say."

Some minutes passed during which Slade seemed to have slumped again and Sugden continued his exhortations to his patient. Eventually Hemingway returned with a dark-green dressing-gown. Sugden propped Slade up on the foundation of chairs and got him into it. Slade was showing signs of relapsing again but the doctor kept at him relentlessly. He threw back the blankets which up to now had served to cover the patient and assisted him to stand unsteadily on the floor. Anthony knew what Sugden's intention was. To keep his patient walking up and down. Anthony gestured to the others and they made a clear lane in the room for the doctor and Godfrey Slade to use. Sugden did exactly as Anthony had anticipated. He kept Slade walking up and down until the emetic acted. Then, from that moment, and gradually, an improvement set in. Sugden persevered nobly and after about a quarter of an hour's intensive activity of backwards and forwards walking he took Slade to a chair and seated him on it. Already Godfrey Slade was beginning to look a different man. The effects of his sickness had worn off. Sugden gave him more coffee and brandy. Then the doctor stood up and mopped his brow.

"That's O.K. As I said—he hadn't taken enough to put him out of mess." He grinned. "Lucky for all of us—himself included. He'll be able to talk to you in a few minutes." Sir Cloudesley Slade went over to his son and sat at his side. The relief that showed on his face was as a sun shining through clouds. He reached across, put his arm round Godfrey's shoulders and half-pulled the young man towards himself. Then as though ashamed of this public display of emotion, he rose, crossed the room to where Doctor Sugden was standing and shook him warmly by the hand.

"Thank you, Doctor. I can never thank you enough. You can guess how I feel."

"That's all right, Sir Cloudesley. Never mind about that. My job! Glad to be able to help. All in the day's work." Sugden grinned again.

Sir Cloudesley returned to his son who was now sitting upright in his chair, rubbing his eyes with the back of one hand and pushing his other hand through his hair. MacMorran went to him and looked anxiously.

"I think he can talk a bit now," declared Sir Cloudesley, "try him, Inspector, will you?"

MacMorran smiled at Godfrey Slade. "How are you feeling, now, Mr. Slade? More like yourself?"

Godfrey Slade smiled ruefully in return. "Just a bit—thank God. For the last few minutes I've been trying to collect my scattered thoughts. And they *have* been scattered—I can tell you."

The Inspector nodded encouragingly. "Start from the time just after the scrap, Mr. Slade."

"The scrap! Good Lord—I can scarcely believe now that it ever took place. How many years ago was that? Seems to belong to oblivion."

"Never mind that. Go ahead, will you, with your yarn. What you're going to tell us will help us a lot."

Slade looked longingly at the coffee-pot. "May I have some more coffee? Does it matter?"

MacMorran looked towards Doctor Sugden for his opinion and lifted his eyebrows in interrogation.

"Certainly," responded Sugden, "you may have as much as you like. Give him some, Super."

Hemingway, always on the alert, poured out another cup for Godfrey Slade. The latter drank some of it gratefully. He put the cup on MacMorran's table.

"Thanks. That's good. I feel a different man now. You want me to tell you what happened to me. After the scrap. Well, when I left the Belfairs Stadium that evening, as you know, I intended to drive straight to Star's—Miss Merrilees—pick her up and come on to my father's 'do' at the Turin as had been arranged. On the way, I thought I'd 'phone her—just to make sure of everything—which I did. I stopped my car, got out and 'phoned from a call-box at Kenriston. That would be, I should think, about eleven o'clock. No—a little before that. Say about a quarter to eleven. That would be nearer. I told Star I was coming straight away and that was that."

Godfrey Slade took up his cup again and finished off the remainder of his coffee.

"Well, I hung up, shut the door of the call-box—you know how I mean—let it come to behind me and started to walk back to my car which I had parked temporarily about twenty yards away by the side of the road. There hadn't been a soul in the village of Kenriston that I'd noticed—beyond the cars that were passing through in an endless stream, of course, and I certainly wasn't on the look-out for or expecting anything in the shape of trouble. But when I got to my car, I was amazed to see a man sitting at the steering wheel. As cool as you like. You can naturally tell how I felt about this! My indignation and so on. I did what any one of you would have done in similar circumstances. I went up to the window and asked this fellow what the hell? At that precise moment I regret to state my recollection ceases for a time."

Godfrey Slade grinned humorously.

"Why?" asked the Inspector—somewhat unnecessarily.

"For the simple reason that somebody came behind me as I was leaning over talking to the chappie in my car and gave me a dough-boy right on the back of the head. A proper fourpenny-one. You can take it from me." Slade rubbed the back of his head reminiscently.

"Go on," said MacMorran.

"The next thing that I can remember was waking up on a bed in a foul sort of room. Like an attic or small box-room. The time was six o'clock. My wrist-watch told me that. I must have been out for about seven hours. My overcoat and my dinner-jacket had gone and my head sang and buzzed like the very devil. I got off the bed and started to prospect a bit. Round the room. There was a door. Locked. On the outside. I shook it. And a small window—through which I could see nothing. It was too dark. So I thought I'd create a diversion. I took off one of my shoes and hammered on the floor with it."

Sir Cloudesley judged it to be the moment for eulogy. "Good!" he muttered—"nice work, Godfrey. Go on, my boy."

"Well—I kept on hammering the floor and after some considerable time I heard footsteps ascend the stairs and the key turned in the lock of my bedroom door. A tall, thin chap came in. Middle-aged. I knew him afterwards as 'Brush.' That's how his gang of associates always addressed him. He put a cup of tea and a plate with some slices of bread and margarine on the bed and told me to shut up making a row or it would be the worse for me. I remonstrated and demanded to know the reason why I had been brought to the place. He pulled out a gun, told me to shut my lip and that if I didn't, I'd go where Bailey, Donovan and Jago had gone. That threat quietened me down a bit. I felt that I wanted time to think. When he cleared out I ate the breakfast which had been brought me—such as it was—and settled myself down to a spot of quiet thinking. It was obvious that I was in a tight spot. For one thing—I hadn't the least idea where I was. Suddenly, for no real reason that I can explain, except perhaps that I wanted to check up on my 'assets' I began to feel in my pockets and in the right-hand pocket of my vest I found a small 'dance' pencil. The sort that are dished out at whist drives. This gave me an idea. Should I be able to communicate in any way with the outside world at all? But I had no paper of any kind to use as a means of correspondence. With a view to redressing this deficiency, I scouted round the room and after a little while I struck lucky! Beyond the bed and a chair at the side of it, the place was empty—stark empty—save for one other thing."

Slade laughed a trifle hysterically. His father was listening to him proudly and greedily.

"In the empty grate had been thrown a cigarette-carton. It was ancient and dirty. As you know, just inside the silver-paper in these packets and folded up with it, is a strip of thin white plain paper. I collared hold of this—a second or so in front of my door being unlocked again. In my excitement in scrounging round on my knees at the grate, I hadn't heard the sound of footsteps coming up the stairs. In came the man 'Brush' again. And there was I with this scrap of paper in the palm of my hand. What do you think he told me?"

All except Anthony shook their heads. "That he was going to make you a grand offer," ventured Mr. Bathurst tentatively.

"No," said Godfrey Slade—"something much more realistic—to hand over all the money and valuables I had in my pockets."

Anthony seemed disappointed at the failure of his shot. MacMorran's laugh did nothing to diminish his disappointment.

"I did as I was ordered. Then he told me I was to prepare myself to go out later—'to an unknown destination.' I told him I had no coat or overcoat. He said 'that can easily be remedied' and cleared out of the room with the breakfast things I had used." Slade ran his fingers through his hair again. "Directly he'd gone away and considering what he had said about my being carted off before many moons, I thought the best thing I could possibly do would be to get my message scrawled while I had the chance. Because that chance mightn't come again. There was just a thousand to one shot that I could get it delivered in some way, but I should have to decide that later on and wait for the opportunity to come. If it didn't—I was no worse off—that was obvious. So I scrawled on the piece of cigarette paper and shoved it in my waistcoat pocket along with the pencil. In the left-hand pocket. Then I sat down on the bed and awaited events. It was damned cold and miserable, I can tell you. I sat there till twenty minutes to ten. Then in came 'Brush' again. Looking ugly and distinctly aggressive. First of all he threw my overcoat at me. 'Put that on,' he said, 'pronto.' I did. I can tell you I was glad to. I was shivering with cold. Then he stuck a gun in the middle of my back and said 'march.' I marched. Out of the door and downstairs— first of all. A squalid staircase it was that I went down—with a sort of sickly brown wallpaper hanging and peeling from the walls. The whole place was as damp as an aquarium. I give you my word—it offended my artistic eye."

Slade grinned at his pleasantry. Sir Cloudesley, almost pompously, leant over and patted him on the shoulder. Godfrey continued with his story.

"When I got into the passage at the foot of the rickety staircase down which I had just been conducted, my friend 'Brush' rapped out further instruction to me—'Left turn. Face the wall.' I obeyed— you bet I did—and to my intense surprise and annoyance I was immediately blindfolded. The gun was still being poked into my ribs, remember, and any resistance on my part would have been foolish. No sooner was I blindfolded than 'Brush' gave me another dose of physical jerks. 'Hold out your right arm. Straight out.' I obeyed him again. What do you think happened?"

178 | BRIAN FLYNN

There was no reply. Even Anthony wouldn't venture a suggestion. Slade went on.

"I was handcuffed to another man. Then a cap was shoved on my head and I was pushed forward along the passage. To the front door and then into a car that had evidently been waiting outside. The car moved off at once. I hadn't the slightest idea, of course, as to where we were going. I could see nothing and for a time nobody spoke a word. The car travelled, I suppose, for about ten minutes in complete silence. Then it stopped—and another surprising thing happened. Two people in the car with me began to argue. From what I could gather, the car had stopped outside a Post-Office. Two things evidently had to be done."

Slade stopped to smile again.

"Each one of these things was eminently prosaic. One was the sending of a telegram and the other the sending of a telephone message."

Anthony interposed a question. "Was each of these to be attended to by a different person?"

"That's it. You've holed in one. It was like this. Somebody called 'Banjo' wanted to 'phone and 'Brush' was the man who desired to send the wire. The other chap they addressed as 'Joe.' For some reason best known to himself, 'Banjo' wouldn't agree to 'Brush' doing his 'phoning for him, and they wouldn't leave me alone in the car with Joe. They evidently didn't assess Joe's powers of looking after me too highly if he were left on his own. So after some minutes of heated discussion my bandage was yanked off and I found I was handcuffed to the man they called 'Joe.' He was a short, lumpish, dark chap, with protruding yellow teeth. 'Banjo' was a proper tough with a large wen on the side of his neck. Couple of pretty dears they looked—I can tell you! 'Joe' took the revolver from 'Brush,' camouflaged it under his overcoat and thus I was marched into the Post-Office. All I know is that the place was on the corner of St. Crispin Street. I spotted the name as I went in."

Godfrey Slade looked unutterably weary but he made a prodigious effort, pulled himself together and after a moment's rest went on again.

"Remember I could use my left arm only. And my scrawled SOS was lying all the time in the left-hand pocket of my vest. It was going to be some job to get at it—especially seeing how well I was being looked after by my captor. Anyhow, I was fully resolved to keep my eyes open and to work on any reasonable chance that might present itself. It came, as I had hoped it would. 'Brush' wrote out his telegram. The man they called 'Banjo' went to the telephone—away from the rest of us—into an apartment. I was left standing near the counter with Joe. With the fingers of my left hand, I furtively undid the buttons of my overcoat—one by one—without him being aware of it and then pushed those same fingers into the pocket of my vest where lay my precious scrap of paper all ready to be disposed of. Where could I put it where my captors couldn't see it but other people might? And *how*! Now Joe and I were standing near the counter and all the time, of course, I knew he had me covered. Near by was a small girl who had come in. I saw her lay a book on the ledge as she asked to be supplied with a postal order. I saw too—and this was a fact that pleased me—that it was a book either coming from or being returned to—a Public Library of all places. You can nearly always tell them by the dirt on them and their uniform binding. In a flash the idea came to me to try to push my message in some way between the pages of this book. I must be quick!" Godfrey Slade grinned again. "It's all a yarn, isn't it, told slow?"

"Go on," said MacMorran, "you're doing fine."

"Well—you can easily see that my main problem was this. To plant my scrap of paper in the kid's book *before* either 'Brush' or 'Banjo' came back and without Joe seeing what I did. I *must* therefore divert Joe's attention some way from myself and from what I intended to do. How could I do it? Inspiration came to me in a flash. I make a habit of carrying a handkerchief in my left sleeve. I worked it loose by gently shaking my free arm and deliberately let it fall from my sleeve to the floor as far away from me as I could and in Joe's direction. I then called Joe's attention to what I had dropped, and requested him as nicely as I could to pick it up for me. To my dismay, he hesitated for a second or so and I was afraid he had tumbled to my little scheme. But I wasn't done with and tried again. I smiled at him graciously and pointed again to the handkerchief, and to my intense satisfaction this time he fell for it. He stooped down, using his right hand, of course (which held the revolver) and in a flash, much more quickly than I can possibly describe the incident, I pushed my little paper message somehow and somewhere into the little kid's book that was lying on the counter. With no more than a handful of seconds to spare! Because 'Brush' came back, 'Banjo' appeared from the telephone compartment and Joe came up again to the surface, to breathe more freely, get firmer hold of his revolver and to hand me back my handkerchief."

Sir Cloudesley beamed at his son again. "Smart work, my boy! 'Pon my soul—I am proud of you. But go on. What happened after that?"

Slade grimaced ruefully at the question. "I'm afraid you mustn't rely on me for very much more. I was, of course, marched back to the car by my trio of captors, blindfolded again directly I was inside the car and driven back to my temporary 'hotel.' The handkerchief across my eyes and the handcuffs were removed; into the bedroom I went again and there I spent the remainder of the day. Twice I've had bread and butter and tea but no more. Once about midday and then in the late afternoon. Luckily I had a few cigarettes and you bet I smoked them. I limited myself to a ration of one every hour. Several times I was strongly tempted to exceed my self-imposed ration but I nobly resisted the temptation. All the time, too, I kept asking myself what these people wanted of me and what eventually they intended to do to me. The more I considered it—the worse I felt. Why hadn't I had the pluck to make a dash for things when I had been in the Post-Office? As I might have done. It was about half-past seven when I heard steps on the stairs. I was sitting in the darkness and the room was horribly cold and damp. My three companions of the morning came in. Joe carried a lighted candle. From the look on their three faces, I honestly thought I was for the 'high jump' as soon as they could hand it out to me and I determined to sell my life as dearly as possible. But I was wrong. My fears were unfounded. 'I want to talk things over,' said 'Brush,' 'important things.' I looked at him stupidly. He turned to Joe and said surprisingly, as I thought, "let's have a drink, you yellow-fanged Dago—bring the Scotch and three glasses or I'll knock seven skittles of muck out of you.' Joe grinned and said, 'don't young Slade getta any, then?' 'You've got me wrong! You're the one that don't drink,' said 'Brush' callous-ly—'get a move on—three glasses and the 'Scotch'—before I flay the hide off you.' Joe went out, brought in the 'Scotch'—he fetched four glasses by the way—the drinks were all poured out from the same bottle—I saw nothing suspicious or anything that raised any doubt in my mind—and I drank the one which was handed to me. Truth to tell I was damned glad of it."

Slade stopped and looked round rather lamely.

"Soon after, I found myself coming over drowsy. Frightfully so! Couldn't keep my eyes open—no matter how I tried to. I don't remember what they were talking about—and I presume that grad-ually I went to sleep. That's the bundle. The next thing I knew was waking up just now in here with all you good people round me." Godfrey Slade reached forward and drank another cup of coffee.

Chapter XXIV
THE SANDED FLOOR

ANTHONY looked enquiringly at Doctor Sugden. "Is he fit enough for me to ask him a few questions, Doctor? I'm in your hands."

"How do you feel, Slade?" asked Sugden. "Pretty fair?"

"Not too bad—considering what I've been through. Tired as hell, though. But you can let Bathurst fire his stuff at me. I'm perfectly well aware that he's dying to. I don't mind. I can stand it."

Anthony grinned at him. "Good man. I won't bother you more than is necessary. I know what you've been through. You've no real idea, I suppose, first of all, as to the locality of the house where you were detained?"

"Merely this. What I mentioned before. About ten minutes fast travelling in a car from that St. Crispin Street Post-Office, say seven or eight miles. But in what direction the house lay or the district it's situated in, God alone knows." Anthony turned quietly to MacMor-ran. "That reminds me, Andrew, something I intended to say before, cover on 8, Florestan Street, Deptford. At once—will you, please?" Hemingway took instructions from the Inspector and went out. Anthony came back again to Godfrey Slade.

"Now tell me this—if you can. Try hard to help. All the time you were held in this house you've told us about—did you hear a telephone ring?"

"Not once," replied Godfrey Slade promptly, "although, of course if such a thing had happened, I mightn't have heard it seeing that I was imprisoned in an upstairs bedroom all the time, with the door shut. But why do you ask?"

"It's not much of a line to go on, I know—but we think we know the name of the man you have called 'Brush.' The telegram he sent was in the name of Chandler."

Slade opened his eyes at the information. "How on earth did you find that out?"

Anthony detailed an account of their activities since Croker reported from the St. Crispin's Library with the book of Marlene Butcher. Slade nodded gratefully.

"I scarcely thought that my SOS would bear so much fruit. Its success has exceeded my wildest expectations. But I'm curious. You mustn't mind. What was that address you mentioned just now to the Inspector? Somewhere in Deptford, wasn't it? I don't think it's possible that I could have been—"

"No," cut in Anthony, "don't make any mistake in that direction—we don't imagine that the place to which you were taken was in Deptford. Don't worry yourself about that. As it happens, we're on to something else. 8, Florestan St., Deptford, is the address to which Chandler sent his telegram from your Post-Office. To a person named Smith. A name you may have heard before. It was by dint of reading and interpreting the real meaning that lay hidden in that telegram that we were able to pick you up on the Embankment this evening. That's telling you." He smiled with a suggestion of success.

Godfrey Slade seemed to be appreciative of the information. "Oh—good! I'm beginning to understand a great deal now that has hitherto been obscure to me."

"Now tell me this," declared Anthony. "When Chandler and his two associates were talking, did you hear them mention the name of 'Asater' at any time?"

"No," replied Slade decisively—"not at all. If I had heard the name of 'Asater' I'm sure I should have remembered it."

"H'm," said Anthony, "not so good. Still if you didn't hear it, you didn't."

MacMorran put a supplementary question to him. "Did you hear the name of 'Smith'? Or any name, come to that?"

"No. All that I heard—I've already told you about." The telephone rang as Slade finished his sentence. MacMorran answered it himself. "Hallo—Hemingway . . . yes . . . what have you picked up? What? You don't say? H'm—pity. Give the place the once-over. Comb it as thoroughly as you know how. Let me know if you get anything. I'll be waiting for you here. Right—get busy." The Inspector replaced the receiver and spoke to the others. "Hemingway's been in to 8, Florestan St. With no tangible results. The Smith bird that we hoped to catch has flown to other climes. I understand that the house is occupied by a respectable couple named Lancaster. They let a bed-sitting-room and this 'Smith' has been their tenant. Hemingway reports that he walked out to-night early on and hasn't returned. Took all his belongings with him, too, I understand. Which weren't either varied or valuable."

"Hemingway, I take it," intervened Anthony, "from what you said, will turn the room out?"

"Ay. He will! A real spring clean. When Hemingway's done with it, it'll look like nothing on earth. He won't miss much, I assure you."

"Much! I was secretly hoping that he wouldn't miss anything. Don't tell me I'm intoxicated with optimism."

"What does he hope to find by doing this?" enquired Sir Cloudesley.

' "It's not what he hopes to find. It's what he might find." MacMorran's reply was terse. "You never know," he added.

"I see," said Sir Cloudesley, though Anthony found himself doubting whether the old man really did.

"How long has Smith lodged there?" asked Anthony—"did the Superintendent mention that?"

"No. But not very long, I fancy. That was the impression I got from him."

"Easy come—easy go—like teeth and money. Well—it fits—it's just what I should have expected."

Godfrey Slade rose and steadied himself by holding on to the corner of MacMorran's table. He passed his hand wearily across his forehead.

Sugden looked towards him anxiously. "What's the trouble? Feeling dicky again?"

Slade nodded weakly and sank into his seat again. It appeared that he might collapse at any moment. His father helped him to more brandy which he took almost greedily. MacMorran appeared acutely uneasy. Inaction and uncertainty were ever his masters. He was on the point of speaking to Sir Cloudesley Slade when his telephone bell rang again. The noise brought everyone to a fuller life. As though eagerly welcoming the mechanical interruption, the Inspector picked up the receiver to answer the call. Anthony stopped watching Godfrey Slade and listened keenly. He was hoping that the caller might well be Hemingway again. His hopes were justified. MacMorran was speaking quickly and his voice was tinged with an undercurrent of excitement.

"What's that you say, Hemingway? Screwed up on the mantelpiece? Good man I What's the address? Sing it out, man, so that I can hear it. Wait a second . . . while I get a piece of paper. I'll put it down. Yes . . . right-o. I'm ready. 37—three-seven—Marlborough Villas—Notting Hill. O.K. Finish the job off then and I'll expect you later."

Anthony saw MacMorran replace the receiver quietly. But there was a look in his eyes that might mean a lot but which certainly boded ill for somebody.

"Hemingway's come across an address. On a piece of paper screwed up on the mantelpiece. This address is 37, Marlborough Villas, Notting Hill. He thinks that it may mean something."

Anthony rose from his chair. "You will agree that there's nothing like prompt action, Inspector? I suggest that I conduct a little party there at once. Bring a couple of revolvers along, will you? As you yourself so wisely said a few moments ago—*you never know.*" He turned and looked at Godfrey. "Do you think you could manage it? In a car? If you could, you know, you'd be tremendously useful."

Slade cocked an interrogative eye at Doctor Sugden. "What do you say, Doctor? Can I manage it or would it be—?"

Sugden grinned. "Lot you care what I say. You know very well you're aching to go."

Sugden addressed Anthony. "How many can you squeeze in your car, Bathurst?"

Anthony looked round the group. "Everybody here—including yourself—if that's what you're getting at."

"You can? Good. Then there's your answer, Slade. Come on now—let's make it."

They packed into the car and Anthony drove fiercely and fast to the house in Notting Hill. MacMorran sat in the seat next to him. The rain was lashing down harder than ever.

"Any exact idea, Inspector?" he asked as they approached the district of their destination.

"Yes. Know the area well. Been there before. In the course of my official duties. I'll tell you where to turn."

"Thanks, Inspector. Say when."

MacMorran very soon obliged him. "Next on the right. The odd numbers are on the left-hand side. I've a good idea whereabouts the number will be. When we get close to it, I'll tell you."

Anthony turned into the stretch known as Marlborough Villas and within a few seconds MacMorran's hand told him what he wanted to know. He stopped the car. The street was desolate and dreary. MacMorran guided them to the desired house.

"Ring the bell," said the Inspector to Anthony. "It's late, but not as late as all that."

Anthony rang the bell. As he did so, he noticed that Godfrey Slade was looking curiously at the front of the little house.

"Do you think you recognize it?" asked his father.

"Well—it's a funny thing perhaps—but I've got an idea that I do—although of course. I've never actually seen it. As I walked up to the porch just now from the gate, the steps I took struck me as a wee bit familiar. I had taken them twice you see when I was blind-folded. That's all. No more than that. Wait till we get inside. Then I'll be able to tell you for certain."

There was no reply to Anthony's summons. "Ring that wretched bell again," ordered MacMorran curtly. Anthony rang again. As he did so, he put his ear closer to the door and heard the rasping noise of the ringing bell as it hit the limits of the house and then came clanging back to him.

"Empty," remarked Anthony—"empty for a certainty. I can tell by the echoes I can hear. Use your key, Andrew. From what I can see of things you'll meet with little difficulty."

MacMorran nodded in understanding and agreement. "Right. Nothing else for it."

He used a key with slick efficiency and swung the door open to them. The five men entered and stood in the dark passage.

"Light," ordered the Inspector. "Find the switch, somebody! Don't stand chattering."

There was an edge on MacMorran's voice. Sugden was nearest to the wall on the left-hand side of the passage. He groped for the light-switch and quickly found it.

"I was right," cried Godfrey Slade in a voice high-pitched with excitement. "I've only been waiting for the light to tell me. This is the place, all right, where I stayed the night. See that foul-coloured paper coming away from the walls—both here and on the staircase? Don't you remember I told you about it?" He pointed to the foot of the staircase. "That's the identical spot I stood when I was blindfolded and handcuffed after they brought me downstairs. Jove—I never thought I should be here again so soon." He grinned at the thought with something like pleasure.

"Upstairs," said Anthony—"if you ask me—we've struck something like an uninhabited house. Uninhabited for some time I mean, but which was temporarily occupied merely for the pleasure of receiving you, Slade. Lead the way for us, Slade, do you mind?"

Slade accepted the order and dashed upstairs with the others quick in his wake. He reached the upstairs landing in a few strides and pushed open a bedroom door that faced him.

"My room," he cried, "this is it—once seen, never forgotten, pleasant view overlooking the sea. H. and C. and all domestic offices. Come in and share home-comforts. I can thoroughly recommend them."

They crowded into the room behind him. "Yes, here they are. My bed and my chair," went on Godfrey, "my floor and my ceiling—companions for a night and day." He demonstrated with quick gesture the parts of the room.

Anthony took a step forward from the others and looked carefully all round the apartment. It was bare and squalid. As he had stated previously, it was plain that the room had not been lived in for some considerable time. He went to the small window which had figured in Godfrey Slade's story. He looked out over the roofs of the other small houses that clustered near in an ugly and sordid huddle. Godfrey Slade called out again.

"Look in the grate—there you are—it's still there—the remains of the cigarette carton from which I scraped the paper for my SOS."

He was right. The crumpled packet lay there still. The outside covering—with the inside contents gone.

"Let's explore," said MacMorran—"there's no knowing with a place of this sort—we may run across something."

He led the way across the square landing into the other rooms. There were but two of these. The larger of them was empty. Dirty, damp and in sore need of many repairs. Anthony and the Inspector in the van, looked it over and quickly decided that it had little or nothing about it that demanded inspection or investigation. The five men made their way towards the smaller room. MacMorran, still leading the way, turned the handle of the door, and the others crowded round him in the doorway. As he entered, MacMorran stopped short and uttered a sharp exclamation. Like the other room at which they had just looked, this room, too, was empty. But when the Inspector called out, the others saw that he was pointing dramatically to the floor. Instead of the bare boards the other room had boasted, on the floor of this room lay a fairly heavy covering of coarse loose sand. This sand was deeper in the corners of the room than round and about the middle. Here it showed signs of moderately recent disturbance. The two Slades looked at the sanded floor in astonishment. Sugden appeared to be merely curious. He bent down as though intent upon making a closer investigation. Anthony stared not only at the covering of sand, but at a mark which showed plainly in the far left-hand corner. For this mark was the impression of a gigantic claw!

Chapter XXV
OPTIMISM FROM ANTHONY

MacMorran had gone as white as a sheet and used bad words under his breath.

"Andrew," murmured Anthony chidingly—"I'm surprised at you. Such goings on. It isn't as though you haven't seen such a thing before. By now—you ought to be getting quite used to it. I feel that I am."

But the Inspector was not alone in his reaction to the sinister mark in the sand. Sir Cloudesley looked as though he had spent the night in precarious isolation in a haunted house. His eyes seemed fascinated by the claw mark on the floor. They scarcely ever left it. If they wavered for a second, they returned to its contemplation. Sugden alone seemed unperturbed.

"Well, I'm damned," he said, possibly in veracious but unintended prophecy, "but what the devil's that? I've never seen anything like it. Has some animal or bird been kept in here? What's your opinion, Bathurst?"

Anthony sniffed the atmosphere in the room. "Don't collect any particular ozone, Doctor," he remarked. Maybe our bird's best friend told her." He smiled and glanced towards Godfrey Slade who was standing next to him. Godfrey Slade looked badly shaken. Worse even than he had looked previously. He had thought of the three men who had died, his three predecessors in the tragedy . . . whose bodies had been picked up . . . and the reminiscences that had come to him out of these thoughts were the reverse of pleasant. Godfrey Slade shivered.

"Expect you know how I'm thinking. I wonder if I was to have made a course—a human *bonne-bouche*—for something frightful which lived and grew hungry in here! Not the nicest of thoughts—is it?"

Anthony replied to him with a shake of the head. "If that had been the case, why did they dope you, dress you up as 'Mother Goose,' and then dump you on that seat on the Embankment for us to pick up?" Mr. Bathurst shook his head as he concluded. "Doesn't make sense to me, any way I look at it."

Sir Cloudesley overheard him. "Unless"—he said slowly—and stopped.

"Unless what, Sir Cloudesley?" interrogated Anthony.

The old man went on and finished his sentence. "Unless something happened during the time Godfrey was held here, to make them change their minds. Isn't that a possibility, don't you think? I must say that it seems so to me."

Anthony shrugged his shoulders.

"I think Sir Cloudesley's right," asserted MacMorran, "circumstances force me to agree with him. Smith cleared from the Deptford address, Chandler and company have given this place the go-by—it all points to the probability that they were scared by something and decided to make a 'get-away.'"

"My knowledge of natural history tells me that birds fly for other reasons than being scared," retorted Anthony with curt emphasis. "They often migrate, my dear Andrew, because it suits them to. And now you know what I'm thinking."

Doctor Sugden nodded in agreement. MacMorran led the way downstairs. "No point in stopping here any longer," he announced. The anxiety on his face had deepened. Anthony grinned.

"Just as well Lilley of Littlehampton didn't accompany us on this little jaunt. The sight of that claw mark on the sanded floor would have just about finished him."

Sir Cloudesley glanced at him anxiously when they reached the passage. MacMorran's example had carried infection. "You seem comparatively light-hearted, Bathurst, considering all that's happened. What have you seen in here that has encouraged you?"

"A ray of light, Sir Cloudesley. Not a lot, perhaps, when you come to measure it up, but a peeping through. I have every hope now that I may be able to draw the enemy into the open. Things are shaping that way."

"How will you manage that?"

A far-away look came into Anthony's eyes as he answered. "I'm not sure—yet. My plans have still to be projected. But we are dealing, Sir Cloudesley, with a crafty, cunning adversary equipped with the qualities of initiative and resource. To gain his ends, he will stick at nothing. He doesn't allow even lives to stand in his way. We must attack him, therefore, with his own weapons. That is what I propose to do—and with as little delay as possible."

Godfrey Slade came into the conversation. "I agree with you, Bathurst. With every word you have just said and all along the line. But isn't the enemy already forewarned? Doesn't this empty house prove that? And being forewarned is being forearmed. I'm not as confident, I fear, as you seem to be."

Anthony found questions for two people. "Did you put your reward idea into effect, Sir Cloudesley? I feel a certain interest in asking you?"

The old man looked at him wonderingly. "It will be in all the papers tomorrow morning. I'm offering five thousand pounds. There won't be time for me to countermand the notice now. But why? Don't tell me you're going to claim the money."

Anthony smiled and shook his head. "You need harbour no anxiety on that account. Although you may have a claim from Croker the librarian and possibly, I suggest, from Richard, the father of Marlene and of brother Warwick. If you should be faced with any other claimants, pass them over to Inspector MacMorran for investigation the moment you receive them. I'm serious about that."

Sir Cloudesley Slade intimated that he would.

Anthony's other question was directed to MacMorran himself. "Remember my putting a query to you some few days ago, Inspector? Two queries—in fact. One concerned a Miss Stella Molyneux once of Northampton and the other had reference to Marcus Secretan Esquire. Remember them?"

"Ay! Well enough. And I can answer 'em now—though I doubt if you'll derive any satisfaction from either of my answers. But I can't help that. I have nothing to report *re* the young lady, and as for friend Secretan, Chatterton's been on his tail for days. From him I get one reaction. And that's 'Nothing doing.' There's naught that's 'phoney' you can pin on Marcus Secretan."

Anthony rubbed his upper lip. "H'm. Disappointing—I must say. You don't seem either grateful or comforting. And I wanted you to be both. All the same—I'm cherishing ideas. Obstinacy on my part. They may take a bit of working out, I admit—I shall be compelled to give 'em my best attention. Listen to me, Sir Cloudesley. I'm out to spread a thick layer of temptation. In that I shall need your help. Even though I may seem to ask for actions that will entail somewhat extraordinary procedures—I want that help which I demand, given without questions being asked or criticisms advanced. Until afterwards and the job's done. Now—is that on, gentlemen?"

"So far as I'm concerned," replied Sir Cloudesley—"every time!"

"And from me, too," added Godfrey Slade with ready enthusiasm.

Sugden looked at Anthony whimsically. "Does that go for me as well, Bathurst?"

"It may do, Doctor. I can't say at the moment. We shall see. In the meantime, thank you, gentlemen. Each one of you."

Godfrey Slade shook him by the hand. "I already owe you a hell of a lot. I know that only too well. In all probability—my life. Anything you require of me—ask and you may command it without the slightest question."

Anthony meditated for a few moments. After a time he spoke. "I may want Lambert and Whitfield to play parts in my little drama. I think that I'm almost certain to. They know so much about the ring and everything connected with it. From henceforth, I must think always in terms of boxing-gloves. The problem started with boxing-gloves, I've a hunch that it will finish with them. So fix up Lambert and Whitfield for me, will you, Slade? That is to say I want them to be ready on the instant they're needed."

"That's O.K.," returned Godfrey Slade—"I'll see to that for you the first thing in the morning. Rely on me."

They left the house. There was no more there that they could do. As they walked towards the car, the Inspector turned and interrogated Anthony.

"What have you picked up, Mr. Bathurst, that makes you appear so confident. Or what do you know?"

"I *know* very little, Andrew. Even to confessing frankly that I don't even know *why*—but I've a hunch! As I said just now. And in a few days' time I shall know if that hunch is a good one. At least I'm hoping so. Get in, Andrew—and I'll warn you—I'm going to drive like smoke. I'm in a bad temper."

MacMorran swallowed hard, crammed his hat on the back of his head and went white round the gills.

"Did I criticize your driving the other day?"

"You did," replied Anthony grimly, "most unkindly."

"Forget it, will you," returned the Inspector as he edged himself into the car.

"I'm going to," said Anthony, "but I doubt whether you'll be able to follow my example."

Chapter XXVI
THE BOYS THAT WERE BORN IN
THE SPRING

ANTHONY Lotherington Bathurst sat comfortably and turned the pages of that excellent newspaper known as the *Sporting Life*. With which, let it be said, is incorporated the *Sportsman*, *Bell's Life in London*, and the *Sporting Telegraph*. Anthony however, at the moment, was not interested in the vaticinations of Augur, the judgment of Solon, or the uncanny wisdom of Warren Hill. He happened to be reading with avidity an account of the careers, short-lived though they may have been, of Ted Bailey, 'Lefty' Donovan, and Mike Jago. The commentator sincerely deplored the untimely demise of three such promising young boxers in such eminently tragic circumstances. Anthony read many details of their various and distinguished performances in the ring against redoubtable opponents of proved reputation. Anthony observed that in the judgment of the particular writer whose opinions he was reading, the finest fighter of the three was Donovan, and who had been by far the most likely of the trio to have risen to the top of his profession. Each account of the three men concluded with a short pen-picture of that man's boxing history, together with other entertaining details of a purely personal nature.

Firstly, Anthony read the story of Bailey. He followed this reading with the account of Donovan. When he came to the history of the Bath fighter, Mike Jago, he was suddenly struck by what he considered to be a most extraordinary coincidence. Bailey was shown to have been born on March the third, Donovan on March the ninth, and Jago on March seventeenth. Why wasn't he more appropriately named Patrick, murmured Anthony to himself? But although he allowed himself this momentary semi-flippancy, Anthony immediately devoted himself again to the consideration of the rather amazing coincidence of birth-month which had reared its incredible head in front of him. But a bare fortnight between the three men from the standpoint of their respective dates of birth! Was it a mere accident of circumstance or was there, by any crooked chance, a so far hidden, unrevealed meaning in it awaiting his investigation and possible solution? Anthony pondered over this new problem which was confronting him. A reminiscence of irresistible insistence came to him of that bizarre case he had investigated some years previously which has been given to the world by his industrious commentator under the title of 'The Spiked Lion.' Were there significant likenesses between that case and the one which was causing him so much anxiety at the present time? If so, could he quickly place his hand on them and drag them into the light? He shook his head as though impatient with his intelligence for harbouring even temporarily a thought that three March birth-dates could possibly mean anything more than mere coincidence of Time.

But Anthony's mind quested in all directions. It had suffered disturbance and was now inevitably reacting to that disturbance. Could the idea that he had been toying with for some days now be reasonably translated through this latest discovery? Even though that discovery was linked with what happened to be nothing more than a coincidence. After due consideration, Anthony thought that it could. Again, he turned idly to the pages of the *Sporting Life*. Racing, football, cricket, tennis, hockey, greyhound racing, coursing, golf, racquets, 'squash,' speedway racing, billiards and snooker were all catered for with varying degrees of journalistic skill and attention. For so much do the modern patrons and matrons of sport demand for their daily delectation! How different it must have been, he thought, in the days of old. Over a hundred years ago, say, when the little Corsican made his camp not many more than a score of miles from the white cliffs of Dover and the beacons had been heaped along the coast of Kent to blazon the tale that English bayonets might soon flash against French hearts. Anthony wondered what the nature of the news had been in the columns of *Bell's Life in London*, that newspaper which had, at some eventful time in the past, surrendered its inky ghost to become a part of the *Sporting Life*. Had *Bell's Life* functioned in the palmy days of the great fighters—Tom Sayers and his like—the Belchers, Pearce, Jackson and Cribb—and even during the times when the famous 'Corinthians' backed the 'Fancy'?

Anthony's thoughts, stimulated by the nomadic urge, strayed still further. He pursued them to 'Brooks's,' the great club of the Whigs, to 'Watier's,' the great gambling centre of the men of fashion who gathered round such famous names as Beau Brummell and the Marquis of Queensberry. Still the old games and sports persisted with a bridge of years of one hundred and a half. The time-honoured gibe of Bonaparte? A nation of shopkeepers? More truly a nation of sportsmen—with our horses, our dogs and our gloved fighting men.

At that moment, a wave of memory surged into Anthony's brain and rolled through it with quick precision. A wave that held a dancing light. A light which he could not fail to see. A thrill of excitement came to him. Of course! Why hadn't he thought of the idea before? The thought of such cold, callous, calculated cruelty made him gasp with feelings of mingled horror and astonishment—but the idea held fast for all that. He refused to be shaken out of it. It was an amazing idea and an affrighting idea and its contemplation brought Anthony standing from his chair. Bellamy, Asater . . . Bailey, Donovan and Jago . . . the gallery fitted. There was no intruder in that list. All high-lights of the 'Fancy.'

Anthony thought of the evening at Belfairs Stadium when Godfrey Slade had so surprisingly beaten his illustrious opponent and of the many figures who had sat close to the roped ring. Besides these, there had been Bradfield and Manning. He must not forget to consider these. He remembered the expression on Bradfield's face and the nonchalance of Manning as he walked from the middle of the ring to harangue the crowd. He remembered, too, how Bradfield had glanced towards Star Merrilees when she had come into the room at the Turin on the night of the fight. Which one . . . Anthony tossed his head and picked up his telephone. For good or ill he had made a quick decision.

Chapter XXVII
INTERLUDE AT MURILLO'S

STAR Merrilees was having supper at Murillo's with Godfrey Slade. Christmas had come and gone with its snow, its wassail and its carolling. Slade had completely recovered from his narrow escape when he had been the guest of Chandler and his compatriots and Chief Inspector MacMorran with his satellites at the 'Yard' were no nearer the murderer of the three boxers than they had been when 'Smith' had accepted the meaning of the danger-signal and slipped away from his rooms at Deptford.

Star, on this evening, looked very beautiful. The table lamp at her left elbow touched her beauty with a soft glow of light and coloured sheen and gave it an added radiance. To Godfrey's mind she seemed strangely aloof and far away from him on this particular evening. He translated this idea into a question.

"Why so *distraite*, Star? You look as though somebody were walking over your grave."

She smiled at his remark and shrugged her shoulders sadly as she replied. "Perhaps, my dear Godfrey, for all I know, somebody is. At this very moment. Why not? You never can tell."

Godfrey adopted his customary technique. He went straight to the marrow of the matter. "What's worrying you? When a fellow takes a pretty girl out to supper and to Murillo's of all places, he expects an adequate reward for his efforts in the shape of sparkling companionship, not to see her as I'm seeing you. You look as though you've been biting on granite."

"I'm all right, Godfrey. Don't worry me. That's all I would ask you. Just bear with me for a time and you'll get your reward all right. You must know by this time that I'm a creature of moods and as such you must treat me with patience."

He grinned. "And I firmly believe that the imperative's the one that suits you best. Also, my dear Star, I'll confess here and now that that's a remark I wouldn't make to every girl."

He suddenly noticed that her listlessness had passed and that her eyes had kindled a look of keen interest. She seemed to be staring fixedly across the apartment at something or even somebody whom

196 | BRIAN FLYNN

she found unusually attractive. Godfrey slightly turned his head and looked across to where he judged Star was looking. To his intense surprise he saw Anthony Bathurst seated at a table opposite to a young man who, to Godfrey, as he looked, was a complete stranger. Even though the man was seated, Godfrey could see enough of him to tell at a glance that he was a completely magnificent physical specimen. He was lean and hard-bronzed and Godfrey knew at his first snatched look that he must be tall with his leanness. His shoulders were well-built and square, and disdainfully careless. His complexion suggested a Viking of old. His eyes were a magnificent blue, his face eminently virile as far as his lower jaw and his mouth gently cruel, with the two qualities alternating with regard to domination, as the exigencies of time and its owner's whim of the moment cared to dictate. Godfrey saw that Star's eyes were fixed on this man as though he had come to her out of another world.

"What is it, Star?" he chided her gently. "Seen somebody you know?"

"No," she half-whispered with a quick shake of her head. "Nobody I know—but what a man! Look over there! At the same table as Anthony Bathurst. See where I mean?"

Godfrey's head followed the line of her indication. "Jove," he said after a moment or so—"I agree with you! A magnificent specimen. And I'll tell you what he is, too! Beyond the shadow of a doubt. He's a boxer. I'd lay a thousand to one on it. Funny—for the moment I can't place him. "

"How can you tell?"

"That he's a fighter—do you mean? Easy, my girl. Dead easy! Notice the deep chest. And so uncommonly well-knit. Those steely blue eyes. Hands so well-shaped. In short, my dear Star, everything about him tells me so. I know the game inside out you see—and the type of man I've met in it."

Star's eyes were still fixed on the subject of their discussion.

"I shouldn't think you've met many specimens like that man with Anthony Bathurst. Why—he's the perfect specimen. He's—he's—gorgeous."

Godfrey Slade winced at the adjective. Then he saw that Star was smiling brightly in Anthony's direction. Slade turned in his chair and half-waved an acknowledgment to Bathurst's table. To tell the unvarnished truth, he felt by no means pleased at the shape events were taking. From the point of view of his own individual pleasure, his evening was most certainly travelling in the wrong direction. Then he saw that Anthony had risen from his chair and was on his way to their table. Mr. Bathurst arrived and bowed.

"Evening, Miss Merrilees. Evening, Slade. Didn't expect to run into you this evening. Last people I expected to see. How are you these days? Quite fit now?"

"Oh—absolutely—thanks. Star and I thought we'd give ourselves a treat. So we broke out for a change. Did a show and then blew along here. Glad to see you look pretty fit yourself."

"I'm not too bad—considering the weather and the festive season. I'm a man, you know, who doesn't mind how hot it is. This cold stuff's not too much to my liking. In a way I'm jolly glad I've run across you. I must say that."

"Why?"

"I'll tell you. I was introduced to a man last night whom I invited to dine with me to-night. I met him in the 'Bishop Latimer'; I've got him over at my table now. He's a fighter. Been in the fight game some years. I took to him rather. He made an unusually good impression on me. That, I suppose, is the real reason." Anthony smiled as he concluded his explanation.

"What's his name?" asked Godfrey Slade.

"'Fingo' Bradshaw," replied Anthony.

"Don't know him," returned Slade, "in fact, I've never heard of him. Where's he from—any idea?"

"Yes. I made it my business to find out. Dagen Bay, New Zealand. That's in the Hawkes Bay district. Walked through most of the stuff he met out there. Hardly ever extended. So I'm told on the best authority. Real class!"

"He's certainly a fine specimen," remarked Godfrey.

"Fine," re-echoed Star Merrilees scornfully—"say 'magnificent' and you'll be much nearer the mark. 'Fine' indeed! What a word to use to describe a man like that. I don't know that I've ever seen his equal. He makes a hungry girl's mouth water." She smiled at her own exuberance.

"What's he come over for?" enquired Godfrey.

"Wants some fights in the old country. So I'm told. I shouldn't think he'd experience much difficulty in getting himself fixed up—would you, Slade. Seeing how things are?"

"I should say not! Some of the managers should be eating out of his hand. If he's as good as he looks—he may turn out a world-beater."

"Introduce us—do you mind," asked Star, "I'd love to meet him."

"Us—or you," queried Godfrey Slade, "I'd love to know where I stand."

There was banter in his voice but Anthony, as he heard it, was by no means certain that there weren't other qualities as well.

"'Us,' I said," returned Star frigidly—"and when I say 'us' I assure you, my dear Godfrey, I *never* mean 'you.' Do tell me that you understand. I should hate to think otherwise."

Godfrey Slade grinned at her and then grimaced to the others.

"If you don't mind I'll bring him over to you," said Anthony, "before we go this evening. And that won't be very long. Promise me that you'll both be nice to him. I can't have him treated roughly, you know."

He waved gaily and departed. To return within the space of comparatively few minutes with the man whom he had named as 'Fingo' Bradshaw. He introduced Bradshaw to Godfrey and Star as he had promised he would. Bradshaw's hand-grip was like iron. Star fluttered beauty's eyes at the new-comer. But the New Zealander was made of sterner stuff. He had not crossed the water to tread the primrose path of dalliance. Without the slightest capitulation of good manners, or natural courtesy, he held himself rigidly within himself and kept most of his emotional outpourings under strict control. Star continued her work. Usually Bradshaw replied to Godfrey fluently and clearly, but to the questions Star Merrilees rained at him his normal reply was monosyllabic. Star, undeterred by Bradshaw's imperviousness, made the running hard. Godfrey bore with her well. Other chairs were handy in close proximity to the table. Anthony and 'Fingo' Bradshaw took them. The cross talk and conversation generally proceeded apace. Everybody contributed with varying degrees of distinction. With the exception perhaps of the man from Dagen Bay. He listened respectfully and well and, which is more, he listened intelligently. When he did speak, his statement was exact and to the point.

"I want to make something of a career in the old country. That's always been my ambition." He paused with a rather embarrassing abruptness and looked steadily at Godfrey Slade. "I'm very much afraid," he said with halting emphasis, "that I'm proving myself a trifle slow on the uptake. When Mr. Bathurst mentioned your name a few minutes ago, I don't think I took it in properly. Aren't you the fellow that caned Phil Blood about a week before Christmas? Didn't I read about it?"

Godfrey grinned. "I got the verdict. That's a much better way of describing what happened. Blood was unlucky. Otherwise he'd have knocked hell out of me. He's really in a different class from me but on the evening of the scrap he was unfortunate enough to break a finger or something."

"A bone in his left hand," amplified Anthony, "and that was during the fight. You can see that Slade is ultra-modest. He put up a wonderful show—take it from me, Bradshaw. I watched every round."

Bradshaw's face was wreathed with the indications of admiration. "That's great," he announced simply. "I wish I'd been there with you. I'd love the chance of a tilt at Blood. But I'm afraid it won't come my way—yet. I've got to walk before I can run, and do a spot of climbing! I suppose you wouldn't feel inclined to—" He paused as though he had a fear or a disinclination, at least, to finish.

"Feel inclined to what?"

The New Zealander flushed as he continued. "I was going to say 'give me a fight.' I don't mean to be over-ambitious or too audacious."

Star put her hand on Bradshaw's arm. "He will *not*! And that ends the matter. So please don't suggest such a thing again, Mr. Bradshaw. For my sake."

Bradshaw turned to her and suffered the full battery of her eyes. They held admiration, appeal, and possibly other conditions.

"I'm sorry. Miss Merrilees. I didn't know that was how you felt about things. Reckon I've put my foot right in it again. I ask your pardon."

Star flooded him with her gratitude. "Thank you, 'Fingo' . . . you won't mind, will you, if I call you 'Fingo' . . . I feel that I can trust you to safeguard my feelings. I think that Godfrey knows very well what I mean so I won't say any more."

Godfrey Slade laughed. "That's all right, old chap. Don't you worry. Your feet haven't done any damage. It's your fists that are going to do that. Don't take too much notice of what Star says. Star's prejudiced against anything in the nature of a sporting 'scrap.' I've done my best to educate her—but she won't be educated. So you see you must treat what she says whence it comes."

At this juncture Anthony intervened. He looked like a man whose plans had been laid for some time and who now saw them approaching fruition. "The conversation seems strangely relevant. I can see in it the finger of Fate. One reason why I asked Mr. Bradshaw to dine here this evening was out of a desire to help him. From what he had already told me, I knew the direction in which his ambitions lay. I brought him here because I wanted him to meet Marcus Secretan, who invariably dines here on Friday evenings. I wanted Secretan to meet him, apparently accidentally. I do not want Secretan to think that Bradshaw, like greatness, is being thrust upon him."

"And of course," commented Godfrey, "as it happens, Secretan isn't here. By all the laws of average and probability, he should be—but the hundredth chance has taken it into its head to come along and Secretan hasn't turned up. That's just the cussedness of things."

Anthony looked at his wrist-watch. "There's still time for Secretan to come. It's not so very late for him. I'm not abandoning hope of meeting him, yet awhile."

Star nodded her agreement. "You are right, Mr. Bathurst. He sometimes comes in very late. I know that—because I've seen him. Been in here and noticed him come in."

She looked at 'Fingo' Bradshaw. "I wish you the very best of luck in your career. You deserve it—having come all the way from 'down under.' I've a strong feeling that you're going to win through."

Bradshaw beamed at her. He looked more splendid than ever. "Thank you, Miss Merrilees. I'll remember that. That's no end good of you. If you'll allow me I'll regard you as my personal mascot." Bradshaw paused and then went on. "English people are different from the people I knew and mixed with at Dagen Bay. At first—when you meet them—you feel that they're strange. But then, after a little while, you feel that in their friendships they're straightforward. And even simple. I should imagine that their enemies must find them very difficult to understand. Almost inscrutable." He flushed and concluded shyly: "I hope I'm not talking too much like a book. I know that English people hate anything like that. But I'm fond of reading and sometimes I'm afraid my thoughts are inclined to run away with me."

"There's something worrying me," contributed Star Merrilees, "This country hasn't been exactly a healthy place for fighters of recent months. But I'm forgetting, I expect you've heard all about that and don't need any reminding from me."

"Why, Miss? How do you mean?"

"Well—there have been no less than three—"

The suddenness of Anthony's voice sounded strange in her ears and brought her to an abrupt conclusion. "Between the acting of a dreadful thing. Miss Merrilees, and the first motion, all the interim is like a phantasma or a hideous dream! Let us therefore, all of us—be merciful to my guest."

"I should prefer," said Star, very much on her dignity, "to afford him, with your permission, justice and a measure of assistance—before I thought of dishing out bowls of mercy. That last seems so incongruous." The hard lines that Anthony had seen before showed plainly round her mouth.

"While you two are bandying words and elegant phrases," intervened Godfrey Slade, "might a mere layman in all meekness oblige?"

"How?" demanded Star curtly.

"Look," answered Godfrey—"Coming along now—straight towards us. The three graces! Lambert, Whitfield and Marcus Secretan himself. See them marching on parade?"

Anthony glanced in the direction that Slade was looking and saw Marcus Secretan.

"Stand up, Bradshaw, will you," he whispered to the New Zealander, "as though we were on the point of going. Just here."

Bradshaw obeyed. Lambert and Whitfield had turned aside towards the tables but Marcus Secretan, from the route he was taking, would be forced to pass Godfrey Slade's table. The necessary moments of time passed. Not one of them spoke a word. Secretan came abreast of them. He bowed to Star Merrilees who smiled at him industriously. He gave Slade a curt nod and something very similar was accorded to Anthony. Anthony returned it to faithful pattern. The sight of Bradshaw, however, affected Secretan differently. His first look in the direction of the man from Dagen Bay was a generous tribute paid by a man who thoroughly understood what he was doing. It was an acknowledgment and a recognition of something valuable and eminently worthy. Given with frankness and admirable candour. Bradshaw himself seemed to sense all this for he flushed under Secretan's undisguised look of admiration. Star saw that Secretan was appraising Bradshaw just as she had appraised him but a short while before. Then Secretan appeared to remember something, pulled himself together and passed on.

There were seats vacant at the next table. Without a second's hesitation he took one of them and very soon a girl joined him—a girl, tall and lovely. With jet black hair and eyes that were raven pools of beauty. Marcus Secretan began to pay her assiduous attention. Anthony addressed himself to the others. Star Merrilees seemed puzzled at his attitude. She looked across at him and her eyes held an unspoken question. Was he seeking a relaxation from what had suddenly come to be an intolerable position? Star went through all the haunting stages of doubt and indecision. As an ameliorative, she tried to exchange smiles with Anthony. But she knew that her own smile was strained and hard. She was an excellent strategist, however, and she knew also that she would gain nothing by inaction. Because she possessed the healthy curiosity of the young she attempted to force the conversation back to the place whence it had originally come. It piqued her to think that there was something going on all around her which she did not properly understand. This was a condition which she had always hated. Suddenly she realized that Anthony was talking to that superb specimen of manhood, 'Fingo' Bradshaw. She heard Bradshaw say in his deep voice, "When am I twenty-four? Not for a couple of months yet. My birthday's on the twelfth of March."

"And that's St. Gregory's Day," replied Anthony gaily, "and also the day when scrupulous and indefatigable gardeners should sow a certain variety of early potato."

He rose to go. Bradshaw at once followed suit. Star Merrilees shook hands with the two men, murmured commonplaces and watched them as they made their way out of the room.

CHAPTER XXVIII
HONOUR FOR DAGEN BAY

ANTHONY again conned the columns of the *Sporting Life*. It may be stated that this was now his practice daily. He had surrendered to the habit for a period of time that had amounted to almost three whole weeks. Anthony was looking for a particular item of news. It concerned the future career of his newly-made acquaintance, 'Fingo' Bradshaw. He was distinctly hopeful that certain news would meet his eye. On the 28th day of January, Mr. Bathurst's patience and persistence were rewarded. His eyes gleamed with satisfaction as he bent forward to read the all-important paragraph.

"We are pleased to inform all patrons and supporters of Boxing that a fight has been arranged between Roger Lebon of Bermondsey and 'Fingo' Bradshaw of Dagen Bay, New Zealand. It will take place early in February at the Belfairs Stadium. Lebon's record is so well known to all patrons of the ring that it needs no reiteration here, but a few words concerning his prospective opponent may not be out of place. Bradshaw, who is not yet 24 years of age, has had sixteen contests of importance. In nearly every one he has conceded weight to his opponent. Of these sixteen fights, he has won no fewer than eleven by K.O. In three he has gained a points decision from the referees and in the remaining two instances, the verdict has been adjudged as a draw. This is a remarkable record for so young a man and when we tell our readers that Bradshaw's list of victims includes such well known names as Trooper Nolan, Joe Prada, Faustino Dellabritto, Battling Callamurra, Danny Preston, Pierre Delevigne and Tom Turpe, it will be readily seen that the Bermondsey lad has no light task to defeat this redoubtable challenger from the land of the Silver Fern. Bradshaw has been fortunate enough to attract as his personal backer that famous sportsman, Mr. Marcus Secretan, than whom, British boxing has had no finer sponsor for many years, and Mr. Secretan is mainly responsible for the arrangements.

"It must be remembered that Bradshaw did not land in this country until early in the New Year, so that it is obvious to all that Mr. Secretan has not let the grass grow under his feet, to have fixed him up so quickly in such an interesting encounter. Let us hope that the contest will attract a bumper attendance and that it will be well up to the standard and traditions of British and Empire boxing.

"We understand on excellent authority that Bradshaw's training-quarters will be at Hornden Park, Essex, and that while he is there he will be under the personal care of Sam Whitfield, the famous trainer, and what Whitfield doesn't know about the game would fill a small egg cup. All communications *re* the fight should be addressed to 'Fingo' Bradshaw, c/o Jack Lambert, 71, Fleet Street. Lambert is looking after the business end of the fight in Bradshaw's interests and from what we know of Jack Lambert, the matter could not be in better hands."

Anthony read the announcement twice—carefully and slowly. Then he rubbed his hands, took down his telephone receiver and asked for Chief Inspector Andrew MacMorran of New Scotland Yard. When he was put through, Mr. Bathurst began to talk . . . slowly and deliberately.

CHAPTER XXIX
LETTER FOR BRADSHAW

'FINGO' Bradshaw sat at his breakfast-table and read a letter. It was of highly-scented, unusually-coloured paper. To be precise—of a delicate shade of pink. The perfume cannot be placed. The writing was in red ink. The New Zealander from Dagen Bay frowned as he read it. The reader is cordially invited to look over his shoulder and share his confidence. The letter ran as follows.

Ingestre Court Hotel, Bayswater.

Dear Mr. Bradshaw,

The writer of this letter to you, is a person who is fabulously rich and who also takes an almost indecent interest in Boxing. This hobby has already led him into nearly all the countries of the world. With many elations and but few regrets. The news of your coming contest with Roger Lebon has reached his ears and it is with regard to this, that he is writing to you. Because, frankly, knowing your record as well as you know it yourself, *he is convinced that you are worthy of flying at much higher game than Roger Lebon. He is convinced, too, that he can put before you an offer which will make your mouth water! If you accept it—and you will be a fool to refuse—not only will you climb to almost instant fame by reason of the programme which he is prepared to place before you, but you will also have your fingers on a fortune. For the time being he must remain anonymous. He can allow no man or woman to proclaim to the world that he or she turned down a business offer which emanated from him. That is not part of the writer's personal creed. He is too proud to have that happen. The address he has given will not help you to identify him. There are many people at Ingestre Court at the present time and one will act as the writer's agent at a later date, if so desired. But if you think kindly of the suggestion, please be outside the telephone kiosk a few yards from the hotel at 7 p.m. tomorrow. The writer knows you . . . he saw you beat Dellabritto at Otago . . . and you will soon recognize him. Yours always, 'Fisticuffs.'*

Bradshaw read the effusion twice. His frown deepened. But he was curious. Curiosity, ambition and a fervent desire for success with her attendant hand-maidens were all clustered in his character, He held the letter, and then the envelope in which it had arrived, to his sensitive nostrils. 'Suppose he uses this sort of stuff because he's a millionaire' thought 'Fingo'—'I wonder.'

He turned up the number of the Ingestre Court Hotel in the telephone directory. Then he closed the book slowly and shook his head. To rise, however, within a few minutes, pick up the receiver and dial a number.

CHAPTER XXX
THE HUNT IS UP!

MR. BATHURST's high-powered car tore down the Kennington road. In its headlong rush, its horn was seldom out of action. MacMorran's face was pasty in the night light and a creamy hue had tinged his gills.

"For God's sake . . ." he said more than once, as he licked his dry lips . . . and then stopped . . . knowing full well that his protestations were useless and that Anthony in his present mood would have none of them and that he might as well save his breath. He was forced to admit that Anthony's handling of the car and the traffic was masterly in the extreme. The car swung right, swung left, turned here, turned there, twisted like a venomous snake obsessed by one idea, but still ruled in the kingdom of its own terrific and insistent speed. Once they stopped. By arrangement. For MacMorran to slide out and use a wayside telephone. The effort was soon over. Back in the car with Anthony he relayed the news he had obtained.

"They passed through Redhill nineteen minutes ago so we're not doing too badly."

Anthony nodded. "Good! They're making for the coast somewhere. Or near the coast. Don't know exactly. Not quite sure which. Rather incline towards the latter. More likely. Hang on, Andrew! I'm going to drive fast."

"Don't you mean faster," muttered MacMorran. Anthony grinned at him and the big car screamed off towards Redhill. Anthony dragged every ounce of speed power from its superb engine. MacMorran clung tight and kept silent. For some miles. He held an utterly absurd idea which he knew full well he couldn't possibly explain were he asked, that to speak would be courting danger.

Anthony said, "How far behind are Townsend and Jessop would you say?"

"I should *think*—probably about a couple of hundred miles."

"Don't be an ass, Andrew. Seriously! Dead seriously! It's important."

"Discipline, eh?" said the Inspector—"well—I'll take it. Not more than five miles. They're in the dark-blue limousine. The newer one. It can move—that 'bus—don't worry."

"Thought you were doing the worrying, Andrew. Sorry if I was wrong. There's Redhill, just in front. I'm pulling up at a decent pub. I'll get some whisky and some sandwiches. No sense in scrapping on an empty stomach. Agree with me, Andrew?"

"Ay. You do talk sense sometimes. It's just on nine o'clock."

"Good. Look out for a pub with a decent parking-place. I don't intend to stay more than the time it takes to cut the sandwiches. We can't afford to."

"They may have some already cut."

"They may, Andrew—but if they have, they'll keep 'em as far as I'm concerned. Here you are! What price this show on the left here?"

Anthony ran the car into a small yard and with MacMorran found the saloon entrance. He gave his orders quickly.

"You have a drink now, Andrew. It may be some time before you get another. I won't. I may have to drive at a fairish pace a little later on."

MacMorran looked at him and swallowed hard. "In that case, then, I'll have a double brandy," he murmured . . . "make it neat."

Anthony grinned again. The barmaid drew the spirit and passed the glass to the Inspector.

"Listen," said Anthony—"our time's right—that's the nine o'clock news that's coming over."

"You won't get Bradshaw's disappearance broadcast yet. I've arranged for it to come over at midnight. Went along and made a special arrangement with the B.B.C."

Anthony nodded. "I was wondering about the time—that was all. I think perhaps you're right. Get going. Here come the sandwiches. Roast beef. You can't beat it."

The smiling barmaid handed over the bag. Anthony took it. The necessary money changed hands. He caught MacMorran by the elbow. "Come on, Andrew—we mustn't waste a minute more. Drink up, man. You swallow your liquor like a cock linnet."

MacMorran shook off Anthony's hand. "Listen . . . man . . . listen. In your hurry—you're missin' all the news. Listen to the name. This is serious—I tell you."

Anthony obeyed.

". . . has suffered a grievous loss. The body of Sir Cloudesley Slade, the famous patron of English sports, boxing in particular, was taken from the railway-line this evening between Redhill and Three Bridges. How Sir Cloudesley came to get on the line at this point is a mystery. Some details of the dead baronet's career may be of interest to our listeners . . ."

MacMorran's face twisted at the thoughts that were ravaging him. Anthony's mind was racing.

"That's *murder*," cried the Inspector . . . "not suicide! There isn't a doubt about it. They've got the old man after all. God . . . this is terrible."

"I think you're right, Andrew . . . in fact I'm certain you are . . . come . . . we must get away at once and wait for the details to come along later. More than ever now, we haven't a moment to lose."

Anthony dashed for the car. MacMorran followed him. "Townsend and Jessop are a little way ahead of us. I shall soon pass them." This from Anthony.

MacMorran looked at him fearfully. He saw that Anthony's face was care-ridden. The news of Sir Cloudesley's death had apparently shocked his composure and struck a heavy blow at his *amour-propre*.

CHAPTER XXXI
THE MAN IN THE SHAWL

AWAY screamed the car again down the Brighton road. To the broad main street of Crawley village after crossing Crawley Down. Anthony slowed down in Crawley.

"Check up, Andrew . . . although I've no doubt . . . there's one just over there."

MacMorran entered a police 'phone-box. To be out again in a matter of seconds. "All right. They've made Handcross and are now close to Cuckfield. The front car is travelling fast. Faster, they say now, than it has been anywhere else on the road."

Anthony nodded grimly at the news. "Do you know the country round Clayton Hill and Pyecombe, Andrew?"

"No—not too well—although I've been here before. Why?"

"I've a fancy that we shall finish up pretty close to there. Something seems to tell me so. Sit tight and hold your breath."

The car flashed on. MacMorran felt a strange and sudden sinking in his stomach. He knew now that he *must* talk.

"They've a fair start of us, Mr. Bathurst. Hope it isn't too much."

"Don't worry, Andrew. This isn't *quick* murder. By an electric shock. It's damned slow, let me tell you. In long drawn out stages. To say nothing of the time taken up in the preliminaries."

MacMorran, rattled more than ever, blurted more words. "Why did they kill the old man differently?"

"Not being a boxer, Andrew! There's your answer in one. Just a stager of scraps but no scrapper himself. Different! *Autres temps, autres moeurs.* Hang on and say ninety-nine. Here's a nasty swerve coming. Hallo! There's a motor-cyclist . . . wants to speak to us. That looks as though I must slow down. Look out, Andrew and see what he wants, will you? It may conceivably be a message for you."

Anthony brought the car almost to a standstill. The cyclist drew up alongside them and spoke to the Inspector. MacMorran bent his head forward to listen.

"The second on the left, you say?"

"Yes, sir. I was to tell you that. Your men will hide their car and then wait for you and further instructions."

MacMorran scrutinized the man's face and then passed on the information. The car flew forward again. For nearly three miles. At length they made the turning. All around there loomed large trees with ghostly swaying branches. The country had suddenly become wild and wooded. MacMorran shivered. Anthony was compelled to reduce pace. The road was not good. The farther they went the worse it became. The car lurched and bucketted. With the night growing older, the wind was rising in fury and whistled in shrill treble through the tree branches with an almost malevolent menace. Suddenly MacMorran leant forward and touched Anthony's sleeve.

"It's been raining here. Not long ago too. But stopped. Notice how strong the wind is?"

The car wheels dipped into a pot-hole and MacMorran's body went lurching against Anthony's shoulders. "Stop," he said, "stop. Townsend and Jessop are waiting over there. I arranged for a signal from them. There . . . there you are . . . look . . . two flashes."

"Perhaps they'll tell us where their car is," muttered Anthony, "for where the merry hell . . ."

He stopped the car suddenly for MacMorran to get out. Anthony waited.

"Follow me," said the Inspector after a few seconds consideration . . . "there's a path of sorts here. And it's not so muddy as it might have been. I can see our men." Anthony took the car along under MacMorran's guidance for some way. At length he stopped. Townsend and Jessop stood there with MacMorran.

"How far's the car you followed?" Anthony asked the question of them immediately.

Jessop answered. "We were well behind it all the way down, in fact, you passed us once. They never knew we were on their tail. When they first turned off the road, we went straight on and then turned back again. According to my reckoning that car's about a quarter of a mile away. Can't be much more than that. I could see its lights about five minutes since."

"Good," returned Anthony. "With me, then . . . and each man keep his eyes open. You lead the way, Jessop, will you? Towards where you think you saw those car lights. Be careful. I don't want to be seen if we can help it." They made their way slowly towards the edge of the wooded plantation. The path was rough and uneven. When they had almost reached the road again, Jessop stopped and motioned the others back. "Somebody coming. Keep well back—everybody."

All four of them halted in their tracks. Jessop was right. Footsteps were coming down the road. Anthony and the others used trees to hide themselves behind. They were now but a few yards from the road again. The footsteps drew nearer. Suddenly a man came into sight. A blurred figure. But of abnormal height. The man came nearer with a curiously swinging stride. In an instant Anthony recognized him. There was no mistaking that height and that unusual walk. The man passed by. Anthony beckoned to MacMorran to break cover from behind his tree. "Recognize him, Andrew?" he whispered.

"Ay," returned MacMorran laconically. "Asater! It's comfortin' to think that we're comin' across auld acquaintances."

Anthony whispered to Jessop. "After him, Jessop . . . but give him a bit of a start first. The darkness will help us and the wind will help to deaden any sounds we make." They made the road, in the wake of Jessop and kept on the way that Asater had taken. Every now and then they could hear his footfalls in the distance ahead of them. Anthony and his companions crept nearer. And then . . . with an almost sinister suddenness, Asater's footsteps ceased to be heard . . . and silence reigned save for the soughing of the wind. Anthony passed Jessop and pushed forward for about another hundred yards before halting his little force. The three men gathered round him.

"He's gone," said Anthony in a low voice, "and I'm hanged if I know where . . . any of you bursting with ideas?"

He obtained no response. There was neither sight nor sound of anything beyond the wind wailing. MacMorran shook his head blankly. There they stood on the rough road that was not much more than a cart-track. Until, suddenly and ominously, there came the sound of a low, dry cough from somewhere away to the right of them. Anthony gestured silently to the three others. They followed him in the direction from where the cough had come. Across broken ground and tangled grass roots . . . until without further warning, they came upon the strangest sight. A man confronted them. He was leaning on some support. Straw-coloured hair hung over his shoulders as a shaggy mane and he seemed to have a violent stoop. Old, tattered grey trousers covered his legs, a dark-blue sailor's jersey went to his neck, and round that neck and across his back, pinned tight to the throat, was a woman's dark red shawl.

As Anthony approached closely to him, he showed ugly yellow teeth . . . like a dog's . . . and he mouthed uncouth noises. It was at that moment when Anthony saw on what he leant for support. There was a square slab of stone, like a mammoth tomb in a gigantic cathedral . . . and at one end of the square slab, Anthony could see a narrow flight of stone steps. And beyond the stone steps . . .

a black pit . . . which looked to be bottomless . . . and as awesome a place in that bizarre setting as the eyes of man could look upon.

CHAPTER XXXII
THE DOMED HALL

As ANTHONY advanced, the man in the shawl made a quick movement towards the steps. Something told Anthony that he must be stopped at all costs. He darted forward, therefore, and caught the man by the shoulder. The shawl was soft and wet to Anthony's touch and the man half-slithered away but Anthony swung him round and MacMorran who was following up did the rest. A blow to the point of the jaw sent the shaggy-maned dolt staggering against the great slab of stone where he fell unconscious. Anthony looked at the steps which led down to the black hole. The steps and the hostile blackness were in front. The wind and the friendly darkness lay behind.

"I'm going down," said Anthony . . . "you others follow me, one by one."

"I'll come next," said Chief Inspector MacMorran . . . "then you, Jessop, and after you, Townsend."

Anthony went down backwards. MacMorran held out a hand as he lowered himself. MacMorran watched him descend into the blackness and shone a torch into the depths. He calculated that Anthony must have descended every one of twenty feet when he saw him step away from the side and apparently stand on something. MacMorran judged that the time had come for him to follow. He trod the steps gingerly and made his way down with an excess of caution. To join Anthony on a square concrete platform. Anthony pointed to a door that faced them.

"When the others come, Andrew," he whispered, "we're going in. It's open! I fancy Asater must have come this way very recently."

They waited quietly for Townsend and Jessop. When the four men had made the platform, Anthony slowly turned the handle of the door. What he saw staggered him. He found himself looking into a domed hall. This hall was shaped like an auditorium. Ventilation came from gratings at the sides. At the end of the hall was a raised stage in the form of a boxing-ring. The hall itself was absolutely empty. The stage was brilliantly lighted. The rest of the hall was in darkness. Not a soul could be seen or heard. In the centre of the auditorium, facing the dais, was a huge chair with a tremendously high back. A chair such as a Mayor might use at a civic function. Anthony made a rapid decision.

"We're going in. Now! I *think* that we've come in time. When we get inside, each man flatten himself against the wall at the back and have his revolver ready at an instant. And take your cues from me."

MacMorran nodded his agreement. The four men sidled through the door and found themselves in this subterranean auditorium. Not a sound could be heard. Anthony motioned the others to appropriate places. He whispered again to MacMorran before they separated.

"See that raised stage, Andrew? That's the place where Bailey, Donovan and Jago were murdered."

CHAPTER XXXIII
SECONDS OUT OF THE RING

MACMORRAN had barely had time to tiptoe to his place when things began to happen. A voice rang through the domed hall. The style was familiar. Directly he heard it, Anthony's fingers closed on the butt of his revolver.

"Gentlemen," said the voice, "the fight to-night is between Asater of America . . . unbeaten throughout his career . . . and 'Fingo' Bradshaw of Dagen Bay, New Zealand. At almost level weights."

Anthony's thoughts raced to that evening at the Belfairs Stadium. The same nonchalance . . . the same technique . . . the same . . . but the voice was going on.

"The fight will be to a finish . . . no rounds and no intervals . . . the stake will be the usual one." Here came a devilish chuckle. "Gentlemen . . . let me introduce the two opponents. On my right . . . Asater." At that moment Asater slipped from the wings in a scarlet dressing-gown, entered the roped space and bowed to the empty hall with its invisible audience. The whole thing would have seemed a nightmare but Anthony could see the brown padded gloves . . . the white lined, soft-soled black ankle-boots and the skin-tight white trunks under the flaming scarlet of the loose gown. But . . . somehow . . . the gloves themselves looked strange!

The voice continued. "On my left . . . 'Fingo' Bradshaw . . . two grand boys."

Just as Asater had done a few seconds previously, Bradshaw came from the wings on the opposite side. He looked pale but confident and his dressing-gown was black, marked with a large silver fern. He shook it from his shoulders. Asater did the same and then, with a clutch of cold horror, Anthony saw that the scarlet of Asater's gown carried the sign of the skull and cross-bones. There appeared to be no seconds present. All to the good, Anthony thought, from the point of view of the immediate future. He craned forward for a moment and then flattened himself back again into the shadows for a figure had come from somewhere at the side of the stage and was walking rather daintily towards the big chair in the middle of the room. Anthony saw the figure raise a hand and sink into the chair and at that precise second, Asater and 'Fingo' Bradshaw sprang to the attack. The powerful light over the ring made every action as plain as though under daylight and Anthony gasped as he realized the dreadful thing that was about to happen.

CHAPTER XXXIV
ANOTHER'S TERROR

ANTHONY'S eyes were concentrated on Bradshaw as he advanced on Asater . . . and suddenly he saw a look of horror come over the New Zealander's face. Bradshaw led with his left and Asater deftly parried the blow. Bradshaw ducked away . . . and Anthony knew that the knowledge had come to him with an appalling certainty that he was facing an ordeal such as three men only had ever faced before him. And an ordeal that would almost certainly mean death . . . death after mutilation . . . unless he could put Asater down as a result of their first few exchanges. Which last proposition, bearing in mind Asater's obvious skill and ring-craft, was well-nigh hopeless.

Anthony saw Bradshaw throw caution to the winds and go right in at his massive opponent. The New Zealander swung a wicked-looking left to Asater's head which was avoided by a piece of superb timing and then, as the impetus of the blow brought Bradshaw forward, Asater darted out his right and chopped at Bradshaw's ear. As this happened, Anthony held his breath and well he might for the blow sliced the top of the ear and the blood spurted viciously and began to trickle down Bradshaw's cheek and neck. The figure in the big chair sprang to his feet and cried venomously in a voice that had become unrecognizable: "Blood to Asater! A hit. A point."

Bradshaw staggered back and the look in his eyes told eloquently of the fact that he sensed his imminent doom. A wicked smile was curling the lips of Asater. Anthony knew that he could not afford to delay action a minute longer. Even now, he was risking Bradshaw's life. He beckoned to MacMorran who crept forward silently out of the shadows. Anthony whispered instructions.

"We must move . . . at once! I'll take the central figure . . . you and Jessop get Asater . . . if he turns nasty . . . wing him without compunction. Tell Townsend to keep his eyes open at the back there. I've a notion that friend Bellamy may be about."

MacMorran nodded, went back to his two men . . . and then . . . in a matter of seconds . . . the quartet moved forward. They were unchallenged. Bradshaw was defending desperately and the shrill voice of the self-appointed referee shrieked from the big chair. About a third of the way down the domed hall, MacMorran and his two henchmen began to run. Towards the raised platform. Asater and Bradshaw heard them. The New Zealander, bleeding profusely, drew back to the ropes, but Asater turned towards the auditorium and swung his arms menacingly.

"Put your hands up," cried MacMorran, "or it'll go hard with you."

Asater, unheeding the warning, jumped from the ring and dashed towards him. Jessop's gun cracked and the giant clutched his wrist and gave a howl of pain. MacMorran and Jessop closed in on him. The scuffle was short. With but one hand in action, Asater was over-powered. Townsend carefully removed his gloves and MacMorran did the rest.

Meanwhile Anthony had dealt with the leading actor in the proceedings. Covered by Mr. Bathurst's revolver, he cowered in the great chair. Anthony beckoned to the Inspector. MacMorran had difficulty in mastering his amazement.

"Take your man, Andrew. I don't think he'll give you any trouble."

MacMorran used handcuffs for the second time that night. "I arrest you, Sir Cloudesley Slade, for being concerned in the murders of Edward Bailey . . . 'Lefty' Donovan . . . Michael Jago . . . and for the attempted murder . . ."

Slade swayed like a man about to swoon. The madness in his eyes died down from a fire to a smoulder. "Blood," he muttered, "Blood to Asater."

"Razor-blades," remarked MacMorran curtly, "fitted into a kind of claw. Foul and beastly."

"I thought so," returned Anthony, "but we'll go into that later. We shall have to . . ."

He paused . . . there was the sound of running feet. "After him, Townsend. Don't let him get away."

A third man had leapt from the stage into the hall and, taking advantage of their preoccupation, was running hell for leather towards the door. Townsend tried to intercept him but failed. Anthony began to run. Jumping over the prone figure of Asater, Jessop sprang towards the runner. The runner dodged and ran on fiercely, but Anthony by this time had got ahead. Turning quickly on his toes, he shot out his fist with vicious force to the point of the runner's jaw. Bellamy, for it was he, taken by surprise, toppled and lurched headlong to the floor.

"And that, my dear 'Banjo'," said Mr. Bathurst, "is where we most certainly cry 'quits'."

CHAPTER XXXV
L'ENVOI

ANTHONY Lotherington Bathurst dined with Godfrey Slade, Star Merrilees, 'Fingo' Bradshaw, and Chief Inspector Andrew Mac-Morran. At a table suitably secluded, and specially selected by no less a person than Murillo himself. Anthony called his favourite Benito to his side and made arrangements with regard to the wine. Star sipped a cocktail and 'Fingo' Bradshaw ate olives with steady determination. Godfrey Slade said little. After a time Anthony spoke.

"I asked you all to come—because I felt you should all be here," He paused.

"I am grateful," said Slade, "there's a lot to explain."

The waiter brought oysters. "Shall I, then, proceed?" enquired Anthony. The others nodded their acceptance of his proposal.

"I suppose," went on Anthony, "that many people, sitting in judgment would call the guilty man a sadist. I would go farther than that. His sadism was allied with madness. Madness that had been handed down to him from a previous generation. You, Slade, probably know more of your ancestor, the late Sir Hugo Slade, than I do. See to Miss Merrilees's wine, will you please—I've ordered *Liebfraumilch* with the *sole meunière*." Anthony lifted his own glass. "I will tell you how the truth gradually came to me. Do you remember the three letters, Inspector, that were received by Sir Cloudesley, Lambert, and Whitfield?"

"Ay," returned MacMorran. "Verra well."

"It struck me that *one* man might very well have posted the letters that bore the *Maidenhead* and the *Windsor* postmarks. The third envelope, with the Basingstoke postmark, might have contained a perfectly innocent letter, sent to Sir Cloudesley and then *have been used again*, by him, to hold *his* 'warning.' I think that idea was my first real starting-point. From there, I cast my mind back. To the occasion of my first meeting with him. He was talking about his great-grandfather, Sir Hugo Slade, and he attributed this remark to that gentleman. 'Put your money on a horse, on a dog or on a—' and he stopped abruptly before naming what the third substantive was to have been. I wondered at the time what it was he had been about to say but it got pushed out of my mind. Until recently—when I had occasion to recall it."

The waiter brought roast chicken. Anthony waited for a few moments. Then he resumed his story.

"I happened to be reading a copy of the *Sporting Life* one day. Not by accident. By design. That estimable paper published special

obituary notices of Bailey, Donovan, and Jago. You know the idea—
with details of their respective careers. I suddenly noticed that they
had all three men been born in the wild month of March."

Bradshaw made a quick movement. "Exactly, 'Fingo'," said
Anthony easily, "that was the main reason why you were chosen
as my bait. I knew that I should have to tell you at some time or
the other."

Bradshaw grinned appreciatively. Anthony went on. "As I read
my sporting paper, my thoughts went back a hundred years and
more, and I tried to picture the early editions of the *Sporting Life* and
to wonder what its columns must have looked like, as compared
with the present day. Its boxing articles . . . its racing accounts
. . . those old prints of racehorses galloping with two legs spread out
in front and two behind . . . what other sports there were . . . and
then, gentlemen, and dear, kind lady, I thought of 'cock-fighting.'
And I *knew* from some strange instinct at work in my brain, that
the word which Sir Cloudesley had refrained from using, *deliberately* refrained, mark you, was the word 'cock'."

MacMorran leant forward with ill-concealed excitement. "Bonny
work, man! I've puzzled my brains for days as to how you got on to it."

"Thank you, Andrew. It all began to fit, too. The 'claw-marks'
for instance! I had always insisted to the Inspector here, that the
claw-marks on the sand at the various places were much too large to
have been made by any known bird. Then I had what I think I may,
in all honesty describe as a real out-of-the-top-drawer brain-wave.
A memory came floating towards me out of the past. Something I
had read at some time in my history. It concerned those boys who
had all been born in March. I 'phoned a pal of mine who, I knew,
was more or less an authority on the subject."

Anthony held up his story once again while Benito brought the
savoury. Then he took a slip of paper from his pocket-book.

"This is an extract from an old book which Meldrum—that's the
bloke's name—read to me over the 'phone. 'In the opinion of the
best Cock-Masters, a right hen of the game, from a dung-hill cock,
will breed the finest cocks from the increase of the moon in February to the increase of the same in March . . . she will hatch those
chickens commonly after one-and-twenty days.' Far-fetched? My

dear people, Sir Cloudesley's mind had gone . . . and when I tell you that Sir Hugo Slade bred the finest fighting cocks of his day in the South of England and that his mains took place in that domed hall on his estate where you and I, Andrew, and Bradshaw here, spent some little time the other day, you will realize the truth of things."

"Amazing," whispered Godfrey Slade.

Anthony went on. "I then endeavoured to visualize how the three men had been killed. MacMorran and I noticed that the cuts and slits were confined, in every instance, to the face, ears, neck, chest, shoulders, and upper part of the body. There were none, in any instance on the hands or wrists! Why? I deduced from this that the hands and wrists *had been covered—protected* in some way! In what way? The answer was comparatively simple. It was obviously boxing-gloves."

Star's eyes shone with approbation. Anthony smiled at her and continued.

"I then began to gasp a little as the enormity of it all came home to me—sorry, Slade. I saw, I thought, the conditions of this modern 'cock-fight.' As arranged by the producer! Friend Asater, fitted into the pattern minus a flaw. I pictured Asater, equipped in some cruel manner at which I could only hazard a guess, and like a sharp-heeled cock, lacerating his victim until he was past the power of resistance. Tell them, Andrew, what you found on Asater when you arrested him."

"The top of the gloves was missing. Instead, strapped to the back of the knuckles, was a sort of comb, fitting tight. The 'teeth', firmly slotted, were razor-blades. Some of the gangs, you know, use razor-blades attached to their finger-nails. Our man had gone one better. Or worse!"

Star Merrilees shuddered.

"The claw-marks on the beach and on the floor in the house at Notting Hill were, of course, faked. Obsessed by the cock idea, Sir Cloudesley had had a huge claw fashioned out of wood for this purpose. Bellamy, I have since heard, is a carpenter of parts. I suspect that it was of his manufacture."

"What was the idea . . . behind it all . . . just blood-lust?" asked Godfrey Slade in a toneless voice.

"I fear so, Slade. He delighted in the sight and sensuality of flowing blood. I fancy that watching an ordinary scrap had become tame for him. He craved for the blood excitement. He met Bailey at Evenino's—at a dinner of sporting celebrities. Bailey was a fine fellow . . . it came out in some way that he was born in March. Full of ancient cock-fighting lore, Sir Cloudesley seized on the idea. It appealed after the macabre to his particular obsession. He would have his own boxing 'cock-fights' just as his ancestor, Sir Hugo had. The venue was already on his estate . . . it merely needed moderniz-ing. So by some means he got hold of Asater and Bellamy. Probably at a low fighting dive in the East End. He frequented such places regularly. Asater had recently arrived from somewhere in the States. They were well paid. Asater—Sir Cloudesley had doubtless seen him fight—was a first-class boxer."

MacMorran intervened with a question. "Do you imagine Asater and Bellamy fell in with the project when it was first put to them? It seems to me rather—"

"No, Andrew, I don't. It was in all probability administered by degrees. I incline to the idea that they were committed up to a point . . . and then found it too late to back out in measurable safety. And—as I said previously—the money was good."

"What I can't understand," said Godfrey Slade, "is the Donovan business. Why was Donovan killed . . . seeing he was fighting for my father against Secretan's man? That all seems so contradictory to me. . . ."

"Your father didn't mind losing that money in the least," Anthony sipped his coffee. "Whatever else might happen, Donovan's death would be bound to divert any suspicion that *might* be knocking about boxing circles, from *him*. He, surely, would be the last person on earth to be suspected. He then employed the same technique with regard to Jago and yourself. As a matter of fact, he spoke to me of Jago with terrific enthusiasm. You were abducted by friends of Asater . . . on your father's orders. You weren't to be seriously harmed. Kept in cold storage for a day or so and then doped. But you threw a span-ner into the machinery when you got your message through to the outside world. He knew this had happened so he sent warnings to the different parts of the gang. That was the reason Chandler and Smith skipped when they did."

"What was their original intention?" enquired Godfrey Slade.

"To hand you over to Smith, I think. Smith would have driven you somewhere in a car and dumped you there to be picked up by somebody, little the worse for wear.

"Tell me this," asked Star impulsively. "Why was Godfrey put into those awful woman's clothes?"

"That's a poser, rather," returned Anthony, "that has given me a teasing to find the right answer. I'll tell you though, what *I* think. That the instructions for you to be dressed like that came from Sir Cloudesley. Seeing a woman lying on the vital seat almost certainly meant that we should *delay* our action for a time at least. Had we seen a man's figure—we should have moved forward immediately. Delayed action on our part suited his book."

"I think you're right, Mr. Bathurst," added Inspector MacMorran.

"You see," continued Anthony, "that Sir Cloudesley was vulnerable from the point of view of suspicion by reason of the fact that his estate was in Sussex. Worthing, Littlehampton, and Lancing . . . coming in quick succession . . . might have made things a bit awkward for him. He reckoned that when you came within the orbit of attack, Slade, that fact alone would be enough to let him out." Bradshaw nodded. He evidently saw the force of Anthony's point.

"Those photos," put in MacMorran, "that were found on the dead men? I'm still a little puzzled about them."

"I think they can be easily explained," replied Anthony. "Bailey carried one of his sister. When he died it was taken off him. When Donovan died they found that he too carried a photo of his wife. With fiendish cunning, the Bailey photo was put in the Donovan pocket and when Jago died the Donovan photo was there already for *his* pocket! Sir Cloudesley argued to himself, no doubt, that the substitutions would be bound to confuse and complicate matters. At least—that's how I see it." Anthony took his liqueur. "Well . . . there I was . . . pretty well confident of what had been happening. I told you I 'phoned a pal of mine after I'd drawn inspiration from the columns of the *Sporting Life*. I wanted from him an introduction to somebody in the boxing world who was a fine specimen and whose birthday fell in the right compartment of the calendar. There I was gloriously lucky. I had produced for me a man I was delighted to meet. You know him. He's sitting next to me at the moment. I met 'Fingo' and I had to dangle him in front of our mad murderer. I felt that a direct contact would invite suspicion. So I held him out to Marcus Secretan. It didn't take long to get Sir Cloudesley interested. The lust for blood was increasing. 'Fingo' knew my plans. I had to outline them to him. He's a brave man and was willing to take the risk. It came. In the shape of the usual letter." Anthony turned to Bradshaw. "You tell them the rest, 'Fingo'."

Bradshaw flushed. "There isn't a great deal to tell. I kept an appointment. Asater and Bellamy put me into a car. The Inspector's men were shadowing me all the time and knew where I was. All the roads were watched. The Inspector knew the car I was in, and its description and number were 'phoned ahead on all the likely routes. He and Mr. Bathurst here and a couple of men from the 'Yard' were on my tail all the way down. Don't call me brave . . . I was in cotton wool, as you might say, all the way through. Except, perhaps, when I saw those wicked razor-blades. Even though Mr. Bathurst had partly warned me—I'll admit they gave me a nasty turn."

'Fingo' Bradshaw laughed at the reminiscence and drank wine.

"Not far out of London the car picked up the old man. He was waiting for it. He was quite charming to me. In fact I had a hard job to persuade myself of the truth, as Mr. Bathurst had given it to me. The car burnt up the road. Near a village, we knocked a man down and killed him. It was a pure accident. He ran right into us. Luckily the road just there was deserted. Bellamy was driving and at first, old man Slade cursed at him like hell for what he thought must mean delay. Then, suddenly, his mood changed. He shoved his own hat and his coat on the dead man, shoved the body in the car, stuffed some papers in his pocket, laughed like a hyena and told Bellamy to make for the railway line. We made it somewhere and Asater in the darkness dumped the bloke on the line. While he was gone on this errand the old man kept on laughing and muttering to himself 'that'll make them think twice about me.' I guess you're acquainted with all the rest."

Bradshaw finished his wine and turned to his Benedictine. "Well," said Anthony, "we're very close to the curtain. And I must pay the bill. For this one evening you're all my guests." He signalled to the waiter.

MacMorran leant over the table. He passed a slip of paper to Anthony. "Something that may interest you. Came to-day."

Anthony read: "Stella Molyneux in New York City. Crossed in the spring of last year. Being married next week to young lawyer—Curtis Singleton." Anthony smiled. "That clears her up. Just as well. Don't like loose ends." He looked round the assembled company. "Well, any more questions? Speak now—or for ever hold your peace."

"Yes." said Andrew MacMorran, "one from me. Why did Bellamy go to the Belfairs fight done up like Mother Machree?"

"Because, my dear Andrew," replied Anthony sweetly, "he guessed we should be there and he didn't want us to recognize him—wen or no wen. We had nothing on Asater but I had on Bellamy, remember."

Godfrey Slade put his hand on Star's arm and spoke to Anthony. "Have a drink with me, Bathurst! I shouldn't like you to think . . ."

Anthony cut him short. "Thanks, Slade. I don't mind if I do."

Finis

Lightning Source UK Ltd.
Milton Keynes UK
UKHW011333010322
399394UK00002B/601